99WAYS
TO DIE

ALSO BY ED LIN

99 WAYS TO DIE

ED LIN

SOHO
CRIME

Published by Soho Press, Inc.
227 W 17th St
New York, NY 10011

Epigraph from Confucius's *The Analects*, translated by D.C. Lau,
published by Penguin Books, 1979.

Library of Congress Cataloging-in-Publication Data

Lin, Ed, author.
99 ways to die / Ed Lin.
Other titles: Ninety-nine ways to die
Series: The Taipei Night Market novel; 3

ISBN 978-1-64129-088-3
eISBN 978-1-61695-969-2

I. Title.
PS3562.I4677 A615 2018 813'.54—dc23 2018027715

Interior design by Janine Agro, Soho Press, Inc.

Printed in the United States of America

10 9 8 7 6 5 4 3 2 1

For the dreamers

It is rare, indeed, for a man with cunning words and an ingratiating face to be benevolent.

—CONFUCIUS (551-479 BCE)

99WAYS TO DIE

CHAPTER 1

When my old classmate Peggy called me I didn't recognize her voice because I'd never heard her cry before.

I'd never seen her shed a tear and now I was listening to double-lung sobs that were clipping out the audio. If my phone hadn't indicated that the call was from her office phone, I would've thought I had a direct line to a cub at the black-bear pen at the zoo.

I clamped the phone against my left ear until the cartilage buckled and stuck a thumb in my right ear. Foot traffic at the night market was beginning to wind down but it was still loud as hell all around me. Honestly, though, I'm usually the noisiest thing in my vicinity, coaxing and cajoling tourists in English to come to my stand, give me money and eat my food in exactly that order if not in those exact terms.

"Peggy," I said. "Catch your breath. I can't understand what you're saying."

I heard Peggy drop the phone, hack out phlegm and blow her nose roughly. She came back on the line and croaked, "Someone kidnapped my daddy, Jing-nan!"

I crouched and felt behind me as I eased into a seat. Her

father, Thomas Lee Tong-ming, was the landlord of nearly every stand at the Shilin Night Market, including the best one, Unknown Pleasures, which I happened to own. On top of that, I've known him for most of my 25 years. Known *about* him, too, what with all the times he's been on TV.

The Lees are incredibly wealthy. They were one of those mainlander families that had sailed from China over to Taiwan on a boat made of gold after the civil war ended and became even wealthier over the last seventy years.

Thomas Lee Tong-ming controlled some of the most powerful tax-dodging entities in Taiwan. He was popular and because he was rich, he was also adored by the media, even by the outlets he didn't explicitly own. His fame made him extremely attractive.

He didn't seem to have much in the physical sense to offer a woman, apart from his relatively tall height, which was enhanced when he stood on his piles of money. He had the natural stoop of a bureaucrat but when surrounded by others of that ilk in a photograph celebrating new legislation, he straightened up to a slouch. He knew he was ugly. He kept his straight black hair parted to the side, making his head resemble a flattened black plum on one side. Dead eyes stared through gold rims. A corporate smile conveyed controlled pain.

None of that mattered, though. The mainlander families of the '80s were focused on alliances for wealth first, politics second. During such times what was on the balance sheet mattered more than what was quivering under the bedsheet. Thomas Lee Tong-ming went on to have five kids, of whom Peggy was the youngest. He had married a film star from a mainlander family whose idea of spreading the wealth was spreading their own wealth by buying up properties around the globe.

You could guess from his compound name that he had one foot in the Western world and one in Asia. When he was making a software deal in Silicon Valley, he was Tommy Lee. When he was lobbying the incorruptible-in-theory members of the Taipei City Council to rezone a commercial block for residential development, he was Tong-tong.

A trashy tabloid, *The Daily Pineapple*, had once declared that Tong-tong had another wife and family stashed in a sub-urb of Vancouver. Such was the power of Peggy's father that *The Daily Pineapple* not only printed a retraction but also ran a center spread of photos of its chairman on his hands and knees, begging for forgiveness from a seated Tong-tong who had his hand outstretched toward the supplicant in a display of grace that evoked our former dictator and deity from the mainland Chiang Kai-shek.

How could a man powerful enough to literally have the media groveling at his feet be abducted so easily?

I LISTENED TO PEGGY sob on. She wasn't calm enough to talk yet. It was just as well, since the crowds were falling off at a pretty steep rate now. I glanced over at my crew of two: the sprightly senior citizen Frankie the Cat; and Dwayne, the tough thirty-year-old who was proud of his aboriginal heritage, his interpretation of which came with a nice shiny chip on the shoulder.

Dwayne shook his closely cropped head at me. "Look at this lazy Han Chinese, sitting down on the job!"

I pointed at the back of my seat to indicate that I was going to be there a while. Dwayne snorted.

"What's that, Jing-nan? You want me to kiss your ass? Frankie, can you believe this guy?"

Frankie adjusted his glasses, pushing the arms deep into his slicked-back hair, and grunted, indicating that he under-stood my gesture to mean that I was stuck on the phone. Or maybe he was merely dislodging phlegm.

A family of Americans came unbidden to the counter. Four

of them—what else?—two parents and a son and a daughter. The boy, an eight-year-old wild child, pressed his nose against the glass and then proceeded to wipe it across the entire pane to get a close-up of the different grilled sausages and skewered organs. Damn it, did we have enough disinfectant spray left? His teenaged sister stood back and grabbed at the insides of her elbows.

"We should have gone to France!" she declared. "The food here is gross!" Her enabling mother put a hand on her husband's arm.

"Honey," she said, "are we sure this is safe? For the kids?"

I wished I could jump in and quip, "Hey, it's safer than Velveeta," or something like that. Dwayne glanced at me, recognized that I was tied up and then took action by leaning over to them.

"Very good, very good," said Dwayne as he moved his hands in a hypnotic circular motion. He should speak English more often. There was an earthy and honest quality to his voice in that language, and he wasn't good enough at it to add a sarcastic tone. "Everything clean." Dwayne gave them a big toothy grin and pressed his hands together at his chest, making him look like a genie ready to grant food-related wishes. Dad smiled. He was into genies.

"Thank you, thank you," the father said loudly in bad Mandarin to Dwayne while waving too much money at him.

Dwayne smiled and replied, "Thank you, thank you." I felt extreme relief knowing that Mr. Tough Guy himself could even knuckle under and extend courtesy to our customers. Sure, we sell them food, but we can't feed ourselves without them and putting up with their occasionally annoying behavior. Dwayne bagged whatever the boy pointed to while the sister wrung out her lips. Maybe she would have been happier at one of Taipei's bakeries, which have more varieties of croissants than you can shake a beret at.

I only know a few French phrases, but my favorite is, *Sourire aux touristes*—smile at the tourists. Smile at the questions that demean your country, your culture and possibly yourself. Smile at the suspicious looks they give you when they think you're trying to cheat them. Smile until it kills you because without them, you'd be alone and crying. The vast majority of visitors are great, but every once in a while, you get someone who doesn't want to be there or doesn't want you to be there.

The son grabbed the bag from Dwayne as his father paid. Inevitably, his sister was now trying to get their mother to make him share with her.

Reassured that my business wasn't in danger of imminent collapse, I fully turned my attention back to my old classmate. Her sobs had decreased in volume and frequency. Maybe she could talk now.

"Peggy," I said as I looked to the wall. "I want to make sure I heard you right. You said your father was kidnapped?"

"Yes," she managed to say. Peggy Lee, who would be nonchalant while standing on a cliff that was crumbling beneath her feet, was having difficulty verbalizing a single syllable. She must love her father more than anything.

I planted my feet flat on the ground, licked my lips and prepared to talk to her in a more sedate manner than I ever have. "Can you tell me what happened?"

I heard her bang her desk drawers open and shut. That was followed by a metallic glugging sound that could only come from a flask. She gasped before continuing. "He was at one of those Double Ninth Festival dinners a few hours ago." The drinking had improved her voice and made her sound more lucid. "You know, they feed the old people, give them some money, put on a little music show and watch them stumble around the dance floor."

I nodded even though she couldn't see. "Yes, I know about them," I said.

Double Ninth is one of those ancient Chinese holidays that have taken on added meanings and rituals over the years to accommodate governmental objectives, cultural considerations and lobbying from agricultural groups.

The holiday takes place on the ninth day of the ninth lunar month and it is a time to honor the elderly, since "nine" in Mandarin also sounds like "old." Chinese tradition doesn't recognize coincidences, so a calendar date that sounds like "old old" must mean that it celebrates "old old" people just as sure as eating cow brains makes one smarter.

Other aspects of the Double Ninth include indulging in *yin* activities to offset the heavy *yang* influence of the day, since nine is the most yang number. One has to manage the opposing and complementing forces yin and yang like balancing tires. You don't want your body to end up deviating from the path, the way, the Dao, the very doctrine of the mean. You could get sick, die and end up a ghost, doomed to a state of sustained unrest forever, which must be like cram school minus the awful fluorescent lighting.

To criminally oversimplify things, I would say that yang is the male element in the balance of yin and yang. Yang embodies overt qualities such as light, heat and substantial physical effort. Yin, the female side, embodies the dark, cool and introversion. One doesn't want to get too much yang, a real danger during Double Ninth. Too much yang is what destroyed the band Van Halen. Not that it shouldn't have been destroyed.

Mountain climbing is a popular choice of activity to maintain stability, as is flying kites, since both things are associated with higher elevations, a yin sort of thing. Drinking chrysanthemum tea also helps boost yin.

In Taipei, local municipalities hold banquets for people over 65 and present them with checks for 1,500 New Taiwan dollars, or almost 50 American dollars. The older you are, the more you get. People 99 and older get NT$10,000 and a gold ring, paid out of the city's coffers.

The gravy train began to bypass Taipei a few years ago when a new mayor gutted the program. Now, one had to present proof of not having much money in order to get an envelope. That was a cynical move because even the most desperate in Taiwanese society have some pride, particularly the elderly. They certainly wouldn't be apt to document their poverty (read "abject failure") to an official a third their age.

Tong-tong had balked at that move. He took out full-page ads in the daily newspapers, declaring that the city was slamming the doors on the elderly and that he himself would provide for them out of his own pocket. Getting older cut across lines of class and background, Tong-tong had written, and reaching a certain age should be celebrated together because we were all one "community." Normally a mainlander using the term such as "community" would come under scrutiny (the public would ask, does he mean "Chinese community"?), but since Tong-tong promised food, money and gifts, his ads were met only with public praise.

Tong-tong was already a big booster of the police officers' union, and when you're good to the cops, obtaining the necessary permits and security for several dozen banquets around town isn't a problem. He followed through, posting sites where banquets open to seniors would be held. I had always felt slightly negative about paying rent to Tong-tong; I was not so hot on the idea of making a rich guy richer. But his actions had made me feel very close to neutral about him. Now? Even if he weren't my classmate's father, I'd wish they'd find and rescue him.

Unfortunately, his kidnapping would be incredibly embarrassing to the Taipei City Police Department if they couldn't solve it before the public knew. One of their most vocal supporters had been snatched from his own event.

I took a breath. In recent years, kidnappings have ended with the deaths of the victims even when the ransom was paid. The guy with the shipping empire paid off the people who had snatched his daughter, but the woman's body was found floating off of one of his own loading docks. Then there was the family that owned that chain of bakeries. The year they expanded to China, the youngest brother was abducted while scuba diving. They followed the kidnappers' directions to the letter, but never saw him again. About a year after the incident, body parts found in a landfill were confirmed to be his upon DNA testing.

Then again, I guess you never hear about the kidnappings that end well. The families certainly don't want the publicity. I hoped that Tong-tong would be one of the stories you never hear about.

I listened carefully to Peggy to see if she had more to add, but I was only rewarded with the sound of her emptying the flask. I rubbed my temples with my free hand as I considered what to say.

"Peggy, you've called the police, right?"

"I didn't have to call them." Her voice was resigned. "The police escorts were right there at the dinner. Those complete losers were supposed to protect my father but they blew it. Who knows? Maybe they were in on it. I wouldn't be surprised."

"What exactly happened?" I asked with caution.

"It was a dinner he had arranged for retired principals and school-board people. My father was seated at the table on stage next to his old high-school teacher, Wang Lao-shi, who introduced him. My dad stood up to give a speech and a bunch of photographers mounted the stage and crowded around the table." Peggy snorted in disgust. "Two of them were fake. The kidnappers threw a net over him and one of our workers and hauled them away like fish. They threatened to stab them while they made their getaway."

Taipei's police don't carry guns.

"What do you mean they got 'one of our workers'?" I asked Peggy.

"One of our media-relations executives who was on hand," said Peggy. "I don't know his name, and it doesn't goddamn matter, okay?"

The stalls across the asphalt pedestrian walkway were closing up. Three kids fast-walked to their parked mopeds, started them and swayed away into the night. Maybe they were going to do something fun. I remembered when I was in high school and I was dying to get the hell away from my family's night-market stall near closing and get back to my life. Now the night market was my life, and my landlord was in trouble.

"What did the cops do when your father was abducted?" I asked Peggy.

"What could they do? They called the station and reported it. Maybe they should have jumped on the kidnappers. You know, all the food they were feeding the senior citizens was soft so there weren't even knives at the dinner. That event itself was so useless and stupid. My father wasted so much money on these banquets. He didn't have to actually go to any of them, but he wanted to be at the one across from his old high school to honor his old teacher. My poor dad."

"I'm sorry, Peggy. I also feel bad for the other guy who was taken."

"Well, obviously, *I* don't give a shit about him! Fuck! Maybe he was in on it, too! Maybe he's the third kidnapper!" Peggy didn't curse on a regular basis, but the kidnapping of one's parent certainly warranted an F-bomb.

"Did the cops tell you to do anything?"

"I'm in my office and there are two of them right here with

me, doing nothing but looking out the window sometimes. They won't even drink with me."

Even if the police are seen as ineffectual in general, Peggy's two minders had to be incredibly patient and yielding in the face of her abuse.

"I think you should give them a break, Peggy. They're trying to help you."

I heard her set down her glass. "And you guys said not to call him or anyone else. Here he is sticking up for you." I heard a man cough lightly. I sat up.

"Peggy, are they listening in on our call right now?"

"One of them is, the man. The woman is just standing there, staring at me like a park squirrel looking for food." A cop had listened to every word spoken so far. Had I said anything insulting about law enforcement? I couldn't remember.

"Hello, officer," I said. "I'm glad that you're there with Peggy. She's under at lot of stress right now."

"I understand what she's dealing with in this situation, Mr. Chen," he replied in a weary voice. Was the resignation in his voice from coming clean on being in on the call or pure exhaustion from being with Peggy? "I'm Detective Huang Tai-ming. I asked Peggy to keep the line clear for any incoming calls but she has multiple lines on her office phone, so who am I to tell her what she can and can't do?"

I glanced over at the people in front of Unknown Pleasures. We always get some pickup as the other stands close. I like to think that that means customers are saving the best for last. If I were working the crowd, our line would be twice as long. Maybe I could wrap up this call. It was absolutely a terrible situation, but I couldn't really help my old classmate, anyway.

"Well, I'm glad the case is in good hands," I said, trying to mark my voice with sincerity. "I'm sure that your dad will be home safe and soon, Peggy. Everything's going to be all right."

"They'd better find him soon or they can all go to hell!" Peggy's interjection was followed by a buzz sound. "Jing-nan, I have to take this call. It could be them."

"Okay, bye," I said. I heard two clicks and then a beep. I could still hear Peggy breathing. I was about to tell her to disconnect me when an electronically altered voice broke in on the line.

"Miss Peggy Lee." It sounded like a cheery children's toy alien. "We want the plan in exchange for the safe return of your father." The voice creeped me out, but how would Peggy hold up? She was already vulnerable. But I should have known that she'd stand as firm as an embattled mayor in a disaster film.

"What plan?" she asked defiantly. The kidnapper on the line seemed taken aback by her tone.

"Th-The chip design!"

"What chip? What are you talking about?"

"You know what chip. The power-efficient mobile chip in your father's files!"

"I've never heard of this chip. How the hell am I supposed to find the plans?" Her steeliness was fully back. Her earlier sobbing episode was all forgotten. Had it all been an act for the cops? Or even for me?

I had to stay on the line, even if I wasn't riveted by the high-stakes conversation. If I hung up, a click on the line could spook the kidnappers and endanger Peggy's dad. I put a hand over my phone mic in case the ambient sounds of the night market swelled.

The kidnapper released an indignant sigh that was rendered comical by the voice-changing device. "He dies in three days if you don't hand over the chip design."

"I couldn't possibly find it in three days. I don't even know where to look. Tell you what. Either you release him so he can find the plans for you himself, or you put him on the phone now to tell me where to find them."

There was a quiet click.

I heard a woman in the background yell, "Goddamnit!" It must've been the female cop. "I told you to agree with everything they said! Are you trying to get your father killed?"

I could picture Peggy turning her cold eyes to the woman. "I love my father. He taught me that one needs to set boundaries and cultivate respect. I don't want the kidnappers to think that I'm some cowering little girl who will knuckle under, which is likely what your superiors think of you, Officer Kung."

Who else in the world can dress down people the way Peggy can? In high school, she had had a confrontation in private with the principal about keeping her phone on during class. When he emerged from his office afterward, the man, a former marine, was reduced to tears. I don't believe in spirits or deities but I do pray to whatever is out there to keep me on Peggy's good side.

I heard shuffling on Peggy's end of the line. I continued to stay as quiet as possible on my end. A stray sound could send the three of them jumping at each other's throats.

Please, Peggy. Just hang up.

"Wait a moment," said Detective Huang. "I'm getting a reading. Does this number look familiar to you, Peggy?" I heard her stomp her feet.

"What the fuck? That's Jing-nan's cell! Jing-nan, are you still on the line?" I squirmed.

"Yes," I said in my nicest voice. "I stayed on because I didn't know when to hang up."

"You just screwed up the tracing of that call!" accused Peggy.

"He didn't," the male cop deadpanned.

"I'm so sorry," I said, thinking that that was the most appropriate thing to say. You can never go wrong by apologizing in Taiwan. "I had no idea when to hang up because you accidentally patched me into a conference call with the kidnappers."

"Oh, I did?" she said, still angry but befuddled.

"I'll hang up now, so you guys can get on with whatever you have to." I had to get back to work, and before I could think of myself as a cold-hearted bastard, I reminded myself that there was nothing I could do to help Peggy or her dad if the cops couldn't.

"Hang on, Jing-nan," said Peggy. "Hey, you two. Are you hungry? We can go get some food at Jing-nan's stall. He makes the best skewers and stews at the Shilin Night Market."

Kung, the female cop spoke up. "We should stay here in case they call again. Leaving the premises would be a dereliction of duty."

I heard Peggy slam a fist against her desk as she stood up. "I've got the line on this mobile phone. Anyway, they're probably not going to call again tonight. They thought I knew how to get what they wanted."

"You really don't know?" Huang asked with a hint of amusement.

I tightened my grip on my phone and curled into the crash position. I tried to keep drama out of the workplace. "Listen guys," I said. "It's been a really slow night and I'm actually thinking of closing up pretty soon, Peggy."

"We'll be there soon, so if you do decide to close, keep something hot." It was an order to be disobeyed at my own risk.

CHAPTER 2

Twenty-seven minutes later, and long after I had filled in Frankie and Dwayne on the kidnapping, Peggy strolled in with the two cops. Dwayne had met each of my sentences with muttered curses. Frankie rubbed his nose once the entire time. Both now gave the new arrivals fake cheery greetings like they were none the wiser. I've trained them well.

Peggy came at me with one arm raised above her head. I thought she was going to hug me with it but instead she slapped my back hard, right on my spine. I cried out from surprise as much as pain.

"Ow! Dammit!" I arched my back to take away the sting and regarded my former classmate.

Peggy would make waves in a crowd, probably because she'd be the one pushing herself to the front. Her facial features, including her thin lips and penetrating eyes, were symmetrical. In other words, attractive. If life were an awful and sexist melodramatic television series, she'd play the hard-charging businesswoman who would discover, perhaps too late, the grief in not yielding her heart to a homely man with no money who truly loved her.

"Jing-nan!" she declared. "We've had the longest night and we need something to eat to sustain ourselves."

We had kept the main grill locked and loaded so we'd be ready for them. I picked out a few choice skewers and stirred the tripe stew that was bubbling on the secondary fire.

Here's an honest tip from a sharp night-market hawker. If it's early in the night, get the skewers because they only become scragglier as the night goes on, and your chances of getting an overcooked one that didn't sell goes up. If it's later in the night, get the stew because it's had enough time to become more tender and absorb what we call in the business "goodness," consisting of spices and flavors fully released only with extended cooking.

Peggy and the cops sat at a table in the back, the same one that I had been sitting at while talking to Peggy.

I eased down a tray of skewers in front of them. I knew they knew what was what, but I figured I'd point out which was chicken breast, chicken butt, intestine, beef and spicy pork. They nodded. Dwayne ladled out three bowls of tripe stew that steamed in my face as I carried them over to Peggy's party.

Both cops were in plain clothes and wore blank expressions. They watched everything and didn't say a word. Detective Huang's large nose had distractingly large pores and looked like a plucked cactus. His hair was cut in uneven bangs that ended in arrows pointing down at his eyebrows. The woman, I had heard her name was Kung, had hard eyes and a scar over her left cheek. She pushed her mouth to the side as she shifted in her seat.

"I've heard of this place," she said casually. "There was a shooting here a few months back."

"You're right," I said. "My name is Chen Jing-nan, as you already know. I'm sorry, I was introduced to you on the phone, but I've forgotten your names."

The male cop spoke up. "I'm Huang. This is Kung."

The female cop made no acknowledgment that that was indeed her correct name. Instead, she narrowed her eyes. "Hey, wait a second." Kung was speaking with a tone that implied I was trying to pull some practical joke. She carefully monitored my face for telling reactions. "You were the guy who almost got shot." Her smile openly mocked me.

I felt I had to respond, reminding myself she was a cop. The humility route was probably the best way to go.

I shrugged and nodded like a simpleton as I passed over a new bundle of napkins. Satisfied, Kung broke away from studying me to slurp up a mouthful of steaming stew. After she swallowed, she tossed me a concession: "It wouldn't have killed you, Jing-nan, but it would have probably punctured a lung."

Huang, having already finished a skewer, threw in an observation for good measure. "More than likely, it would have only bruised a rib," he said out the side of his mouth as he licked his fingers.

I couldn't believe these guys were downplaying the most dangerous event of my life. I considered it a minor miracle that I was still here and personally serving them food free of charge. I folded my arms and asked, "Are you sure?"

"I saw the gun," Huang said. "We all saw it. Pictures of it were going around. It was a cheap, small-caliber knockoff."

"Well, it looked scary," I said, holding out my hands in a "Gimme a break!" gesture I had picked up from Americans.

"Everything looks scary to the untrained eye," said Huang.

Kung took another skewer and leaned away from both of us. I took that as an opening to walk away and attend to paying customers. People who would worry if I were shot.

Cops sure liked to eat their food. Peggy did, too. She must have burned all those calories with her insatiable drive to own a piece of every business in the world because she was slim and looked good in her uniform of choice, the pantsuit. Maybe it was also her drinking that kept the weight off. I had a cousin who had interned with her who said Peggy was a functioning alcoholic, but then again my young relative's lies-to-truth-telling ratio was materially greater than 50 percent.

The food I placed at their table dissolved before my very eyes, leaving behind only wood, bone and utensils.

"Don't worry, Jing-nan, I'll pay for everything," said Peggy. Her declaration sounded like a threat.

"Everything for you is free," I said. "You're my classmate." I turned to the cops and added, "It's always an honor to serve the police who serve us so well." I had nothing against Huang and Kung, but cops hadn't always been very nice to me. Peggy put on a cultivated expression of damaged honor.

"No, let me pay!" She rose from her seat and pointed both index fingers at me. "I am somebody who supports my class-mates in all their ventures!"

I heard Frankie cough. He was cleaning up the prep area. "Money," he barked just loud enough for me to hear.

Dwayne leaned over the counter to better display his tat-tooed biceps. Now it was time for him to pull his simpleton act. "We don't often have the pleasure to serve you, Peggy," he said. "Well, we don't know what to charge you, since we've only been giving you our leftovers and the mistake skewers that Jing-nan made. I'd say five hundred NTs should more than cover it."

Mistakes that I've made? I don't make mistakes. None of us did. Well, it was part of the setup for the payoff so all I could do was smile sheepishly.

"Done!" said Peggy. She slammed an NT$500 bill on the counter.

"Jing-nan," said Dwayne as he lifted a final tray of skewers to the counter, "if you'd be so good."

"Of course," I said, taking up the tray. As I set it down before Peggy, Kung and Huang, I said, "Well, it's looking like the night is coming to a close soon. I hope this is enough and you won't leave hungry."

Peggy leaned over to whisper in my ear. "I'm gonna go to the can now." Peggy ducked into Unknown Pleasures' most coveted night-market treasure: a private bathroom. I cringed as she slammed the door behind her.

I went back to the front of the stall and tried with mild success to entice the last few tourists around to buy our past-prime skewers. My phone buzzed in my front pocket. It was a text from Peggy.

—I DON'T TRUST THOSE COPS FOR SHIT. THEY THINK I'M A SUSPECT.

I looked over at both cops and smiled.

—THEY'RE TRYING TO HELP YOU, PEGGY.

—THEY BOTH HAVE ABORIGINAL HEADHUNTER BLOOD. I CAN TELL.

—ARE YOU BEING RACIST, PEGGY?

—DON'T WORRY, I'M DELETING THIS CONVERSATION. JUST WANTED TO LET YOU KNOW HOW I FELT.

—YOUR FEELINGS ARE CREEPY, PEGGY.

I put away my phone and felt it vibrate with some parting shot from Peggy, but I didn't bother to check it. More slyly this time, I checked out the cops again. Huang's face was in his phone while Kung's eyes wandered with no clear purpose. The cops didn't seem to be taking the kidnapping seriously. If they did, they'd be peeking around corners and kicking in doors, right?

Maybe keeping tabs on Peggy as a suspect really was their main purpose. I eased my way over to their table to see if

I could glean more from a casual conversation. Maybe if I understood them better, I'd be able to avoid running afoul of them.

"Say, Detectives Huang and Kung," I said as carelessly as possible, "it's none of my business, but shouldn't you guys be out running around, searching for the kidnappers?"

Kung's cheek scar pulsed red and her mouth clicked as she opened it only to snap, like a predatory fish: "It's being addressed right now."

I quickly counted my fingers and straightened up. "In any case, I welcome both of you to return to my tiny stand any time you're free because I'm sure you'll find Tong-tong soon. Right now, though, I know you're both having a tough night, so if there's anything else I can do to help, please let me know."

Huang looked up and regarded me with a measured look. "Thank you," he said.

I cleared my throat and decided to push things a bit, since they'd eaten here at a discount. "You both may also want to consider leaving me good reviews online," I said, drawing bemused looks from them. Well, I had to ask. I'm a businessman.

Peggy returned from the bathroom with a fresh coat of lipstick on.

"Where were you?" accused the male cop.

Peggy smiled sweetly. "I had to freshen up, jackass!"

Huang pointed at his partner's nose. "You're supposed to follow her into the bathroom!"

Kung raised an eyebrow. "And you're supposed to keep the station posted about our whereabouts." She raised the other eyebrow. "Before we change locations."

Huang's face and neck reddened. "I'm going to call it in right now, then."

"Let's do that, huh?"

Huang stood up and, after throwing an exasperated glance at me, walked off to make his call.

Peggy slid into a chair and asked me right across Kung's line of sight as if she weren't there: "Who do you think would want to kidnap my dad, Jing-nan?"

Kung knocked the table hard three times with her midfinger knuckles. "You are not supposed to talk about the case out in public, Peggy! You're putting your father in danger!" Peggy angled her head and stared directly at Kung's scar without an ounce of discretion.

"Jing-nan already knows what happened. He was on the call, Detective Kung." Her sentence dripped with condescension, as if she were talking to a child interested in police work. Kung ground her teeth as Peggy twirled her phone and continued. "The two guys who work here know, also."

Kung's shoulders collapsed in resignation. "They do?"

Frankie tapped his ring to coax a ride cymbal sound from the ventilation hood above the grill and called out, "Yes, we do."

Dwayne puffed out his chest and his T-shirt went taut. "Jing-nan told us about it, but we would have gotten the gist of it anyway from listening to his side of the phone conversation. No one's got any secrets here." Frankie kept tapping his ring, adding a touch of a jazzy Japanese noir film to the proceedings.

Kung rose and stared us all down even though she was the shortest one. Damn, this really was turning into a Japanese noir film. "All of you better keep your mouths shut." Her words were hardened rubber bullets. "If any of you compromise this case, I won't hesitate to throw you in jail!" Huang was trudging back toward Unknown Pleasures. "Everybody here knows what happened to Peggy's dad!" Kung notified him. Huang responded by raising an arm, anticipating someone would pass him the basketball.

"The case has been compromised in a big way," he said with a relieved sigh. "Everybody everywhere knows. It's out all over." Huang displayed his phone with one hand and in the other he clutched a frozen fruit drink he had procured on the sly from elsewhere in the night market.

The mobile version of the homepage of *The Daily Pineapple* screamed, "Tong-tong Abducted by Knife-Wielding Maniacs!"

Kung stomped her foot like a substitute elementary-school teacher who had been pushed to the limit and rubbed the back of her neck. "*Ma de*," she said. I knew female cops were tough, but it was the first time I heard one say "motherfucker." She was already breaking the female stereotype of flawless faces by not covering up the scar. Why not curse, too?

Huang put away his phone, sucked his drink and stared down at his nose. After he swallowed, he asked Kung, "What should we do now?"

Peggy spoke up. "Once again, the cops have failed to keep wraps on their investigation."

"Hey," I said. "Anybody at that banquet could've tipped off the *Pineapple*."

"Impossible," said Huang. "All those guests, including many dignitaries, were ordered to stay silent."

Peggy smoothed down her sleeves, brushing imaginary lint into the faces of Huang and Kung. "Do you at least have a list of suspects that you're tracking down?"

Huang's face hardened and his eyes iced over. "We do. And it's a long list."

"He must have a lot of enemies," I offered.

Peggy picked up the second-to-last skewer and pointed it

at me. "Everybody loves my father, Jing-nan. It sounds like you might have a problem with him, for some reason."

"I don't, but the people who rent booths in this area do. You know, your dad increased the rent by five percent last week. It doesn't bother me because we've been doing well, and we can absorb the cost, but a lot of people were pretty mad."

Kung pried open a leather-clad notebook. A pen appeared in her hand as suddenly, a venomous barb. "Who was mad, Jing-nan?"

"Uh, eh-everybody was," I stammered.

Huang gave me a death glare. "Eh eh?" A cruelly contemptuous smile spread across his face.

Kung's eyes opened with concern. She went into nice-cop mode. "Was there anybody who seemed unusually angry, Mr. Chen?" She was even addressing me formally.

"Not really," I offered. "Just the usual grumbling."

"What do Dwayne and Frankie think?" asked Huang. Dwayne was taken aback the cop knew his name. Frankie had no visible reaction. "Yeah, I got your names from the online reviews of this joint."

Frankie took a step forward and kept his hands at his side. "It's just like Jing-nan says. Nothing really out of the ordinary, officers. Most of the people who operate stalls here wouldn't have anything to do with a kidnapping. They're cowardly merchants by nature." Frankie dipped his head and appraised the floor tiles. They were all cowards except for us here, he meant to say.

Dwayne jerked his thumb at Frankie and nodded. "I agree two hundred percent with what the Cat said."

Huang clicked his tongue, shook his drink and turned back to me. "You've said Tong-tong has a lot of enemies, Mr. Chen. Who do you mean?"

He couldn't be serious. Maybe Huang was pissed that I

was on the line with the kidnapper. One thing I knew for sure was that if I didn't forcefully reject any suggestion that I knew anything about the kidnapping I could end up in an interrogation room. Again.

I've had bad experiences with cops in the past. I wanted Huang to know I wasn't soft, even if he didn't think much of the gun I had had pointed in my face.

"Hey, you don't need me to tell you who Tong-tong's enemies are," I said as I looked directly into his eyes, seeking the weaker man that surely was cowering somewhere inside. I stuck my right hand into my pants pocket and rolled it into a fist. I didn't need him to see my resolve. "Tong-tong is on the pro-unification bandwagon. He's a mainlander who talks a lot and loudly about how Taiwan is a part of China. So that doesn't exactly endear him to at least half of the people on the island."

Peggy dropped her empty stick on the tray with a clatter and picked up the last skewer. It's common courtesy to check with everybody at the table before taking the last of anything, but there was nothing common or courteous about Peggy. "Tong-tong always has a certain level of hate mail," she said of her father. "But like I told you cops earlier, there was nothing extraordinary recently and no real threats that the family didn't handle."

Interesting choice of words. Because the Lees were prominent mainlanders, they had strong ties with the military. Off-duty and retired air force and army guys often moonlighted as muscle for hire. Any time the Lees had protests at one of their construction sites, they'd break up relatively quickly.

As I contemplated this, something else bothered me. I thought about the kidnapper's demand. "Isn't it weird that they didn't want money?" I asked Peggy. "They kidnap one of Taiwan's richest men but they only want some plans for a chip."

Peggy nodded enthusiastically. "Yeah, I didn't know what the fuck that was about. A low-power chip sounds like something he might feasibly have, somewhere. He has a wide portfolio and not everything's monetized yet."

Huang hunched his shoulders. "It may not seem like it's about money on the surface, but it is. All crimes are based on money, in the end. These chip plans can be converted into cash if you know the right people to sell to. We'll see."

Kung scribbled something in her notebook and secreted it back into a pocket. "What did the commander say?" she asked Huang, checking if any clues floated to the surface.

"With the story out, he said we could use our discretion. For tomorrow."

"That is," Kung reasoned, "we're off the clock now?"

"Exactly," said Huang, hoisting his cup to get the last of his drink. "Actually, we've been off the clock."

Kung exhaled and turned to Peggy. "Well, boss, what do we do now?"

I also looked to Peggy, unsure what was happening.

She opened her mouth to mock me. "Don't be confused, Jing-nan," said Peggy. "The Lee family is hiring off-duty cops for our private security." To Kung and Huang, she said, "Let's all wash up and then you guys escort me home, if you would be so kind."

I guess military guys weren't the only ones who moonlighted.

CHAPTER 3

I met my girlfriend, Nancy, back at my apartment, which is about a five-minute walk from the Shilin Night Market if I cross against the light. It's not an amazing apartment, but it's close to work and it has what I need and more. I have a magnificent view of a poorly maintained neighborhood park. My landlord is an investment company, not a *jiaotou*, a local criminal, like my old landlord, so when something goes bust, a repair guy comes over to work on it, not a low-level hood on a probationary period.

Nancy was sitting on my couch, and by sitting I mean nearly sliding off, her bare feet against the coffee table's edge the only things preventing her ass from hitting my patchy living-room rug.

She had shoulder-length hair with the ends cut straight across, making her head look like a perfect sphere. Her ears stuck out on the sides of her broad and beautiful face. She was two years younger than me but decades ahead in terms of human achievement.

An overwashed and stretched-out Psychedelic Furs shirt, one of my castoffs, disguised her athletic build while declaring

"Love My Way." I did like the Furs, but by the time that single from their third album was released, they had already started losing what made them cool.

The television was tuned to the Meilidao cable news channel but was on mute, which was the best way to watch it if it had to be on. "Tong-tong Is Gone Gone!" scrolled across the top of the screen while real-estate listings scrolled across the bottom.

"I'm so glad you're back," she said with a sigh. "I've been waiting for the leftovers." Her feet nudged a bowl half-filled with rice that was waiting for me to top it with a heap of grilled meats and vegetables from Unknown Pleasures. Also splayed across the coffee table were the biology and biotech journals that Nancy read thoroughly and obsessively. I'm sure she knew more than many of her professors at Taida, which is Taiwan's top university. Nancy's the best asset in its biochemistry doctorate program, and they know it. Why else would the department make her the liaison for foreign undergraduate students if they didn't think she reflected well upon the school, Taipei and the country?

The genius was crankily hungry now, however, and all bets on her behavior were off.

"You don't have anything good in your fridge," she moaned. "How is that possible? Aren't you supposed to be a food guru or something?"

I slid in next to Nancy and put my right arm around her shoulders. "It's true, I don't have much food right now. You've caught me between personal shopping trips. But I have some bad news for you, honey. First of all, you know that that's Peggy's dad that's been kidnapped, right?"

Nancy stretched and pushed her shoulder into my armpit. "Yes, I know. Peggy's face keeps popping up every fifteen minutes when they do a slideshow of Tong-tong's family pictures."

"Well, Peggy and her police escorts came by late and they ate so much, I don't have any leftovers tonight."

Nancy retracted her legs and whirled her body around, slamming her knees into my side. In Taipei, being hungry and not having access to any good food was a serious emergency. "You didn't bring *anything*, Jing-nan? Nothing at all?"

I folded up my legs and placed them between us in a defensive move. "It's all gone. They were hungry because they were waiting so long at Peggy's office for a ransom demand from the kidnappers."

She drew a breath and shifted her jaw. "Ransom, huh?"

"Oh, shit, I shouldn't have said that."

Nancy's eyes rolled up and to the right as she picked up her bowl and took a mouthful of plain rice. I couldn't help but twitch. How can people eat rice with nothing? Texture's no good without taste.

"Do you want some soy sauce or sea salt on that, Nancy?"

"Nah, it doesn't matter, Jing-nan. This is just nervous eating now." She swallowed and took in a sharp breath. "How much money did they want? A million NTs? Or maybe a million American dollars?"

In her voice, I heard the fascination and apprehension of the United States. They reminded me of someone else, my old high-school girlfriend. Curiously, though, she had no qualms about going to the US for college like I did.

"That's the thing, Nancy," I said. "They didn't want money. Can you believe that? They want a chip design that they claimed Tong-tong had stored away. A special low-power chip."

Nancy chewed another spoonful of rice. "That could be worth a lot of money," she suggested. "If you own the patent and license something like that to an international company, it could bring in big money for years."

I couldn't help but rub my hands. "How much are we talking about?"

"A few million dollars. American dollars. Look at the royalties phone makers or even drug companies pay to license intellectual property. You get a patent on a whole new platform of technology that everybody ends up using, it could even be a billion dollars."

As rich as they were, Peggy's family didn't have that kind of money. There was something that felt wrong, though.

"Well, let's say the kidnappers manage to get the chip design. What company is going to pay to license stolen technology?"

Nancy rubbed her nose as a faraway look appeared in her eyes. She had entered a deep-think zone and it was a state from which she wasn't easily aroused—in any sense of that word. I focused on the television to wait it out—her processing of the information.

The sound was still muted, but I was able to pick up the timeline of events leading to the kidnapping from the pop-up text along the bottom of the screen. Tong-tong had just enjoyed a surf-and-turf dinner when Wang Lao-shi, his high-school teacher, was introducing him to speak. Wang's hair was completely white but it wasn't thin and the guy continued to wear it in a crew cut. The old man raised a hand and shook a finger at a smiling Tong-tong and noted that his old student was always the first to speak when a mistake had gone unnoticed in class. Even if the teacher had made the mistake. The room erupted in laughter at that remark because what sort of student would be dumb enough to correct a teacher in front of an entire class?

"Aha!" said Nancy as she slapped my shoulder. "I've figured it out!"

"Ow!" I said, rubbing the point of impact. "What have you come up with?"

"What if it's not a company that licenses the technology? What if it's the Chinese government?" She greedily shoved more rice into her mouth and talked through her food. "It's China, Jing-nan! It has to be!"

China. Taiwan's political arch-nemesis even though many of us shared common ancestry. Those ties are ancient history for most people. From the Chinese government's view, however, Taiwan was a toy that it desperately wanted to grab, and like a toddler, China would rather destroy it than let it get away.

"I hope you're wrong, Nancy," I said.

"I could be," she said, although the pull in the pitch of her voice said she was right. She worked her tongue around her teeth to loosen a stubborn grain of rice.

"Wait," I said. "One thing I don't understand. If the chip is already patented, how can anyone else steal it and expect other people to license it from them?"

"Is the chip patented?"

"I don't know."

"I'll bet it's not," said Nancy. "I'll bet someone offered Tong-tong some or all of the patent for money upfront."

"Well, they don't know Tong-tong," I said. "I don't even know him that well but I know he's too cheap to lay out cash like that." It took the guy a million years to repave the pedestrian walk in my area of the night market. Is there such a thing as waiting for a sale on asphalt?

Nancy ran a finger along her right eyebrow. "It's a little odd, the timing of this thing. Peggy's dad was supposed to come to Taida next week to announce a major donation."

"He didn't even go to Taida," I scoffed. I didn't attend the school either, but I loved someone who did. I could've probably gotten in, too.

With the back of her hand, Nancy rolled a stray rice grain from her chin into her mouth. "Anybody can give money to the school. You don't have to be an alumnus. You don't even have to be a good person."

A few years ago, the CEO of a Taiwanese company that made parts for the Apple iPhone referred to his factory workers as "animals" that were a "headache" to manage. He had been donating hundreds of millions of NTs to Taida—right in biomedical engineering, Nancy's field. She had considered not taking any of the research money, but in the end she chose to be agnostic about it.

I support every choice my girlfriend makes in life. Every single one. But I don't think I personally could've taken that guy's money. Well, my fake night-market alter ego Johnny could. I slip into that guy every night and he doesn't take offense to anybody bearing money. Actually, there's one thing I definitely couldn't do, no matter what persona I slipped on. I couldn't call my workers animals. Dwayne would probably break me in half. If I ever made a truckload of money, I wouldn't let it go to my head.

I imagined what it was like to be rich, as rich as the Lees. Once you had all that wealth, how could you be so insecure that you had to put people down as "animals"? At least Tong-tong was hesitant in speech, as Confucius instructed. Not that I admired Confucian ideals. No one followed them to the letter, but the man's teachings sure seemed to be profound when taken piecemeal and out of context. The devil could cite Confucius to his purpose, after all.

My hand came across a rice grain on the couch and I palmed it. Nancy really must be hungry. She wasn't usually a sloppy eater but now rice was going all over the place.

I chucked the rice grain in the general direction of the kitchen sink and was rewarded with a ping sound as it struck the metal. "Is Taida going to name a building or an autonomous car after Tong-tong?"

"He was planning to establish fellowships for eight students to study and do anthropology research in China. I found out about it from my friends in the student council. They have sources in the president's office. They're all so gossipy."

I cracked my neck. The fellowship was the kind of thing that was a headache for the national consciousness.

A large part of the population, particularly the *waishengren*, the mainlanders, who were predominantly in the northern part of the island, believes that Taiwan is a part of China and should eventually join the motherland, one way or another.

Others, including many *benshengren*, people of Chinese descent whose ancestors had moved to Taiwan centuries ago, feel that Taiwan had separated from China in antiquity, and is an island nation in its own right.

Then there are the Hakka, people of Chinese descent who could be mainlanders, *benshengren* or a combination. Their identity is a cultural one, not ethnic, and Hakka have their own customs and language whose origins are obscured by the passage of centuries and the many migrations of their history.

Meanwhile, Taiwan's indigenous people, of both officially recognized and unrecognized tribes, want the *waishengren* and *benshengren* to stop developing on their ancestral lands.

Lost in the mix are the newer immigrants from Vietnam, Indonesia and Burma, and the Southeast Asian brides introduced to Taiwanese men through marriage brokers. These men have typically had a hard time meeting a potential mate because they aren't upwardly mobile enough to attract the women who will indulge them in their misogynistic fantasies.

I'll bet Tong-tong never had a problem like that.

TONG-TONG'S FINANCING OF A Taida fellowship to study in China could be seen as a soft-power move to reinforce ties with The People's Republic. Tong-tong was the ideal tool of the Chinese Communist Party: A charismatic and filthy rich Taiwanese from a mainlander family who could smooth out public apprehension at closer ties and eventual reunification.

But those attributes also made Tong-tong the perfect target for Taiwan-independence-minded kidnappers.

I pumped my left leg in excitement. "Nancy, who knew that Tong-tong was going to donate money to your school?"

Nancy chewed thoughtfully. "A few students, the administrators and I guess Tong-tong himself and the people who run his foundation."

"Let me guess. This anthropology research will only reveal more cultural ties between the people of China and Taiwan." There are often reports in media outlets run by mainlanders that Taiwanese customs have their origins in Chinese culture. That's as ridiculous as saying that American traditions have their roots in Great Britain; everybody knows Americans drink coffee, not tea.

Nancy pulled a few strands of hair behind her ears and let them slip out. "I don't think there are restrictions on what people can study and conclude. Otherwise it wouldn't be honest research."

I rubbed my right ear. "Maybe Tong-tong's upcoming donation is a clue."

"Jing-nan, you should probably tell the cops. They should know."

"You're right." I knew where I could find at least two.

I called Peggy. As the phone rang I watched Nancy lope off to the kitchen. She scooped the rest of the rice out of the bowl and into the garbage.

"Hello, Jing-nan," said Peggy. I heard the television in the background and it was the audio to our muted station. "Did you have a sudden realization or something?"

"You know I never get those, Peggy. Is Huang on the line, too?"

"Yes, I am, Mr. Chen," he grunted.

"Well, I just heard that Tong-tong was going to announce some Taida fellowships to China." I heard a tinkling sound coming from my kitchen. Nancy was shaking corn flakes into her emptied bowl. Then she jerked open the fridge and grabbed a carton of mango-flavored milk.

"Hmm," said Huang.

"This is news to me," said Peggy. "Not that he would tell me about it. What are the specifics?"

"He was going to sponsor students to study anthropology. In your homeland, Peggy."

"It's your homeland, too, Jing-nan. If you only admitted the truth to yourself." She sighed. "You heard this from Nancy?"

"I did."

She gave a satisfied grunt before talking because she had me all figured out. "Hey, Huang?"

"Yes."

"Jing-nan must have heard this from his girlfriend, Nancy, who is some Taida superstar. My dad might have just floated the idea to see what sort of response he would get. Maybe he was fishing for an honorary degree from Taida or trying to get them to name a campus lake after him. He went to Ohio State in America, and even though he did well there, it's not a real prestigious degree to have in your bio."

"It's no New York University," I said, citing Peggy's alma mater.

"No, it's not," she sang back. "It's no UCLA, either. Huang, did you know that Jing-nan went to UCLA?"

"Oh, yeah?" asked the cop without a trace of interest.

"I didn't graduate. Well, that doesn't matter, anyway. What about the Taida thing, Huang. Does it interest you at all?"

He inhaled slowly. "This is new information. I don't know if it's useful."

Nancy returned to the couch, and I angled away from her cereal-crunching sounds. "Despite what Peggy says, Taida took the offer seriously," I said. "The students are already chatting about it."

"The guy talks a lot of shit, Jing-nan," said Peggy, almost exasperated. "Especially when there aren't cameras in his face. His mouth is like an old hair dryer."

Huang grunted lightly. "I'll have some of our people look into it. I'm sure one of the boys or girls could give some attention to this." I hoped he meant lower-level cops rather than high-school interns.

"Thank you. Peggy, I feel terrible about your father. I hope we get him back soon."

I heard her suck in her lips. "Thank you, Jing-nan. I'm not really that worried. I'm sure he'll be rescued, one way or another." She was trying hard but her voice wavered. "Listen. Jing-nan, your food was really good tonight. Have you ever thought about opening a real restaurant?"

I stretched my legs. Was she trying to annoy me? "Unknown Pleasures is a real restaurant."

"You know what I mean. Being in the night market is, well, kinda scuzzy. You should have a nice, big place with banquet rooms and everything! Do you know how many famous people you could be rubbing shoulders with?"

"I already have Nancy to rub my shoulders." Nancy looked at me and raised an eyebrow.

Peggy clucked her tongue. "I'm glad I'm not in a relationship. It robs you of your ambition! Huang, are you married?"

"Yes."

"Are you happy?"

"Yes."

"Well, you probably don't spend much time with your wife, as a cop. That's why you're happy."

Huang gave a warning laugh. "Say whatever you want. You're paying me to be here."

It was time to go. I had gotten the Taida info to the police and subjected myself to Peggy's annoyances. With those tasks done, I said good night and hung up.

"Did I hear that you wanted a shoulder rub?" asked Nancy.

"I wouldn't mind one."

She formed a pair of chopsticks with her index and middle finger and made like she was eating something out of the bowl with them.

Of course Nancy was still hungry even after the cereal.

"I get you food and then you give me a shoulder rub?" I asked. She nodded.

I left the apartment, jogged around the corner to the nearest Family Mart and scooped out a passable bowl of beef noodles from the hot bar. Who knows how many hours the noodles had sat in hot water? A chef should never treat a starch like that. Then again, anyone who considered himself or herself a chef wouldn't work at Family Mart.

As I was paying, I overheard a snippet of conversation from a straight couple in their early twenties, immersed in their respective phones at an eat-in table.

"Did you hear about Tong-tong?" the man gasped with his mouth full of food.

"Yeah, I did," muttered the woman. "Fuck that prick. He got what he deserved."

"Still, it's embarrassing for Taiwan."

The woman smacked her lips in contempt. "He should

have thought about that before he started throwing his money around for the Double-Nine holiday. What a publicity hound."

I turned my head but couldn't bring myself to walk away just yet. I thought I could say something like, "Hey, I'm classmates with his daughter and you're being incredibly disrespectful." But confronting strangers won't do in Taiwan. Here, you can only tell off people close to you. On the way out I waved to them to get their attention, and then nodded. Let them wonder what it meant.

When I returned to the apartment, Nancy bounded off the couch and confronted me even before I had both shoes off. "Oh, thank you so much, Jing-nan!"

I held the bag up, out of her reach. "Well, hold on, now. How are you going to compensate me for getting you this food? I sorta went through hell for this, after all."

She strutted to the couch, ran her fingers through her hair and delicately put her feet back on the coffee table. "I will allow you to feed me, little boy." Nancy opened her mouth comically wide and clapped her hands in a call for service. I could only comply.

IN THE EARLY MORNING we showered off the crust accumulated from sleep and sex. It was a little after 5 A.M., but no sleeping in today for either of us. Nancy had to do some lab work and I was hitting the day market.

We dressed in front of the TV. There wasn't anything new in the Tong-tong coverage. His photos cycled through the screen, the same treatment given to newly dead celebrities. Tong-tong looked triumphant and only a little smug in each one, whether declaring a vow at his wedding, walking as one of the bearers of Mazu's statue in the birthday pilgrimage of Taiwan's top Taoist goddess (another bearer, behind Tong-tong, was the vice president of Taiwan), or sitting courtside at a Los Angeles Lakers home game.

As I did a standing breaststroke into a tank top, I thought about that couple back at the Family Mart. I could see how they could casually dismiss Tong-tong. He had money. He was comfortable. He was worthy of contempt by those who were stumbling at the yoke end of our country's gross domestic product.

Taiwan's economy was sputtering along and the job market sucked for my generation of twenty-somethings. We were a people born in the years following the Tiananmen Square crackdown, and for the most part we wondered what we could possibly have in common with the government and events in China, which is what many non-businessmen in Taiwan regard as a foreign and hostile country.

That mindset didn't stop people from going to China to try to find jobs. Didn't the Beatles have to go to Hamburg, Germany, to get decent gigs when they were starting out? If your parents were mainlanders and if you had no problem using "Taiwan Compatriot" forms of identification (China doesn't recognize Taiwan passports), you could. Australia was another destination for young people. Supposedly you could make more waiting tables in Sydney than sentencing yourself to a sixty-hour workweek in a Taipei office cubicle with no paid overtime.

I was fairly lucky. Well, as lucky as an orphan could get. Yes, my parents were dead, and yes, I never got to finish my degree at UCLA. But look what I had. My own apartment, for starters, which was a big deal because most young people in Taiwan unfortunately lived with their parents until they were married. Sure, I had to pay rent, but think of all the money Nancy and I were saving by not paying for a love hotel on a regular basis.

I had my own business, too, the old family stand, and we were kicking ass. I created food and got paid for it. Quite a bit, at times. Locals may not like the Shilin Night Market because its offerings run too touristy, but the work-alter ego I have cultivated for myself loves the foreigners. Johnny loves hearing their stories, fielding their questions about Taiwan and all Asians in general, and giving prefab answers about his personal history—all up until they pay and for maybe a minute after, depending on the size of the ticket.

The real me is an introvert willing to engage with strangers with little else apart from the topics of proto-punk, punk and post-punk bands of the 1960s through the 1990s.

I will talk to anybody wearing a Joy Division shirt, no matter how damaged and/or deranged they look. We'll light up to talk about our favorite band and debate which of the studio albums were better, *Unknown Pleasures* or *Closer*. I loved the debut album enough to name my stand after it. Maybe Peggy was right. Maybe I should think about opening a big restaurant and naming it "Closer." Then again, that sounds like "close," as in my restaurant could do badly and close. Certainly it was an ill-omened name.

I've already committee a major faux pas by naming my business after a Joy Division album. One aspect about the band that I loved was that they shied away from anything that could be even remotely construed as commercial. They didn't put their name on the front cover of their albums and their individual names or pictures didn't appear anywhere. The pre-Internet listener of the early '80s had no idea who they were or what they looked like.

That was cool.

Then again, I had read in bassist Peter Hook's autobiography that they all had gotten screwed out of money. Actually, they continued to be screwed because the band's members had signed contracts they hadn't read, much less understood, and had missed out on millions. Surely, that was no way to conduct oneself in business, even if it gave you a superhighway of street cred.

I wasn't one to talk about pure artistry. I sort of sold myself out by assuming my Johnny persona, but I hadn't gone further with it. Would it be egregious to take the celebrity chef route and open a place nice enough to have candles on the tables, the kind of place with ambiance, where a person might pop the question? I couldn't ask Nancy to marry me in the clammy confines of Unknown Pleasures, could I?

Nancy closed the pearl snaps on her blouse and the sharp sounds jolted me out of my anxieties thought piece. I actually twitched. Then I felt ashamed about being selfish in my thoughts, wondering if I was cool enough while my old classmate's father had been kidnapped.

"Are you all right, Jing-nan?"

"I'm just a little shaken up about Tong-tong." That was true.

She touched my shoulder. "We're all worried about him. He was trying to do a good thing, too, for the elderly on the holiday." She sighed with a measure of futility. "Tonight I have to write something for our department website about the Double Ninth. How our research is connected with respect for our elders."

"Shit," I said. "Why do you have to write garbage like that?"

Nancy raised an eyebrow as she adjusted her belt. "My advisor wants it online with a special acknowledgement to Best Therapeutics for supporting our department."

I waited a few moments. "You don't have any recent Double Ninth experiences to draw from."

She evaluated what I said. "I don't."

"When do you think you're going to see your mom and the rest of your family?"

Nancy looked into the corners of the room. "It's not entirely up to me. Anyway, what families don't cut each other off for a few years?"

"Or a few decades."

"It hasn't been that long."

"I wasn't talking about you in particular," I said, reaching down to scratch my knee. "I was just saying, you know, some people are like that."

She nodded. "I know. This thing I'm writing, though, it's more like a service piece to thank the drug company for its support under the guise of the holiday."

"What holiday are you going to soil in order to thank Tong-tong for his donation?"

She tucked her shirt into her slacks. "I would never do that. I don't want anything bad to happen to him, but I would draw the line at thanking him. At least Best Therapeutics is saving lives, so it's more than just a business."

Did Tong-tong ever save someone's life? Probably not. A Buddhist would say, maybe that's why his life was in danger now.

Wait, did I ever save anyone's life? I sort of saved Dwayne and Nancy, but actually it was Frankie who saved all of us in the end. I wondered if it would come down to Frankie saving Tong-tong. No way. The cops would handle this one.

Nancy was already dressed. "I'll be back here before you." She kissed my forehead. "This time, bring back food."

I shoved a few cloth bags into the biggest one. "You're still mad about me not bringing leftovers last night?" I asked.

She dismissed me by tousling my hair. "Don't be silly. If I were mad, I wouldn't even be talking to you."

CHAPTER 4

We caught the first MRT train just after six in the morning at the nearby Jiantan station and rode south with sleepy business people who had sleep-inducing real jobs. Four stops later Nancy had to transfer to get to Taida.

"Watch yourself," I said. I gave her a little shoulder wipe as she left. Taiwanese frown upon public displays of affection. That's why she kissed me back at the apartment. We didn't even hold hands in public. Why would anybody? Two people walking close together already meant they were in love. No need to spell everything out to the general public and embarrass yourself, your parents and your ancestors. You never knew who was looking and who would gossip about it, after all.

I transferred two stops later to get to the Gongguan Day Market.

The day market is held in the same blocks as the Gongguan Night Market, which in all honesty is a half-decent enterprise, even if it can't hold a fried drumstick and thigh to the Shilin Night Market. The day market, with all the fresh produce, is where the action's at.

My strategy at the day market is to walk through every block before buying anything. It's the best way to find the lowest prices and also the most interesting things on offer. A guy can only carry so much, after all.

A while ago, before I'd taken my vow to be circumspect, I'd regrettably filled my bags with mundane but good produce before coming upon the sexiest small pumpkins I'd ever seen. They would have looked beautiful cooked, bursting with orange and branded with grill marks. On social media, these pumpkins would have racked up their own fan page. The vegans—and there were more of them every damned month—would have loved them. Strangely, the vegan tourists all seemed to be rich. Maybe they were saving a bunch of money from not eating meat or buying leather goods.

I stood at the curb to fortify myself mentally before I entered the day market. I took a deep breath and said to no one and nothing in particular, "Please let me find something great." It was the closest I ever came to praying with sincerity, since I didn't believe in any of Taiwan's legions of goddesses and gods. I used to think less of people who knelt down before these idols and asked for help. Now I know that they are only seeking comfort and there's nothing wrong with that.

My own "prayer" is really meant to address my subconscious and encourage my creative process. Seriously. I mean, once in a while, the image of my high-school girlfriend flashes through my head, but apart from that, there are no otherworldly presences in my life. She's dead now, after all, and the dead don't come back.

I rubbed my hands in anticipation and strolled to the first two stalls. I noticed that buckets of chrysanthemums adorned nearly every corner. What better way to celebrate the Double Ninth than to wear flowers and decorate the home with them?

I heard a rattling and focused on Buddhist beads dancing on a woman's wrist as she sliced lotus root for samples. The scene gave me an epiphany.

I should offer a vegan option every night.

Unknown Pleasures could be highlighted by travel blogs as a joint that has vegan fare. It could be a whole new revenue stream.

I had to find something inspiring for the stall's first vegan offering. Something distinctive. Something great. Something that could be liked and shared infinitely online. Nothing's dumber or more tasteless than random vegetables spiked on a skewer. I needed something to really stand out.

Broccoli? Blah. Cauliflower? Double blah. Could I do something with spinach? Nah. It cooks down to soggy clumps. Useless and ugly.

I picked up a bundle of asparagus and tapped my fingers on the tips. Still fresh. Asparagus doesn't last long once harvested. I liked the shape of the vegetable. They are the noble columns of the palaces of the plant kingdom.

The vendor, a man in his mid-forties, ambled over to me and pushed back his Yankees baseball cap. "I just cut them this morning. My best crop ever. These asparaguses are good enough to offer to the gods!" Whoa, guy, let's not overdo it. Don't make me rethink this purchase before we even begin to bargain.

I saw a boy, no older than ten, sitting on a crate, bundling asparagus and snapping rubber bands around them. He was already in his school uniform and probably did this every day before classes. I was like that kid, only I had had to help in the night market after school, and I hadn't been able to keep my uniform as clean.

The boy was eating something with relish. It wasn't candy. Every few seconds, he'd pick up a piece of fruit that looked like a light-brown apple and take a huge bite. What was it? I gingerly put down the asparagus bundle.

"What's that your son is eating?" I asked. "It looks like something really good and special."

The vendor smiled but his eyes narrowed. "Everything I have is special, what are you talking about?"

"I rarely see kids eat anything but junk food. While I'm sure you're forcing him to work with you, he appears to be happily eating something voluntarily. Tell me what it is." The boy smiled mischievously behind his father's back.

The vendor ran his tongue over his teeth and sighed through his nostrils. "I have some really good spinach you might want to look at. It's great in soups and so nutritious."

"Ah, spinach isn't going to work for me." I glanced down at the asparagus bundle again. Now that I had lost interest in them, they resembled a bundle of crooked green crayons.

The boy spoke up.

"Dad, why don't you sell him the jujubes? They're better than you think."

The man turned to his son. "I don't think this guy cares about that."

The jujube is a fruit that comes in many shapes and sizes. Some are grown to be dried for tea. Some are eaten fresh.

The sort of jujube that I was most familiar with was the green jujube that resembled a Granny Smith apple only it was sweet and had an olive-like pit. Also, it was way too early in the year for them to be harvested. They usually don't show up until December.

"What kind of jujubes are these?" I asked.

"They are a new variety they experimented with down in Kaohsiung. They're ripe, but they're too sweet for me, even though the kid likes them." He pulled his cap back down to cover part of his face. "I made a bad trade."

"Can I try one?" I asked.

The man peered at me to see if I was serious before handing me one from under the counter. "If you want to spit it out, use a garbage can, not the street," he warned. "There's no spitting allowed at the market."

It was the same size and shape as a green jujube but the skin was a purpled chocolate color.

I took a bite. The smooth skin snapped and a syrupy film coated my lips and tongue. It really was way too sweet, but I chewed through the entire fruit. It was still fibrous enough to be grilled. Then the sugary glaze that it yielded would be even better with something to enhance the taste and texture. I had to figure out what I would add, but first I had to have those jujubes.

"How many of these have you got?" I asked.

The vendor was knocked back. He couldn't believe his fortune and/or my stupidity. "Xiao Ping," he respectfully addressed his son, since he was the one who had spurred the sale. "Bring those jujubes over here."

The boy swung to his feet and lugged over two tied-up burlap sacks one by one. Xiao Ping stood them up against a box of untrimmed asparagus.

Seeing the sacks leaning against each other, I thought about Tong-tong and the other guy who had been kidnapped. I wondered if the cops were as attentive to the other man's family as they were to Peggy. Or was he expendable?

I untied the two sacks and pulled out two from as deep as I could reach. I sniffed them for good measure. The jujubes were comparable with the one I had.

"How many have you eaten?" I asked Xiao Ping.

The boy cautiously glanced at his father and then looked me right in the eye. "Five," he said.

"Were they all good?" He nodded. "I'll bet you can eat

some more." He looked worried as I handed him two more. "Don't worry," I told his father. "These two are on me."

I LUGGED THE SACKS through the market, thinking that maybe I had overpaid for the jujubes, and I certainly didn't have to buy all of them. Once again, I had been too impulsive. Maybe I saw the boy and had projected my life broadly upon his. Maybe that had been the plan and I had been played like a sucker.

Now I had enough fruit for a few nights of vegan skewers and then some. If the jujube specials crashed and burned, then there'd be plenty left for Nancy and me to snack on.

I trudged on through the market. I noticed some people reading newspapers with Peggy's dad on the cover. "Where Is Tong-tong?" the *World News* plaintively asked. It was paired with a photo of the man laughing.

I pressed on, picking up scallions, parsley, onions, garlic and some secret ingredients. I worried about Tong-tong and felt worse and worse about the jujubes. Maybe I shouldn't have bought any at all.

Shit. Second-guessing myself again. I should think positive thoughts.

Surely there were nutritional properties of the jujube that I could freely expound upon and exaggerate. People love to eat things with health benefits.

I walked by a woman casually flaying pineapples with a machete as long as her forearm. She ended each motion with a flick that gave each spiny rind flap just enough power to wing into a mesh bag strung open at the end of the table like a net.

My thoughts again turned to Tong-tong. How much danger was he in? Would his kidnappers really execute him as they'd threatened to if it came down to it?

If I could do something to help Peggy's father, I would. She hasn't always been the greatest person in the world to me, but she had never really hurt me.

Peggy might even be a real friend. We were certainly close enough to yell and scream at each other.

We were also probably close enough relationship-wise for her to sic one of the cops on me. I was blithely unaware, as I breathed my jujube breath, that I was about to be accosted on my way to the train station from the day market.

DETECTIVE HUANG CAME UP from behind and grabbed at the bag handles I had in my right hand. I fought him for a few seconds until I recognized him. He looked happier than I had remembered.

"What the hell are you doing?" I asked as I let go. The cop staggered back as he tried to balance the five bags. The jujube sacks had to be 10 kilograms each.

"*Ma de*, is this how you keep in shape? You should thank me, Mr. Chen, for helping you carry these. Well, you should thank Peggy. We're going to give you a ride back to your apartment. C'mon." He stalked off.

As I followed him, I looked to the curb and saw a black stretch sedan. That was Peggy's chauffeured company car.

I considered making a run for the MRT, but I needed that produce that Huang had walked off with. Besides, if I could help Peggy, I wanted to.

I followed Huang to Peggy's car. As we drew closer, the trunk door majestically lifted like a giant clam yielding its pearl to a sea god in dragon form. Huang stowed away all my bags quickly but with care, a skill likely derived from handling live weaponry. "This looks and smells great, Mr. Chen. You have a real talent at picking the best ingredients. I can see why your food is so good and I appreciate the trouble you go through."

That was the nicest thing a cop had ever said to me. I reached in and loosened one of the burlap sacks.

"Please call me Jing-nan," I told Huang. "You've already helped me carry my stuff, so you're a friend now. Go ahead and grab a bunch of jujubes. Take as many as you want."

"Isn't it a little early in the year for them?" said Huang as he scooped one up and cautiously held it at arms length. "Or maybe it's too late in the year. What's up with the color? Why are they brown? Are these diseased or something?"

"It's a new variety that's been bred to be especially sweet," I said. Man, I was fast when I was trying to sell food. "Take a bite."

"I trust you," he said. "I'll eat 'em in the car."

Like Buddha, the man could hold an infinite number of items in his hands, and he made full use of the crooks of his arms. How had he managed to snag a dozen of them? I heaved the trunk shut for him.

"Thank you," said Huang.

I caught a jujube as it slipped out of his embrace. "I can hold more for you," I said.

"I'm good," he said.

A door next to the curb popped open. Huang gestured for me to enter first. I pulled out the door, all the way, ducked down and stepped in. Peggy and Kung were sitting in the back seat. "Good morning, ladies," I said as I shimmied like a crab and dropped on the shorter side seat. "This is for you," I said to Kung. I showed her the jujube before tossing it to her.

"What the hell is this?" she asked as she handed it to Peggy.

"It's a new kind of jujube," I said.

Kung frowned. "What's wrong with the color?" Peggy displayed no curiosity in the fruit at all and handed it back to Kung.

"It's a new variety," Huang gurgled with his mouth already full of mashed jujube. He dumped the jujubes into an empty magazine holder and sat next to me with a satisfied grunt.

Kung turned the jujube carefully over in her hands as if she was searching for a port to plug in a USB cable. I turned to Peggy, who crossed her arms and craned her neck at an odd angle to emphasize how disappointed she was with me.

"It would be so easy to kidnap you, Jing-nan," Peggy sighed. "You live your life on such a predictable schedule!"

I shrugged and lay back as the car eased out. "How did you know I'd be here?" I asked. "You've never been out shopping with me."

"You put up pictures of what you picked up from the day market on the Unknown Pleasures page on Facebook. I know you go to Gongguan because you told me it was your favorite. Based on the timing of the pictures, I figured you leave the market around nine in the morning and head back to your apartment to take pictures and post them."

Satisfied, Peggy took the jujube from Kung and bit into it. Her expression registered only that Peggy was pleased with herself, and didn't reflect how the fruit tasted.

I was still blocking Peggy on Facebook from my personal account, but I couldn't stop her from viewing my business page.

"Listen," I told her. "I don't go to that market every day. Anyway, if someone wanted to kidnap me, they could just show up at work or come in the middle of the night to my apartment."

Kung put her elbows back. "We stopped by your place this morning, but you weren't there. You wouldn't open up your stand until nighttime, but Peggy knew where you probably were."

Huang covered his mouth with a tissue and spat a pit into

it. Kung pointed at the pile of jujubes and he tossed over two of them to her in rapid succession.

"Don't get any juice on my goddamned car," snapped Peggy, even though some jujube juice was leaking down her wrists.

"We're professionals, Peggy," Huang said. Was that some spittle I felt? I edged slightly away from the detective.

"If you guys wanted to find me," I said, "you could've called. We could've just talked on the phone."

"We didn't want to make you worry," said Kung. "We figured we'd let you go about your routine and then interrupt you after you shopped." She rubbed a jujube across her left sleeve to clean it and took a healthy bite before her face took on a mildly grim expression. All three of them looked that way.

What did they want from me? Was I possibly a suspect or something? Maybe I had said something that wasn't positive about Tong-tong a while ago to Peggy, and she had turned it over and over in her mind, making something out of nothing.

I had mentioned that her father was greedy for raising the rent. In the past I had said mainlanders should all go back to China. When we were in elementary school, she had given me a jade pendant as a token of her affection, but I handed it back almost immediately. I didn't think it was wrong for me to take it, but I didn't want it. It was ugly, one of those hybrid fish-turning-into-a-dragon things. She hadn't said a word and only glared at me, but maybe a part of her still resented me for that.

The car slowed and stopped at a red light. Kung and Huang leaned over to each other for a private conference. An inquisitive look came over Peggy's face as she mimed holding a cup and tilting it back. I shook my head but raised my empty hands in a gesture that asked, "What am I doing here?" She held up an open palm to me, signaling that I needed to wait.

The light changed and the car went ahead. We seemed to be heading toward my apartment so I played it cool and bided my time. I wasn't under arrest or wanted for questioning, was I?

The cops had ended their tête-à-tête and Huang was now writing something down in his notebook. An inventory of everything I had in my bags? Questions for an upcoming session with a lie detector? Kung stared hard into my eyes as she chewed.

Despite her earlier warning to her fellow passengers to keep the car clean, Peggy dropped her jujube pit on the floor and recklessly tore off the paper wrap of a package of haw flakes, a snack made from dehydrated and processed hawthorn berries. They are sort of like the Pringles of Asia.

Peggy ripped out one of the thin disks from the package and held it out to me. Purple haw crumbs scattered everywhere.

"No thanks, Peggy," I said.

She flipped it into her mouth. "Suit yourself."

I turned to Huang and Kung. "Can one or both of you tell me why you've picked me up?" I asked.

Peggy licked her fingers and worked out another haw flake. "Should I play him the message?" she asked.

Kung held up a hand. "There's no need, we'll just tell him what it said. Tong-tong managed to leave a short message on Peggy's phone earlier this morning. We weren't able to take the actual call because the ringer was off despite several reminders to keep it on."

Peggy grunted with contempt. "Turning it off before going to sleep is a routine action for everybody. You can't blame me when you should've double-checked."

Kung, without looking at Peggy, resumed. "Tong-tong said that a certain man had the chip design the kidnappers were looking for."

Huang picked up a jujube and held it to his crotch before speaking up. "We've sent our hacking unit after the man's email and phone records. They came up with nothing. Well, nothing directly related to the case." The tentative tones in their voices and their distracted glances at the floor made me uncomfortable.

"If you know the man, why don't you bring him in for questioning?" I asked. "He's not dead, is he?"

Kung let out a small laugh. "No, he's not dead. He's incarcerated at Taipei Prison at the moment." People doing hard time for murder and high-profile financial shenanigans were locked up there. It had originally been built by our Japanese rulers during Taiwan's colonial years in the first half of the 20th century, so you knew it had to be a serious place to serve out a sentence.

"We won't be able to reach him in a timely manner," said Huang. "The corrections department gets bureaucratic with the police when white-collar criminals are involved. They want everything by the book. Warrants, court orders and all."

Kung rolled two jujubes in her left hand in a meditative action that I found impressive. "We were thinking that maybe you, Mr. Chen . . ."

"Again, please, call me Jing-nan," I said. "We're already close enough to share car rides and fruit."

"Okay, Jing-nan, we were thinking that maybe you would want to go visit this man and ask him where the chip design is. It would help us so much."

"This is a pretty high-profile case," I said. "The prison wouldn't want to help out the cops?" I asked.

"Lemme put this way," said Huang. "A lot of people in the corrections department are people who wanted to be cops but didn't make it, so they resent us. Yeah, it is a big case, but it also means they would want to assist us even less. They want us to look badly in the public's eye." He cleared his throat. "We need a civilian, like you."

I pressed my shoulders into the back of my seat. So they needed my help. I wasn't so sure I was ready to be generous.

"You mean you want me to pose as a visitor and get him to tell me where the plans are? Sure, I could do that. I'd do anything to help Peggy. But tell me, why do you want me in particular to go see this guy? Because you trust me so much with this information?"

"We do trust you Jing-nan," said Huang. "We know you'll go the extra distance to help Peggy."

"We wouldn't want to send just anybody into this jail," said Kung.

"The guy in jail is Nancy's former sugar daddy, Ah-tien!" blurted Peggy.

I felt my scalp tingle. Nancy had been a mistress to Ah-tien when she was an undergraduate. She was poor and he was an executive at a tech company. He had rained money on her before going to jail for bribing government officials to buy his company's laptops for Taipei's public schools. Nancy had described him as "a nice guy."

"Fuck that motherfucker!" I yelled. Kung gave me an admonishing smile that a school nurse wears for a kid who was sick because he hadn't done what she had told him to. "Peggy, your father had some business dealings with that loser?"

Peggy tossed another haw flake into her mouth. "I looked over my father's notes. Ah-tien really had approached my father, looking for an intellectual-property licensing deal or a joint venture. Things didn't work out in the end, and my father doesn't have the actual chip design in his files."

Kung chimed in. "Ah-tien had a mobile phone that he only used to call Nancy. A line with only one contact means either spying or an affair."

"Turns out, it was the latter," said Huang.

"No shit," I said. "Listen, guys, I'm not going to see that piece of shit unless I can slam a brick on his head."

We all swayed as the car turned onto an exit ramp. Peggy tapped her foot on the floor. "I already know there's no way that Nancy would want to go see him, so I'm asking you as an old classmate to go visit Ah-tien in order to help my father." Peggy touched my shoulder in a rare act of reaching out for compassion. "And you did say you'd do anything to help me and my father, right? I am begging you, Jing-nan. Help. My. Father."

How else could I respond?

"*Gan!*" I yelled. "Okay! I'll go!"

"You don't have to tell Nancy," Peggy suggested.

"I'm going to tell her," I threw back defiantly. I didn't need her relationship advice.

"Good."

"Very good," said Kung.

"Thank you very much, Jing-nan," said Huang. "We all really appreciate your service to your country because that's what this is."

"I don't know how I'll do it, but I'll manage," I said. "Anything else that you'd want me to do would probably be much easier. Is there anything else I could do instead? Anything?"

Kung's eyes flashed. "Maybe there is another thing you can do. I mean, not instead, but in addition to the jail visit." She leaned forward and pointed a blood-painted fingernail at my heart. "We know you have a family member involved in organized crime, Jing-nan."

"Allegedly involved," I said. My statement neither confirmed nor denied what I knew about my uncle.

Kung continued. "You have an uncle named Big Eye. He might know something about the kidnapping because he's actually met Peggy before. Am I understanding this correctly?"

Peggy stuffed haw flakes in her mouth and rolled her eyes to the ceiling.

Goddammit, what had she told them about my gangster uncle?! Well, her father's life was hanging in the balance, so maybe I should cut her a break. She had to tell them everything and explore every avenue.

I opened my arms to Kung to indicate that I was going to be completely forthcoming, as well. "Yes, I have an uncle named Big Eye who knows some *heidaoren* people. Of course he isn't involved in the underworld himself. He's a legitimate businessman." Peggy stifled a guffaw. "And, yes, he's met Peggy before, but he hasn't had any contact, for personal or business reasons, with her family since."

Peggy crumpled the haw flakes wrapper in her hands and tossed it to the back of the car. "Okay, Jing-nan," she said. "You can say whatever you want about Big Eye. And, no, he hasn't been in contact. I just want to know one thing for sure. Is there any way he can help get my dad back?"

"I'll have to ask him." To Kung and Huang, I added, "I myself haven't seen him in a month and I don't hear from him on a regular basis. He doesn't live in Taipei, after all. He lives in Taichung." That city was a good two-hour drive southwest from Taipei. I know this because I recently enjoyed a few trips down to see him at his insistence.

Peggy slid back a panel in the door, extracted a flask and swirled it thoughtfully in her hand. "How about we make that call now, Jing-nan?" she asked.

I took out my phone and hid it in a fist. "I don't have much power left right now."

Huang pressed his leg against mine and I could smell the cloyingly sweet jujube on his breath. "Well, why don't we go down to the station and use one of the phones there? I'm pretty sure all our lines are working."

Every cop I'd ever met had sooner or later put the squeeze on me, no matter how friendly a conversation had started out. This was a good thing, though. At least they were predictable and clear in a country and culture where people are never direct about what they expect from you.

"All right," I said. "I'll call him, but all of you need to be quiet. It might spook him to know that I'm with some cops and Peggy." The cops nodded and Peggy put her hands together in a thankful gesture.

I fumbled through my contacts list. I didn't have many personal friends in it. Most of my contacts were people I knew who ran travel sites and blogs, and probably half of the info was out of date, as turnover and laziness has felled many a former great online page. I needed to do some major purging. My uncle maybe should be included in that purge.

To say the truth, the whole truth and nothing but, my uncle was a lousy human being. I didn't know that when I was a kid, when he was pushing candy and pastries on me. Earlier this year, however, I found out that he was a rotten parent, a racist, a murderer and a homophobe. What else did I know about the kindred soul who lurked inside? Oh, he has a kidlike fascination with koi, the decorative carp that rich people keep in their ponds.

I touched his name on my screen and put the phone to my ear. Kung tapped my wrist. "Put it on speakerphone," she warned. I shrugged and complied. The other three leaned in to me.

As we listened to the rings, I remembered that Big Eye had invited Nancy and me to come down to his house for the holiday and I'd responded with some bullshit excuses about why we couldn't. The weather forecast didn't look good or it was a friend's birthday party. Stuff along those lines. It wasn't nice of me to do that. After all, despite everything, he was the only family I had left, and family ties in Taiwan were more bonding than any legal contract.

I heard a scraping sound when he took my call.

"Ah," he exhaled languidly with a strain of menace. "Jing-nan! My favorite nephew!" I was his only nephew. "Have you changed your mind, I hope? Are you and Nancy coming down for Double Ninth?"

Big Eye's voice was loud and the way it probed for weakness reminded me of a principal I once had. The guy would yell and beat you at the same time for perceived infractions. I was one of the good students so he only got me twice. Kids have it so easy now because school beatings were outlawed in 2007.

I crossed my legs and hooked my fingers in my exposed right sock. "Hello, my favorite uncle," I managed to say smoothly. He was my only uncle. "I am really sorry, but no, we still won't be able to make it down there. You know we want to see you for dinner and all . . ."

"That is such a shame, Jing-nan," Big Eye interrupted without an ounce of regret. "How about the big kidnapping? Tong-tong, head of the goddamned Lee family!"

Peggy, Kung and Huang all drew in closer.

"Yes, I find it quite troubling. Nancy and I are both really shocked."

"Yeah, that's your friend Peggy's dad. That poor girl. Don't know if I mentioned it before but she's got nice tits. I mean, I think they're fake, but, still, they look pretty good. Of course, when you're grabbing them, you want the real ones. They just feel better."

Kung looked up and rubbed her chin. Huang tightened his mouth, narrowed his eyes and turned to Peggy, who didn't visibly react.

I cut off my uncle. "Hey, Big Eye! Could I ask you a few things about the kidnapping?"

"How can I help you, kid?"

"Uh, do you know anything about it? Do you know who could be behind it?"

His breath whistled noisily through his teeth. "Who's behind it? I have no idea. Tong-tong has more enemies than me! Good luck figuring out who. Anyway, it's stupid to kidnap someone for ransom. So many things can go wrong. It's so much easier and more lucrative to make fake ATM cards or trick people on the phone into giving their bank and credit-card information, not that I would know. Anyway, our clueless police probably don't have a chance of finding Tong-tong on their own." He provided a big yawn that ended with a doglike whine. "I guess everyone has a purpose in life, even the stupid and useless people that end up as cops."

I heard Kung's knuckles crack as she tightened two fists.

"My dearest uncle," I blurted out. "Please, if you know anything helpful, tell me. Tong-tong may not mean anything to you, but he is the father of my classmate."

"Listen, I don't know anything." He was getting annoyed. I shouldn't press him anymore.

"I'm sorry I had to bother you and I want to say again how sorry Nancy and I are that we can't get to your house."

"How many fucking times are you gonna say you're sorry? I get it. You don't wanna associate much with me. I know I haven't been there for you all the times I could've been. As a matter of fact, I've been pretty shitty to you. I understand why you don't respect me as your elder. I haven't earned your respect."

The nearly genuine sadness in his voice almost got to me. "But I do respect you, Big Eye."

He couldn't restrain a second yawn. "You do? Then why are you calling me at nine in the fucking morning?"

"Your favorite nephew can't call you to say hi?"

He scoffed. "You're lucky we're related. Later." He hung up.

Huang sucked his lips in distress. Kung crossed her arms and legs. Peggy rubbed her hands.

"They're real, Jing-nan," she said. "Tell him when you can."

"Sure, I will."

Huang straightened up and hooked his fingers into his belt. "He knew we were listening," he said.

"Oh, do you think?" said Kung.

I glanced at my phone and clamped it against my leg. I cleared my throat. "Hey, guys, I did what you asked of me. How about taking me home now?"

"You're not off the hook yet, Jing-nan," said Kung. "You're going to see that guy in jail. Tomorrow morning." I thought I was doing them a favor, but now it had become an order. It was like being back in high school where the only path was one of acquiescence.

"I know, I know."

Huang nudged me. "We'd pick you up and take you there ourselves, but it's better that you just show up like a civilian, which you are." He picked up a jujube and furiously rubbed it with his fingertips. "And tell your uncle I said 'Fuck you.'"

I nodded and pocketed my phone.

"I'm not the only avenue you're pursuing to find Tong-tong, right? There are other leads coming in and sources that you're humoring and threatening, I hope?"

Kung twisted her face, making her scar more prominent in the morning light. "Sure there are, Jing-nan. That's no reason not to put the screws to you, though."

"Of course," I said. I remained quiet for the rest of the ride, containing my glee that none of them had seen the text from Big Eye. He wanted me to call him back when I was alone.

CHAPTER 5

I got my bags up to my apartment, locked the door and retreated to the kitchen, the room I felt safest in.

If Big Eye were mixed up with this kidnapping I would just die of embarrassment.

I stared at my phone. If I called him, I would probably find out something I would have to eventually relay to the cops in a way that wouldn't implicate Big Eye.

What did my uncle know? What were the chances that Tong-tong was hog-tied in the basement of my uncle's house?

I took up the phone and tapped Big Eye's name.

"Are you alone this time?" He barked out the question.

"Yes, I am. I'm sorry about before."

"I could hear that you were in a car and even if you didn't have me on speakerphone, you had this stupid lilt in your voice that told me others were listening in. It was cops, right?"

I couldn't help but cringe a little. "You're right."

"*Ma de*! You know very well that I've never been convicted of anything, but still they treat me like a criminal. Peggy was on the line, too?"

"Yes." He gave a short and lusty laugh as if he were a pirate on a tight schedule.

"I knew it. Nobody will ever get anything past me. I'm too careful. Not even using my dearest nephew as a tool can trick me."

I swallowed the insult and moved on. "Big Eye, you wanted me to call you. Can you help with Tong-tong or not?"

"I can maybe sort of help you," he mused. "It's not really up to me, though."

"What do you mean?"

"You'll have to ask your very good mainlander friend, Frankie the Cat. He could probably help you find the guys responsible."

"Frankie?"

"You bet your ass. He knows more *heidaoren* than me. He spent quite a few years locked up on Green Island back in the day. All of his old prison buddies are high-ranking brothers now. They're all elder gods compared to me."

I knew that Frankie had contacts in shady places, but I hadn't thought of using him as a source. Obviously the cops hadn't either.

"Thank you very much, Big Eye. Um, happy Double Ninth Festival."

"Oh, no problem. And fuck you, favorite nephew, for trying to set me up," he growled.

IN SOME WAYS IT was harder for me to ask Frankie for help than my uncle. I've known the Cat for as long as I can remember; I've seen Frankie every day of my life, with rare exceptions. Sometimes we don't say much. We don't have to. We know our jobs. We know what we have to do. In Taipei, your work is your life, and working together created blood bonds.

I see Dwayne all the time, too, and while I'm as close with

him as a brother, he's different from Frankie. Dwayne almost can't hold a thought in his head. He has to say what he has on his mind. He's like social media on two legs. "Did you hear about so-and-so who was caught leaving a love hotel with so-and-so?" he might interject randomly. At the end of every night, it's always, "See you tomorrow." Frankie doesn't bother with the small talk, or any talk, at times.

Frankie's role at Unknown Pleasures is like that of the bass player in a boringly conventional rock band like The Clash. He's a steady worker who stays in the background but also controls the tempo and holds the rhythm.

I don't know much about his life outside of work. Then again, did anyone in Taipei have lives outside of work? My father told me years ago that Frankie had married a woman from Vietnam but I was never to ask him about her.

What Big Eye had said was definitely true. Frankie knew people in the criminal world and it was through some of his connections that we got the best meat at the best prices. I gave Frankie the money and didn't worry about the starting point of the supply chain. Everything was high in quality and fresh. My concerns ended there.

Incidentally, I also like Frankie a lot and appreciate him as an integral part of my livelihood. I would be completely screwed without him both in business and on a personal basis. He's bailed me out in big ways and has saved my life, both figuratively and literally. All things considered, he is a lethally dangerous and incredibly capable senior citizen who I am on very good terms with.

I have never sought to test my relationship with Frankie and asking him to help rescue Tong-tong could prove formidable.

I tried to recall his expression while Peggy and the cops were seated at Unknown Pleasures. Did he feel caught between the cops and the criminals, wondering which side to tip off? Frankie had betrayed none of his thoughts that night even though I know he was taking in everything that was being said.

I WASHED THE JUJUBES and shook them dry, leaving plenty of luscious water drops for the pictures on social media. They glistened in the sunlight like buns on a nude beach.

I posted the pictures, adding the hashtag #nofilter just in case people thought their unusual color was something that was digitally enhanced. I'll admit that sometimes I've helped pictures look more appetizing, but not today.

I also added the #vegan hashtag to bring in another demographic that wouldn't be roped in with #beef or #bbq, my constant top two tags.

By the time I had moved on to posting pictures of a stack of strategically chopped spring onions, I noticed quite a lot of likes for the jujubes. I was glad that the meat eaters weren't turned off by the vegan tag. In fact, the comments were supportive of having such an option.

I was pleased with most of what everyone had to say with the exception of one commenter who suggested we have a special skewer named after Tong-tong to be served in a net and tied up. Two people actually liked the comment.

I'm not a fan of big money or major corporations. I suppose I'm not even a natural ally of Peggy's father. But there is such a thing as going too far, and I've blocked users for such infractions. For example, someone once said that Unknown Pleasures was the McDonald's of night-market cuisine. No matter how you feel about the American chain (I love their fried pies but their burgers suck), it was a dig at both our businesses. I couldn't allow it.

In this case, however, I didn't want to merely block the

user. I wanted to take a public stand here, something that I couldn't do when that couple was bad-mouthing Tong-tong back at Family Mart.

"Tong-tong is my landlord and my friend's father," I added to the comment. "Without him, there wouldn't be an Unknown Pleasures. All of us here are praying for his safe return."

By the time I was slicing sugarcane into pointed sticks for their photo op, the user had deleted his mean comment. Victory! I had prevailed by using the treasured passive Taiwanese way of shaming bad behavior.

I ARRIVED AT THE night market fairly early, at around five. Frankie had been there for about an hour, judging by the volume of cleaned intestines ready to marinate overnight for tomorrow. Most of our prep work at Unknown Pleasures was for the next day, not the night about to fall.

I set down my jujubes and other day-market finds, and washed my hands in the sink. I dried my hands and approached him, thumbs in my pockets.

"Hey, Frankie," I said.

He gave me a brief nod and remained seated straight in his plastic stool. Frankie hadn't bothered looking at me fully, and kept his eyes on his hands running unclean offal under water streaming from a hose. Waste and water ran down a drain set in the asphalt.

"Frankie, can I ask you something?"

He looked at me. "You just did." His face twitched, showing flashes of humor and concern.

I shifted my feet and gave a fake laugh. He didn't show off his wit too often, but Frankie was quick with the teasing. I think it's a mainlander mannerism meant to keep the younger generations in line. At least he was gentle about it. I grew up seeing some *waishengren* parents just ream their kids loudly in public simply for perceived infractions.

I pulled up a stool next to him and just to show that I was somewhat serious, I began to take up the same work. I grabbed a choice pig intestine and cut away the membrane that held it together. Once freed, the small intestine spooled out to several feet in the tub.

"Frankie," I said as casually as possible, "I need help with a problem I'm having."

He pointed his feet at me and looked into my face. "A problem, huh? What can I do for you?"

I hunched up my right shoulder and wiped a corner of my mouth against it. "You know a number of *heidaoren*," I said. Frankie didn't so much as blink but he also didn't cut me off. I should tread carefully from here.

I pinched salt from a nearby bowl and began to rub down the sides of the intestine in my hands. You only need a little bit to help scrub off the slime and the stink. I rinsed the intestine thoroughly before continuing.

"I was wondering if you possibly knew who was behind the kidnapping or if you could think of anyone who could help the situation."

Frankie heaved an exhausted sigh and grabbed the intestine out of my hands. "You're not doing it right," he said, his voice devoid of emotion, making the statement an even harsher assessment of my work. It came off as, "You've never learned how to do it right, and you'll never do it right!"

I stood up and stupidly watched Frankie work. I pulled back both my arms and held my hands behind my back.

"What do you say, Frankie? You know that Peggy's dad is in serious danger."

I saw his right foot turn slightly. "Have you heard anything new since last night?"

"Tong-tong managed to leave Peggy a voicemail. He gave her the name of a guy who might have what the kidnappers are looking for."

Frankie's fingers flew through the limp organ, playing the supple flesh like a concert pianist. He considered what to say for a few measures.

"His circumstances aren't that bad if he can get to a phone," he ventured. "Or his kidnappers are pure amateurs. Either way, he's in a bad spot, but it's not the worst possible scenario." He tossed the intestine without looking and it landed squarely in the bucket. "What exactly did he say?"

"He told his daughter the name of the guy who has the chip design that the kidnappers want."

Frankie measured his breath as he inhaled and exhaled. "Then get the design from the guy, take it to the kidnappers and they'll release Tong-tong. Every delay, every move to try to outsmart them jeopardizes his life." He shrugged while his hands continued to work. "You don't need me to tell you this."

"It's not that easy, Frankie. I'm gonna visit the guy in jail tomorrow, but what if he doesn't have it anymore or refuses to hand it over? Things might be easier if you could help the cops rescue Tong-tong."

Frankie closed his mouth and ran his tongue over his teeth behind his smiling lips. "Look here, Jing-nan. I have known my friends for a long time. We only talk about old times and funny things that happened in the distant past. Stuff that's beyond the reach of the statute of limitations. If I asked any of them about Tong-tong, they would take it as me implying they had something to do with it." He set aside another clean intestine and looked at the ground. "I would rather die than insult any of my friends by giving them the impression that I was accusing them of . . . doing things." He lifted his head and regarded me from an angle.

I pressed my hands together in a gesture that I hoped Frankie found deferential. I returned to sit down on my plastic stool so my eyes were level with his.

"You don't have to accuse anybody. Maybe you could phrase it in a way that couldn't possibly cause any offense."

Frankie exhaled as if he had just taken a long drag on a pipe. "Even if I found out exactly who the kidnappers were and where they were holed up, there could be a serious price to pay if the cops attempted a rescue. There would be a lot of blood and Tong-tong might not make it out alive. Just by asking, I might provide information that my friends could tip to the kidnappers. There could be blowback if they come after me." He looked through me. "And you, too, Jing-nan. My way could be the way of death and misery. It should be your last resort. Try talking to your guy tomorrow. Sometimes jailbirds can be more helpful than you think."

I didn't appreciate until that moment that I employed a man who had the potential to be a person of interest should I be found murdered. I always knew Frankie was familiar with a dangerous world, but I had thought that he could protect me. Now he was telling me he couldn't.

"Well, thank you, Frankie," I said. "I will talk to the prisoner. Just, please, keep your eyes and ears open."

He turned on me as if I had insulted him. "Do I ever close them?"

I scrambled for the words. "No, you don't. But if you could pay extra special attention, I'd really appreciate it." He didn't seem appeased but he didn't get up and quit, either. "I forgot to mention, happy Double Ninth."

He hunched his right shoulder to rub his face. "Thank you, Jing-nan." Most of the tension was gone from his voice. "Are you going to give me an envelope because I'm a senior citizen?"

Please smile again so I know you're joking and that you're not mad at me, Frankie. Please.

"Do you want an envelope?" I asked.

Finally, both ends of his mouth curled up into its familiar form, reminiscent of the Cheshire Cat. Everything was fine.

What would I do if Frankie ever left Unknown Pleasures? I'd be working longer and harder for less money, that was for sure. I would have to hire more help. It would probably take at least two people to replace Frankie. I'd have to find a new meat connection, too, which would certainly cost more. The thought of less and less money coming in unnerved me.

My hands shook as I opened up one sack of jujubes and washed them in the metal sink. As the water swirled down the drain, I thought about the turnover at other stands that eventually destroyed formerly thriving businesses. It's hard to find the right chemistry that allows a group of people to come together and work hand-in-hand every night without wanting to kill each other. It's even more difficult to find workers who are talented and driven, and yet lack the ambition and measure of self-worth to leave and start their own businesses. People with strong backs and weak spines are in high demand at the night markets.

My guys could each easily strike out on his own. Honestly, I think the main reason why Frankie and Dwayne stick with me is out of loyalty to my grandfather and father for giving them a place to work when they were each down on their luck. They would probably be racked with guilt if they left me, the orphaned child of their old bosses. Then again, even guilt has its limits. I remembered that kids never felt bad about shoplifting from stores whose owners were mean, making them even meaner, creating a negative feedback cycle until the store closed.

I shook off water from the jujubes and placed them on

a towel to dry some more. I went to my phone to see what papers I needed to bring to visit someone in prison.

DWAYNE ARRIVED IN DUE course and swung a small duffle bag off his shoulder in an exaggerated motion. Did Dwayne also bring a special ingredient for the night's menu?

"It can't be that heavy," I said. "Unless you brought coconuts."

His eyes narrowed. "I just hit the gym again for the first time in weeks. I'm in serious pain." That was my cue to slap his right shoulder hard. "*Ma de*!" he cried. "Lay off of me, or I'm gonna sit out the night and won't your ass be in a sling?"

Frankie slapped Dwayne's left shoulder and the big man nearly crumpled to his knees.

"I never ask for mercy," Dwayne panted. "Please don't hit me, just for tonight."

"It's like you're doing a scene from a prison movie," I said.

Frankie scoffed at my remark. "You don't know what prison's like, Jing-nan. Your little visit tomorrow is going to be like going to jail in Monopoly." He sized up Dwayne's agony. "Well, I'm glad there won't be any horseplay tonight," he said without masking a tone of satisfaction. "When you two goof around, I half expect one of you to end up on the grill."

"We need to keep our traditions alive," I said. Dwayne and I had play-wrestled since the night we first broke even under my watch a few years ago. It's the closest thing to a religious ritual that I'm willing to participate in.

Dwayne pointed a finger at my nose. "Your ancestors killed my people's traditions. You stole our land and our languages. Now you want to dig up our graves!" He was referring to the latest news that the government planned a new highway that ran through sacred burial grounds of the Paiwan people.

"You're Amis, not Paiwan," I said.

"I represent all the legitimate Taiwanese," Dwayne countered. "It was a mistake to let all you illegal-immigrant Chinese in. Some day soon, we're gonna load all of you on to a boat and send you back to China where you belong. Wait and see."

"Are you gonna send Frankie back, too?"

Dwayne raised an eyebrow. "The Cat can stay. He's one of us. He hates Chinese people, too."

Frankie made a guttural sound that could have indicated agreement or disgust.

My phone buzzed in my hand before I could think of a comeback. It was a text from Peggy.

TURN ON THE TV, it said.

WHICH CHANNEL? I texted back.

ANY.

Dwayne must have seen the look of worry on my face. He came closer and cupped my right elbow.

"What's going on?" he asked.

"Not sure yet," I said. "Let's go to Beefy King."

Beefy King was the steak place in the night market. Business was good for the King. It took up the space of three standard stalls and it offered a royal deal: Eat ten steaks in one sitting, and they were free. If you fell short, however, you had to pay for them all.

In all honesty, I had a hard time eating just one of its pedestrian steaks. If you absolutely had to have the taste of a dirty grill and the mouthfeel of soggy cardboard, look no farther than Beefy King.

It was actually difficult to look farther than Beefy King because it blared its menu from three huge flatscreen monitors mounted outside. Usually they displayed the menu while strategically cutting in loops of meat in flaming hell, but the inputs could be switched to cable television, when needed.

It was early, but Uncle Bing, the guy who ran Beefy King, was already having a pretty good night, judging by the fact that there were two lines: one waiting to order and the other waiting for their orders.

Uncle Bing was middle-aged and normal-sized, which suggested he didn't get a lot of red meat in his diet. Dressed in a "Got Beef?" T-shirt and sipping a bitter-melon shake, Uncle Bing stood off to the side and watched his staff sweat it out. I approached him with my head bent in deference.

"Uncle Bing," I said. He nodded to me and Dwayne while continuing to sip. "I was wondering if you could do us a favor." He raised his eyebrows but said nothing. "Could you change one of your monitors to a cable news station?"

He glanced at his lines. They were already at capacity for a while. Uncle Bing had a pretty good business because he was pals with a guy who owned a bunch of hotels. The hotels sent over tourists who got 10 percent off their steaks in exchange for some kickback, I'm sure. Uncle Bing picked up a remote control and shook it once at the rightmost monitor because he couldn't simply push a button without a grander gesture.

The picture changed to a darkened image of what looked like two dogs in cages. Then the brightness adjusted—the footage was apparently from a phone camera. It was two grubby men in cages. The image gradually came into focus. Tong-tong was on the left, his face wracked by stress and embarrassment at being filmed. The other man, a heavyset cubicle creature, seemed to be having a harder time. His noisy mouth-breathing was the only sound audible and took on an orc-like quality as Uncle Bing turned up the volume of Beefy King's PA system.

A scrolling message along the bottom read, *This is recorded from an Internet feed. There are disturbing images. Sensitive viewers are cautioned.*

A muffled off-screen voice declared, "Peggy Lee. We know you've gotten the police involved. We could've handled this safely and quickly but that's all over now. If the chip design isn't handed to us in forty-eight hours, we're going to kill one of these animals."

The camera veered away from the caged men to a handgun hanging loosely from a gloved finger looped through the trigger guard.

The camera dipped and then slid back to frame the two men. A foot swung out and kicked the fat man's cage and he screamed like a bird. The off-screen voice barked again.

"Forty-eight hours!"

The screen went black. Two seconds later, a clearly rattled news anchor appeared. She was in her mid-twenties and seemed more attuned to happy news for happy people and entertaining news about weird people, but certainly not anything as disturbing as the live feed. The woman took a deep breath, squared her shoulders and said, "That is the latest information we have regarding Tong-tong's kidnapping. As you've heard, there's now a forty-eight-hour deadline before he or his underling is shot and, presumably, killed."

A second camera angle took over and she looked over her left shoulder into the camera.

"We will continue to replay the feed. All other programming will be on hold until further notice."

Uncle Bing pointed the remote at me. "You want more, or is that enough, Mr. Chen?" he asked. The way he said "Mr. Chen" reminded me of an old principal.

"I don't need to see it again," I said, glancing at Dwayne. I could recognize the small, scared child inside him, and seeing fear in his eyes made it palpable.

"That was so fucked up, Jing-nan," he said as he pressed his closed fists against his jaw.

"Yeah, I know," I said.

Uncle Bing swung the remote to the screen. "I hate repeats," he said. A miniature lightning strike went across the monitor and the merciless scroll through the hellish beef landscape resumed.

"Hey!" called a man as he held an injured steak sandwich to his mouth. "Put the news back on!"

"I want to see it, too!" called a woman who had just picked up her order. Uncle Bing observed them coldly and drummed his fingers against the bottom of his bitter-melon drink.

"Get back in line and order more food," he told them. The man and the woman exchanged incredulous looks. Uncle Bing searched their faces. "It's going to look better up there than on your phone," he added. The two returned to the line. Uncle Bing changed back to the news station and went to the order counter himself to speed up the repeat orders. Dwayne and I walked away, lest Uncle Bing pick on us next.

"That was a no-joke real gun," said Dwayne. "It's a military issue. I have a cousin who had one."

"Do you think the kidnappers are ex-military?"

"They gotta have some training and access to weapons. Pretty tough to learn kidnapping skills on YouTube."

My phone buzzed.

48 HOURS WTF, Peggy's texted. I'M COUNTING ON YOU TO GET THAT DESIGN TOMORROW, JING-NAN.

OK, I typed. What the hell else could I say? I'M SORRY ABOUT YOUR DAD. I HOPE THIS TURNS OUT ALL RIGHT.

On the walk back to Unknown Pleasures, I told Dwayne that I was going to visit Nancy's former sugar daddy in prison, get the chip information from him and save Peggy's dad. The plan sounded stupid to me as I was saying it.

Dwayne shook his head and sighed. "Jing-nan, this

whole situation sounds so twisted, it will have to work out somehow."

"Do you think so?"

"Absolutely. It's the simple things that wind up as disasters."

Simple things. Like jujube skewers.

We stopped talking after we walked to our respective stations, Dwayne to the secondary grill and me to the prep area. The washed jujubes were arranged in pairs and eyed me with caution.

Before I explained what I envisioned to Frankie and Dwayne, I cut up one myself and laid out the slices. I gave it a minute and then flipped them. I was glad that the grill marks were easily visible. People are hardwired to love them. They must be Jungian archetypes. I picked one up with silicone-tipped tongs, blew on it and bit off half. I pushed the fruit around my mouth before chewing it.

The warmth brought out a caramel quality in the natural sugar. I should salt them slightly. This would be so good with crispy, salty bacon. Wait, what an idiot I was! I had to keep it vegan! Maybe rolled with some crushed nuts. No good. People are allergic to nuts.

I had it. A light dusting of powdered dried chili. Just for taste, not enough for tears. What would alternate well with grilled jujube slices on a skewer? I popped the rest of the grilled jujube into my mouth and got my answer.

The skin. I should peel the jujubes and grill the skin separately, creating a crunchy alternate layer between jujube slices.

I made three test skewers and gave the best one to Frankie, the second-best to Dwayne and I ate the ugly one.

"This is the vegan option," I declared. "We could end up doing this on a regular basis."

"If it doesn't suck," said Dwayne.

"It doesn't suck," I said forcefully. "It's delicious."

"I mean, if the sales don't suck."

I straightened myself. "People will buy them."

Frankie looked over his skewer. "They look good," he said.

"Try it," I said. I watched them begin to eat and waited for sounds of approval before eating mine. I was completely right about the chili. The overall profile tasted like a caramel apple with ice cream and some heat.

Now that I had something perfect, I had to find a way to get the usually reticent masses to properly appreciate my art by paying for it.

I made a bilingual sign for the jujube skewers with VEGAN SPECIAL at the very top. I handed out samples on toothpicks, something I almost never did, but I had no idea how this thing would go. It was against my nature to reach out and give things away, but I was rewarded with their stunned and silent smiles.

I cajoled English-speaking tourists to get at least two because these fruits were only available for a short time. Which was not a lie at all. Nancy accuses me of flirting with the women but if I am, it's just an aspect of my friendly alter ego.

On the back end, Dwayne pleasantly scorched skewers on the main grill while Frankie stirred and seasoned the stews on the back burners. Frankie cast a mildly sorrowful look at my customers from time to time, pitying the people paying for food that didn't even include any meat.

The jujubes exceeded my cynical expectations and rewarded my deep-seated need to create by doing great. Some meat-eaters picked one for dessert. After two hours, I made back what I had spent on the two sacks of fruit.

And they were still moving!

I cycled through my three mostly truthful pitches that addressed the most popular afflictions. For the people worried about their weight, I told them that skewers were low in fat. For the people a little timid about eating foreign foods, I told them that if they were already familiar with barbecue and stews, those methods of cooking originated in the Caribbean and the Middle East, respectively. For those who wanted to try the most Taiwanese thing I had, well, I'd pick whatever was lagging.

Ordinarily, I'd be thrilled about the night we were having, but I was slightly sick inside. I wanted so badly to feel my phone buzz with a text from Peggy telling me that everything was over and the cops had rescued Tong-tong.

I became antsier as the hours ticked by. The more I thought about jail, the more I didn't want to go—not even to visit. After all, I had seen *The Silence of the Lambs*. I saw what that guy did to Jodie Foster when she passed by his cell!

We hit an inevitable lull and I decided to take the initiative. I came around Dwayne and pinned his arms back while he struggled to keep his head up.

"Hey, not fair!" he howled. "I told you before, I'm in pain!"

I managed to hold on as he thrashed. Wow, wrestling was relieving my stress—as long as I had the upper hand.

I had a good view of Frankie's face. His typical reaction to our horseplay was silent amusement as long as the equipment was out of harm's way and there were no customers waiting. Tonight, though, instead of watching us, he rolled his eyes and washed up in the sink.

I worked a hand free and pulled a dirty move by tickling Dwayne's left armpit. The big guy could take anything but being tickled.

"Oh, shit! Oh, fuck! Get away from me!" Dwayne

scampered back to safety behind the grill. He picked up a pair of greasy, blackened tongs and snapped them at me like a dirty crab claw. "Back off, Jing-nan, or I'll rip off your face and throw it on the grill!"

"Hey!" yelled Frankie in a tone that seemed too harsh. "Are you guys working tonight or not? Did we run out of food to sell? Jing-nan, get out front and do your stuff!"

Dwayne and I were both stunned. I raised my hands.

"Okay, Frankie. We're sorry. We're going back to work."

I couldn't help feeling that Frankie's irritation was rooted in the fact that he knew a lot more about the kidnapping than he had let on earlier. Seeing the news clip of the men in cages on Dwayne's phone probably dribbled more sand into his shell.

About fifteen minutes went by before a decent wave of tourists approached. I leapt into them like a bodysurfer.

CHAPTER 6

Frankie sidled up to me as the night was winding down, choosing a moment when Dwayne was in the can.

"I might know somebody who might know someone else who knows something." Frankie looked defeated. I looked down at his hands. He was trying to pick a hangnail.

"If it's any imposition," I said, "please don't bother looking into it. After all, let's see what my friend in jail says."

He grabbed my arm loosely. "I'm doing this because *I* need to know. I don't want to have this feeling that I could have helped even a little bit. Things are more serious now." He tightened his grip and when our eyes met he nodded.

That scared me. Frankie is an unflappable sort of guy but now, with the release of the video, he thought that things were dire enough to tap his criminal network for a route to save Tong-tong's life.

AT THE END OF the night, Dwayne went home to soak in a tub, I went home with a bag of leftovers for Nancy, and Frankie went shrimping to connect with his old acquaintances.

Shrimping places are open twenty-four hours a day. Most of the time, families with small children and even some tourists try to catch shrimp in stocked pools using baited fishing poles. You pay by the hour and you get to salt-roast your catch in nearby ovens.

After midnight, the clientele changes a bit and becomes a bit less family-friendly. Sure, there are harmless drunk kids hanging out after a night of partying but you'll also notice a contingent of older guys in shades, looking a little comical sitting on plastic stools and holding those playfully colorful fishing rods. They are the old-school gangsters, the ones who remember how the grudges began and how easy it all used to be. There's no retirement from the criminal life, however, and they stand by waiting for a call that might never come, and ready to provide alibis as necessary.

Why, Mr. Officer, they might say. Lee was with me that night. We were shrimping until five in the morning—here's the receipt!

I hoped Frankie could hook something more substantial than shrimp and war stories.

I CALLED PEGGY AS I made my way through the closing night market. I dodged people using their backs rather than their legs to lift and carry boxes—some empty, some full— to their cars. We were right up against midnight but I knew my classmate would be up.

"Jing-nan," she said.

"Peggy, I know it's late, but I wanted you to know that Frankie is looking into matters. Have the cops found anything yet?"

"They found their fingers up their asses," she spat.

"I'm sure the cops are doing their best."

"They're both asleep now. Drunk."

"You got them drunk?"

"I didn't force 'em to drink. Anyway, I've been going through their stuff. Emails and notebooks. Looks like everyone out in the field is just playing wait-and-see instead of being proactive. Even after that video."

Cops probably don't take too kindly to people rifling through their belongings. Nobody does.

"You'd better leave their stuff alone."

"There should be agents out there busting in doors, but instead they're watching the video again and again!"

I envisioned a buzzed Peggy wandering around her apartment, carelessly kicking around the contents from the cops' bags and wallets. With her guardians passed out, she was a danger to herself and the investigation.

"Listen, Peggy, keep the blinds down and stay away from the windows."

"Okay, Mr. Paranoid."

She hired two cops to be her security detail and had the nerve to call me paranoid.

"Don't insult me when I'm doing all I can to help. I'm going to Taipei Prison tomorrow morning for you. That's already beyond what I think is reasonable."

"Feel free to use force on him, Jing-nan. If he wants to shake hands, bend his middle finger backwards until he tells you where the chip design is."

"That's not my style."

"Then just show up and put your head down and mope. You're pretty good at that. After a minute or two, he'll be so frustrated he'll do anything you say."

My grip on my phone tightened. I had to remind myself that her dad was in danger and that her judgment was currently impaired. She wasn't aware that the words she was using were hurtful, but was she ever?

"It's time to say good night, Peggy."

At the entrance to my building, I had to shake my entire body to get rid of the bad vibes as I fished out my keys. I went up to my apartment and proudly held up the bag of leftovers to Nancy as if I were returning from a successful hunt. She nodded and looked at me tentatively. She must have seen the video. Most of Taiwan probably had.

I had brought her favorite skewers, the chicken butts, but maybe her appetite had been ruined already.

Nancy tilted her head and crossed her arms. "Did you see that video clip, Jing-nan?"

I put down the bag and let her hold me to comfort herself. "I did. It's terrible. What an awful thing."

She patted my back and withdrew. "Do you think they're going to kill Tong-tong?"

"I don't think so. They're just trying to scare Peggy into giving them that chip design."

She opened the bag and unwrapped the skewers. So her appetite wasn't ruined. "They scared half the country!"

"The cops will save Tong-tong in the end. I'm sure."

"How can you be sure?"

I stepped back and put my hands on my waist. This was an opportunity for me to tell her. "For one thing, I'm going to be helping them."

She picked up a chicken-butt skewer, took a big bite and talked through chews. "How are *you* going to be helping the police?"

"I'm going to see a man tomorrow who has the chip design that the kidnappers want."

"Why do you have to go? Who is this guy, anyway?"

"I'll tell you once you've swallowed that bite."

Her eyes narrowed. "Why?"

"Please, just swallow."

"All right, I just did."

"It's your former sugar daddy, Ah-tien. I'm going to visit him in jail."

Red patches appeared at the tops of her cheeks and began to spread all over. "Are you kidding me, Jing-nan?"

I put my hands together in a pleading gesture and lowered my head to show her how serious I was. "I wish I were joking around. Believe me, Nancy, he's the last guy in the world I want to see. You know that."

She continued eating the skewer automatically as her eyes rolled upward to review a memory. "I feel so bad for him."

I said what popped into my head. "That guy can go straight to hell!"

The red patches grew larger and made the leap to her ears. "He was never anything but good to me, Jing-nan. Do you understand that?"

I had to bite my tongue. The last time we "discussed" Ah-tien, I ended up sleeping on the couch. I took a deep breath and felt the inhaled air move down to my spleen, where mental fixations are stored, according to an herbal-medicine infomercial that plays continuously on every channel.

I could use a dose of that now, if it worked. I wished I had no apprehensions about meeting Ah-tien. I wished he meant nothing to me. Well, maybe he should mean nothing to me. After all, I had still been in love with someone else when Nancy was briefly entangled with him. It's not like he had stolen her away from me. It's not like she had chosen him over me. He was just someone out of her past.

And yet, just thinking about him made me want to punch him out. That just wouldn't do well for a jail visit.

I regarded Nancy. She was annoyed with me but I could see that she was also sad that I couldn't get past this. Why couldn't I? Even if I claim to be stubborn and idealistic, which I am, I couldn't let that be a line in the sand between my girlfriend and me. There probably shouldn't even be sand between us.

"It is not the first choice of either of us for me to visit him," I said with caution. "But Ah-tien may be the only hope to save Tong-tong."

Nancy nodded. "I'm glad you said that," she said. "I think he will help you."

"Really?"

"Sure. I mean, Ah-tien has nothing to lose, at this point. Maybe they'll reduce his sentence for helping the investigation."

"How long is he in for?"

Nancy bit into the skewer and twisted her head slightly to tear away a chunk of meat. She chewed a few times before pushing her food into one cheek so she could talk. "You should do some homework before you go meet him. Ah-tien will be much more amenable if you show him you know his story."

She brought me to the couch and swung up the lid on her laptop. The screen lit up and she typed in a video-sharing service. We reached a thumbnail picture of a guy behind bars and Nancy hit play.

"This is from last month," she said.

A middle-aged prisoner dressed in a white T-shirt with long sleeves rolled up to the elbows and faded blue shorts sat alone at a table. His crew cut looked like a white mold that covered most of his scalp. He had been eating well but his eyes looked like hell behind his glasses. Ah-tien's face glistened as if brushed with egg yolk. His nose twitched rabbit-like as he awaited the decision of an off-camera judicial board.

Despite his timid looks, Ah-tien had been designated a class-three prisoner, one class below what a convicted murderer would be. He was attempting to have that lowered to class two, which would give him more personal freedoms, a chance to move to a less-restrictive facility and an earlier shot at parole.

I took in another deep breath for my spleen. I had never tried to picture Ah-tien. I preferred to think of him as a faceless, Gollum-like creature confined to a cell. He was Nancy's sugar daddy for about a year. He had bought her a sports car and a swanky apartment that turned out to be in the same building as Peggy's. Then his corrupt dealings caught up with him. He was convicted of paying an official to circumvent the normal bidding process in order to get his company's laptops into New Taipei City's school district. The official later decided he was getting lowballed so he turned in Ah-tien.

Let that be a lesson to the business community: Always bribe more than what the government is offering to whistle-blowers.

There wasn't much movement in the video, apart from seeing Ah-tien wipe his forehead or his mouth. I couldn't help but feel bad for him. I have often thought about physically hurting him in many different ways, but now I couldn't even make a fist as I watched him sitting in his chair, drooping like a neglected plant whose owners were on vacation.

Someone offscreen announced that due to the seriousness of Ah-tien's conviction, he would remain a class-three prisoner. He actually straightened up slightly and nodded. It was his expected result. His lawyer drank some water and swished it in his mouth.

The system had really made an example of Ah-tien, the poor bastard. If I were in high school, I'd be terrified to end up like him. Jailed, old, resigned and fated to dress like shit to the end. He was serving a forty-year sentence, which effectively looked like a life term.

As the camera focused on his face, I reached out and hit the spacebar, pausing the video. He looked resigned to whatever fate had in store. Maybe that included handing over the chip design to me.

"I feel terrible for him," I said. "That's a really long sentence for a nonviolent crime."

"Murderers have gotten less because they can claim insanity," said Nancy. "But you know what? Business crime destroys the lives of multiple people. Remember Bernie Madoff in America? He destroyed entire institutions, including charities."

"I think it will do some good if he serves out his sentence. Seeing what Ah-tien looks like will scare people straight."

She adjusted the angle of the display. "He's lost a lot of weight."

He used to be ugly *and* fat, I thought but didn't dare say. I licked my lips.

"Nancy," I said. "Please try a jujube skewer. I saved it for you. It was today's vegan special, our first."

She took a few bites. "It's good, but maybe it could be spicier," she said, putting me on the defensive.

I took a small bite to see if it was an outlier of tonight's batch. "It's got the right amount of seasoning," I said. "It tastes different when it's hot." I sat down and raked my tongue over my top teeth. "You're right, though. The spices could be better. Not hotter but it should be more coarse. Something granular to make the mouthfeel a little rougher and more pleasurable."

"Um," she said. "It's really good as it is. I've never tasted anything like it. The skin is a great touch. What kind of skin is it?"

"It's the actual jujube skin."

Nancy looked puzzled. "What's wrong with the color?"

she asked. Why was everyone in Taiwan obsessed with skin color—even that of fruit?

MY BEDROOM HAS AN excellent view of a patch of dirt where stray dogs used to gather and fight. I had always assumed that something was supposed to be built in the neighborhood park but that the money had run out.

At around six in the morning a cataclysmic sound came from the park, waking both of us up. It sounded like a giant child's toy chest had been dumped.

That was actually close to what happened. I rolled out of bed to my feet and stared out my window. A truck had just unloaded brightly colored pieces of a ready-to-assemble playground. I had no idea such kits existed.

I stood naked in the shadows as I watched three men in hardhats, T-shirts and flip-flops pull out giant plastic tubes from the pile. The workers had wiry appearances, with darkly tanned and lanky arms and legs. Judging by how ill-equipped they were, these men were immigrant contract laborers, probably from Indonesia, Thailand, Vietnam or the Philippines. The men seemed a little stiff, probably because this was their second or third job in the last twenty-four hours for the same boss. I watched them sort out the pieces with their bare hands and it reminded me how privileged I was to be a citizen of the Republic of China on Taiwan. I was wealthier than my Southeast Asian neighbors but the tradeoff was that my country didn't officially exist in the global community. We had money but not fame, and wouldn't we have chosen that if we could?

These migrant workers chose to come here because it offered more money than jobs back home but with a lot more negatives. Taiwanese construction contractors and fishing boats exploited them, especially if they were undocumented or otherwise not officially allowed to work. Every few years, advocate groups for the workers agitated for better pay, equipment and training. Then the business community would push back, saying market wages were already fair, because if they weren't, then why do these people keep coming in? Why, these people loved coming to Taiwan to work. They even paid job brokers outrageous fees to find the most menial jobs on the island.

If Taiwanese employers were expected to spend more on salaries, stifling regulations and unnecessary safety equipment, then there'd be fewer jobs, and that certainly wasn't in the interest of those people. In so many coded ways, however, lurked the idea that only this lower strata of society was open to working-class foreigners, and part of it was because something was wrong with their skin color.

You'd hear about the protests for the migrant workers, then promises that bills would be passed, and then nothing. I don't know if any legislation was ever ultimately passed because the same things seem to happen again and again. The latest outrage on behalf of labor activists was when a group of Indonesian men accused a Taiwanese fishing captain of holding them as virtual prisoners while at sea by working them for long hours and withholding food. One man had even died and was buried at sea, a move that was apparently legal.

I don't visit nursing homes, farms or factories. Construction sites are blocked from public view and fishing vessels are out to sea. I haven't actually seen migrants at work until now. I could tell they were exhausted but they pressed on.

Nancy's pale arms and legs writhed on the bed and she held a pillow to one ear while pressing the other against the wall.

"Ugh, so loud!" she moaned. "How am I supposed to sleep through this?"

I took a seat on the bed. "They're finally building a playground there. You know, so our kids will have some place to play."

Nancy slammed the pillow against my head. Then she reached down and swung one of her house slippers at my face. She wasn't fully awake but I was barely able to duck the assault.

"Hey, now! I'm only joking."

"Don't talk about children in the morning. That's not a casual subject for me!"

"All right. I'll wait until lunch." The other slipper glanced off my chest. "Oh, wait, you're still mad at me for making fun of Ah-tien for so long."

Nancy sprung herself off the mattress to come face-to-face with me. "Thanks for reminding me!"

I put my hand on my heart. "I told you, I'm letting go of my negative feelings about him." Yet I couldn't help but add, "He took advantage of you."

She crossed her arms over her chest and heaved the bony ends of her elbows at me. "I'm going to say this again, Jingnan. We got what we needed from each other. Without him, I would have been screwed." I thought of a wise remark right then but I exercised enough self-control to merely nod. "I never loved him, he never loved me and what we had is over and has been for a long time now, all right?"

I shifted on the mattress, making us both wobble slightly. "Did you ever visit him in jail?" I asked.

"No. Why would I?"

"Have you written to him?"

"No way." Nancy scratched her right ear. "He said that if he was ever arrested I should cut off all contact with him, otherwise I would get dragged into the news stories."

"I'm glad you weren't all over the news. You could have been made infamous."

She shrugged. "I was scared at first, when he was taken away from his office in handcuffs, but nothing happened to me. No reporters or lawyers ever called."

I grabbed her hip and pulled her to my side. "I'm glad you didn't have to live in the spotlight."

A new horrible sound came from the park. A cement truck was noisily lurching to the playground. Was the driver new at this or was the vehicle on its last legs? I turned to Nancy and swept the hair behind her ears.

"I have to get going," I said. "Visiting hours start at seven-thirty." I picked up yesterday's boxers from the floor and shimmied into yesterday's pants.

"You're not going to shower or put on clean clothes?" Nancy asked.

I couldn't help but laugh. "I don't need to clean up to go to jail. I need to look as rough and dirty as possible!"

IT MAY HAVE BEEN a mistake not to. The visitor's office was clean enough to withstand a health inspection. The walls gleamed like well-brushed and flossed teeth. Even the black floor tiles shone like the surface of an unplayed vinyl record.

I walked with some trepidation up to the counter. I tried to smooth out my hair, which was now permed in the shape of the inside of my safety helmet. Luckily I only had about three people in line in front of me.

As I bided my time, I scrolled through the news on my phone. There were stories about the video accompanied with enlarged screenshots of Tong-tong and his fellow captive, who was identified only as an executive at the Lee family's holding company. The gun was indeed a military issue. Dwayne had been right about that.

In order to really help Tong-tong, I decided to review a little more about Ah-tien, and there was plenty to read. His case had inspired many hand-wringing editorials in Taiwan's leading and lesser media outlets that I had been completely unaware of. The only people who really keep up on business news are the ones who expected to read glowing things about themselves and their companies.

"How far has Taiwan's democracy backslid to allow such brazen corruption?" howled one editorial. "We are teaching our children that cheating is acceptable!" declared another. A third cried out, "Taiwan's global reputation will suffer!" I seriously doubted that it had. Most people in the world think we're "Thailand," anyway.

Seeing older pictures of Ah-tien made me realize how badly he had aged in the last two years. Or maybe he no longer had access to hair dye and skin lotion. Ah-tien had pled innocent and stuck to it, but a placard can only hold up for so long in a country with a nearly 100 percent conviction rate.

It didn't help that his lawyer, in what everybody agreed was a terrible misstep, never allowed his client to testify before the court. Ah-tien's only comments were in the form of quickly stifled courtroom outbursts that the jury was told to disregard. When he was found guilty, Ah-tien became so disruptive he was dragged out of the courtroom on his stomach. He banged his handcuffs on the floor so hard that his wife later had to pay for the tiles to be replaced.

I HAD ADVANCED IN the line and now only one person stood between me and my favorite prisoner. Ms. Chen, the woman behind the desk, was about forty and had no soul inside. She was sipping tea from a glass bottle to fill the void.

"You can't bring that in," Ms. Chen told the woman in front of me, pointing to a box in her hands. The woman was here to visit her son.

"Why not? You allow cakes." I could feel her heart speed up.

Ms. Chen tapped her pen against her desktop with joy. "You could be concealing something in it. You'll have to celebrate his birthday with a hug, not a cake."

"Can't you x-ray it to check that there's nothing in it?"

"No. In fact, I'll say that your son has been gaining weight, so cake isn't good for him at this point. I'm sorry you've brought it all this way."

The woman stepped aside and heaved the box into a garbage can. "There," she huffed. "Are you happy now, you hussy?"

"No, I'm not," said Ms. Chen, "but you should be because you can visit your son now." A door buzzed and the woman hurled herself through it.

I stepped up confidently to Ms. Chen. "Hello, officer," I said. I placed my national identity card on the desk. She glanced at it before turning her checked-out gaze to my face. "We're both Chens, so you should be nice to me in case we're related."

"There are too many Chens in this world," she snapped. "Now, who are you here to visit?"

"I'm here for Wu Ah-tien. He's a class-three inmate."

I thought I saw a distant shooting star in her infinitely black eyes. She picked up her phone and although there wasn't a glass shield between us, I couldn't pick out a word in the stream of her tense whispers.

Ms. Chen put down the phone and stood up, smoothing out imaginary wrinkles on her dress. "Please excuse me. Someone else will help you soon."

The lock buzzed. She shoved the door open with far more force than was necessary and left the room. I became conscious that no one was behind me in line and I was alone in the room. I guess I had come at the end of rush hour for visiting.

The door through which Ms. Chen had exited now opened haltingly as a man awkwardly pushed his way through it. His arms were overburdened.

I crossed a white line on the floor on my way to help him out.

"Get back and stay at that desk," he said firmly, before adding a menacing, "Please."

I walked back my steps and watched him extricate himself fully from the door. He was an average-sized man, about fifty or so. His off-center nose and lumpy forehead indicated that he had been a boxer or street fighter who enjoyed repeat bouts. The man dumped five three-ring binders on the desk. "Sorry," he said in an accusing tone as he took a seat. "I didn't want to take a chance that you were going to rush the door. That would be a very bad thing."

I put my hands in my pockets. "I am not a guy who does bad things. Who would rush to break into jail, anyway?" I asked.

He raised his eyebrows. "Some people want to come in and attack the inmates. Some want to sneak in drugs." He paused to look me in the eyes and search my thoughts for certain keywords. "I've seen it all."

I nodded and pointed at the desk. "That's very interesting to hear. Well, that is my national identity card right there. You'll see that everything's in order."

He leaned over and narrowed his eyes. "Why do you want to visit Ah-tien, Mr. Chen Jing-nan? You're not related to him, are you?"

"That's true, I'm not."

"I don't remember you coming to visit before. Why are you coming here now? Do you even personally know Ah-tien?"

I hadn't expected being questioned. I thought my visit

was simply going to be some procedural rubber stamp sort of thing. "I know people who know him," I offered like an idiot. His nostrils flared. I had said the wrong thing. Well, saying anything to him except "Thank you and goodbye, sir," would be wrong in his eyes.

He flicked up my ID card with his fingernails and palmed it in his right hand. His left hand pointed an accusing finger at me.

"I know what you're up to. You're writing a book about him, aren't you?"

I almost laughed in his face. Me? *Write* a book? I didn't even *read* books! "No, you've got me all wrong. I swear."

He tore open one of the notebooks and began copying the information on my card. "Ah-tien hasn't had a visitor in a few months. He used to be on every website. People he didn't know were signing up to visit him. But Ah-tien's not so hot anymore. Now his wife shows up on his birthday but not for New Year's or Double Ninth." He raised an eyebrow at me. "Are you visiting him for Double Ninth?"

I kept still and quiet, refusing to give him a reaction apart from a simple, "No."

The man twisted his lips. "You're not allowed to bring in any writing instruments, Mr. Chen. You're not allowed to give him anything or receive anything. You will be monitored on camera the entire time. This camera does not record audio. However, we do have a few staff members who can read lips." He tossed my national identity card at my neck and I snatched it out of midair before the market closed. "Oh, and no physical contact is allowed, no matter how tempted you may be to give him a big sweetheart hug."

I'm guessing this guy wasn't supportive of marriage equality.

"Sir," I said, "I didn't get your name."

"It's Wang. You know, as in royalty." Although the

surname literally meant "king," it was a common one. There might be a metaphor in there.

I tapped my ID back into a wallet slot.

"Are you ready?" Wang asked me.

"I'm ready."

He buzzed me through the door. When I made my way inside, a lanky string bean in uniform guided me down the hall to a windowless meeting room. Inside were a desk and two chairs, all made of polished aluminum. He directed me to sit in one of them and left. A camera squatted in the far corner near the ceiling. The air was a little cold so I rubbed my hands and knees. Then I thought about Ah-tien and I felt warmer.

Was I jealous of the shared history of him and Nancy? I really shouldn't be. Was I mad at him for being married and having a mistress? Yeah, I was mad about that. I guess I was angry in general at the whole convention of rich old men doing whatever they wanted.

I stood up and began to pace the room. Man, I could just punch that guy in the face. I wondered how many I could get in before the guards grabbed me. Then I'd be in a fix. It would feel so great to hit him but the price to pay would be steep. I'd probably be convicted of assault and with the camera right there, I couldn't say he started it. I'd end up losing my business and maybe Nancy, too.

Not to mention Tong-tong. Shit, I need to get a hold of myself. I swung my fist a few times to get the aggression out of my system. I stretched my arms to the ceiling and wiggled my fingers.

A few minutes later, the infamous Ah-tien was led in by a solid-looking man who undoubtedly had aboriginal blood.

"Please sit down," the officer said softly to me. "You have ten minutes for this meeting. If you want to come out earlier, knock on the door."

I sat down and said, "Thank you."

When the door was shut and locked, I focused on Ah-tien. He wasn't a big man. He wasn't even an average-sized man. He'd once been a high-ranking corporate executive, but his time in jail had sapped calcium from his bones. His posture was now indistinguishable from any other hapless office worker with a heart full of ashes of dreams that had been incinerated like so much joss paper.

He caressed the knobs of his right wrist. "Young man," he said, "why did you want to see me? You're Chen Jing-nan, right? We don't know each other, do we?" His voice was searching and not devoid of hope. It seemed a little too high to be a man's.

I made sure both of my feet were flat on the floor and braced myself by grabbing the edge of the desk with both hands. "Well, sir, thank you for seeing me, a complete stranger." I managed to keep my voice even. "I'm not sure what sort of access you have to media in here, but have you heard about Tong-tong?"

His mouth twitched. "I saw on the lounge TV that he'd been kidnapped. They want a chip design for his ransom."

I stretched my right leg until that foot was slightly behind me. "I was told that you have that design, sir."

Ah-tien tilted his head. "I don't have it with me in here, that's for sure."

"Maybe you can tell me where it is. Maybe you've stored it in the cloud somewhere?"

He leaned back and I heard some of his joints crack. "You can't trust the cloud with something like that," he said, shaking his head. "Nothing's really safe there. All it takes is one disgruntled employee to penetrate the security layer. So many companies outsource now to save money. Some of them use contractors they don't fully vet. That was how Edward Snowden got his foot in."

"I've heard the name, but I don't know exactly what Snowden did," I said.

Ah-tien sucked in his cheeks. "You don't know anything about computers, do you? Are you a member of the Lee family?"

"I'm a family friend. I'm here to see if you could help Tong-tong."

A change came over Ah-tien's face and he seemed to gain confidence. "So the family sent you, huh? They didn't want to send their lawyers because that would raise too many red flags in the system. I'll bet the cops told you to come see me, right?"

I didn't like the defiant tone to his voice. I preferred the beaten-down old man. He was becoming aware of the power he wielded over me.

"If you want to put it that way, Ah-tien, you can. I'm just trying to save a man's life."

He slapped an open palm against his own thigh. "Nobody saved me! Nobody even bothered to scratch their ass to even help!" He folded his hands on the table into an angry pile of dried knuckles. "Why am I in jail?"

I had to stifle a laugh. "Ah-tien, you were convicted of bribery of a government official. That's why."

He let out a deep sigh. "I was the pencil," he said. "The fall guy! I had nothing to do with government contracts! I was an engineer before they moved me up to management. Look at me! Do you think they'd send a guy like me around to schmooze with officials and sell our laptops? I don't know how to socialize and show people a good time."

I leaned back and tried to imagine what the pre-prison man looked like. Being completely objective, I'd have to say that Ah-tien was not an attractive guy. He oozed the charisma-less functionality of a light switch. Yes, he had a purpose. No, he wasn't memorable. There's a reason we forget if we shut off the lights or not. It's a pedestrian task we perform with a simple device. Ah-tien's eyes pulsed with resentment. His lights were switched on now. I cleared my throat and tried to find a way forward.

"Before your present situation, I understand in the past that you approached Tong-tong for an investment to make a new chip. I assume that the design in question is the one that you had presented."

His fingers snuck under the table. "That wasn't for my company. It was for the new startup I was planning. The current industry just wants to make marginal improvements every year. It's the safest way to grow profits reliably. My new chip was going to fuck everything up in a major disruption."

Ah-tien crossed his arms and cocked his head thoughtfully. This was the man who made chips. "I designed a central-processing unit that required so little power, if it were used in a typical phone with today's battery and the brightness at fifty percent, it would only have to charge once a week." Ah-tien held up a single finger to illustrate his point. "If it were scaled up in a laptop, it would only have to charge once a month." The finger now wagged. "That's with heavy usage, as well."

He shoved his hands into his armpits and fell silent. The faintest smile rippled his lips. That chip sounded great. If it really worked. I took in a breath and coughed to clear my throat.

"Sir, can you tell me where the design is? I need it quickly to save Tong-tong's life. You know we're facing a deadline."

His face twisted into a cruel circle of blood-red lips and teeth, like a lamprey's mouth. "Yeah, I'll gladly give it to you," the lamprey chortled. "I need something from you first, though."

Did he already know about Nancy and me? Did he want

something sick like her used panties or naked pictures? That would help him cope with being in jail, right?

"What do you want?" I asked.

"I want a new trial!" The answer relieved and confused me.

"How can I do that, Ah-tien? I'm not a lawyer."

His nostrils wheezed as he took in a sharp breath of air. "You don't know anything about technology or law. What do you do?"

"I work at a stand in a night market."

He didn't bother to cover up his disgust. "You work in a night market?" He threw his hands up and spoke slowly in case I was too stupid to follow otherwise. "I thought I was talking to an educated person here!"

"I am educated." That sure sounded stupid.

He smiled and spoke with the firm condescension of an elementary-school teacher to a student repeating a grade. "Listen, boy. You tell that super-rich Lee family to prove that my lawyer sold me out. They could get a mistrial declared. I have a friend, Liu Ju-lan, who worked at a rival chip company. Do you know the characters? 'Liu' as in 'Liu'—even you would have to know that one—and 'Ju-lan,' like 'chrysanthemum.' She has copies of all the emails that prove that I wasn't the guy who met with the government officials. I sent them to her when I thought I was being set up to take the rap. Ju-lan was supposed to send them out to the press but she didn't. I don't know what the hell happened.

"You got all that, Chen Jing-nan?" He stood up and knocked on the door. "I hope you don't leave cooking-grease stains on the chair! We're the ones who have to clean up everything, you know."

Now, I would never deny that my ass is greasy at the end of a night. But it does take a while to build up. Sure, I was wearing the same jeans from yesterday, but they still smelled of cheap laundry detergent that hadn't washed out completely.

I could hear a corrections officer approaching from down the hall. I couldn't let this conversation end this way. I decided to say what I was going to say in order to put Ah-tien in his place, even though it might not help Tong-tong.

"I know about you and Nancy," I said as I stood up slowly and casually rolled my neck and both my shoulders. "You know, Ah-tien. Your mistress."

I'm unfamiliar with the specifics of what a heart-attack victim does when stricken, but Ah-tien's physical reaction hewed close to what I imagined. He slumped against the door, eyes bugging out, instant sweat streaking his whitened face.

"She doesn't know anything about any of this," he gasped. "Leave her alone!"

I kept a stoic face. "Where's the chip design?" I asked.

A key rattled in the lock. He swallowed hard. "Get me a new trial. That's all I care about."

The door swung open and a corrections officer stood aside, allowing Ah-tien the dignity of walking to his cell without being cuffed or manhandled.

"Mr. Chen, please head back the way you came," said the man as he headed off with Ah-tien.

I turned the other way and wondered what sort of legal representation Peggy's family had. Their lawyers had to be awesome because the Lees were able to throw their money around effectively. No one in Peggy's family would ever come close to getting snagged by the legal system the way Ah-tien had been. Maybe they could get him a new trial easily, but could they do it quickly enough?

Suddenly a door swung into the hallway, nearly slamming into my face. Wang with the lumpy forehead blocked my path.

"You have a good talk, Mr. Chen?" he asked. "About power-efficient chip designs, by any chance?" He checked me as I tried to walk around him.

"We might have. What do you care?"

"If you found anything out, don't hold out on me." He leaned in to my face. "Is it true? Did the cops really send you?" So he had been listening in on me. Well, fuck this guy.

"How did you end up in this shithole, Wang?" I challenged. "Couldn't pass the tests to become a cop, huh?"

Red blotches surfaced all over his face and began to seep into each other. He banged on the door he had come out of.

Two men, younger and less-verbal versions of Wang, appeared.

"Go ahead and search him," Wang spat.

I was accustomed to wrestling with one big guy at a time, but not two. They easily rolled me up and carried me into what turned out to be an empty interrogation room. Before the hydraulic-pump door had swung completely shut, my gut had already been shoved into a table edge as each man used one hand to search my back pockets and my armpits. In no time at all they had removed my shoes and socks.

With a practiced move, they flipped me around and groped around in my front pants pockets, making sure to finger behind my scrotum sack.

Wang entered and the men released me. I stumbled.

"He's not carrying anything," said one of the men.

"Nothing exceptional in the wallet, either," said the other, who tossed me my wallet. I missed and had to retrieve it from the floor. I came back up and adjusted my belt.

"I feel dirty," I said. "Thanks for that illegal search, Wang. The Generalissimo would have fully approved."

He turned his eyes to the ceiling. "I was perfectly within my rights, Chen Jing-nan. After all, I was watching you on

camera and I thought I saw you take something from him."
He looked at me and shrugged. "Whoops. Honest mistake. It
will definitely hold up in court if you'd like to sue me."

"Cavity search?" the first officer hungrily suggested. "We
might find a memory card."

Wang twisted his mouth. "Now, that is going way too far.
I would never allow an unwarranted violation like that in my
institution."

I crossed my arms. "I'm leaving," I said.

"Just a second," said Wang. "If you hear anything or
manage to find that chip design, how about you give me a
call, hmm?" He stepped away from the door, giving me just
enough room to get by.

I brushed past him and stomped out. I don't remember
the moped ride back home. The thick, angry fog in my head
didn't dissipate until a realization came over me.

Peggy! I had to tell Peggy to get Ah-tien a new trial as soon
as she could. Definitely before the deadline was up. Were
the kidnappers really going to kill one of the men on a live
stream? A death stream?

I pulled over to the side of the road and called my old classmate. I told her and whichever cop was listening in about the
visit and the appropriate adult version of the aftermath.

"No way can I get him a new trial before the deadline,"
Peggy huffed. "Mazu couldn't even do that. It would take
days to even put the paperwork together." If Taiwan's top
Taoist goddess couldn't, no one could. "I'll track down Liu
Ju-lan but in the meantime, watch your ass, Jing-nan."

"What do you mean, Peggy?" It came out a little meaner
than I had planned. I still hadn't had breakfast. She cracked
up a little bit.

"Isn't it obvious? The guards, the corrections officers,
they're after the chip design, too. I'll bet it's worth a lot

of money on the black market. I mean, even the cops, the unscrupulous ones, would probably want to get their hands on it. They wouldn't hand it to the kidnappers to rescue my father. They'd rather straight up sell it to the highest bidder. Right, Huang? Kung?" The moonlighting police officers were on the line and both assented with wordless sounds.

"If the prison guards want it so badly, why don't they go in and beat up Ah-tien until he gives it up?"

"You idiot, they can't touch him after all the prison reforms. But his visitors, who can bring things in and out, they're up for grabs." She cleared her throat. "Or gropes."

"Listen, Peggy. Call your family lawyer and start the process."

"Yeah, I'll get the balls rolling," she said. "Just like how the guards got your balls rolling."

Kung couldn't stifle a laugh. "I'm sorry, Jing-nan. That was funny."

"No problem, officer. And Peggy, when you hear any good news, go to Taipei Prison and tell Ah-tien himself what's going on."

"I'm a little too famous right now, Jing-nan. You don't want to feed a media circus, do you? I'll need you to go again on my behalf."

"There's no way in hell I'm going back there, Peggy. Send a lawyer. They like getting probed."

CHAPTER 7

I went back to work. What else could I do? I was just one citizen in a nation of workaholics. A job was a source of pain, comfort and confirmation of one's identity. Yes, I work at a night-market stall.

Working sure beats sitting around and feeling helpless. A man was going to be killed at 7 o'clock the next day unless some jerk in jail got his retrial. I told the guys about my visit to Taipei Prison and it worked on one level as an episode of comic relief for us all.

"You should've farted in their hands," said Dwayne.

"When I was in prison," said Frankie, "the guards didn't stop there."

I kept checking my phone. *The Daily Pineapple*, Taiwan's morally bankrupt media outlet, suggested that the online broadcast of a live murder could be a generation-defining event, as big as the day news broke that Chiang Kai-shek had died and everyone was forced to mourn.

"Tong-tong certainly is not in any way as admirable as the Generalissimo," the column read. "However, it could prove to be a tragic loss of one of our most prominent businessmen in a truly bizarre public execution. It may be prudent to trim stock positions tomorrow, ahead of his murder."

Dwayne was on his phone as well. We kept swapping phones to show each other new stories and rumors popping up.

An anonymous blogger was claiming that Tong-tong hadn't been kidnapped at all and the whole ruse was cooked up in order to trick the chip designer to hand over the architecture.

If Tong-tong had in fact planned this, he hadn't told his daughter. The panic that I had seen in her eyes couldn't be faked because she had never panicked before.

Some tasteless jerk autotuned the ransom video and made a song out of it. I regretted being its 23,023rd viewer.

The jujubes were having another hot night but I was feeling frayed from my jailhouse rock. Luckily, Frankie was cool as usual and helped keep our menu items well-stocked. He also encouraged me to lure in particularly indecisive large groups, which needed attention before they split up and half of them went elsewhere. He warned phone-surfing Dwayne when skewers were beginning to char too much. The Cat was as alert as ever, and yet I could tell that even he himself was weighing things carefully in his mind.

LIKE A LOT OF relationships in Taiwan, the one that I share with Nancy is guided by restraint, even with our phones. We don't regularly text or call each other while she's in class or I'm at work. Generally, we meet up at my place and we update each other as needed.

I hadn't told her yet about my treatment in prison and was looking forward to doing so after work, but Frankie came up to me as the night was winding down and asked me to go somewhere with him. He literally said "somewhere."

"Uh, Frankie, *where* are we going?"

"Just come. There's a car waiting."

I scratched my right ear. "I have to make a phone call first."

"Go ahead."

I picked up my phone and pressed my only favorited contact. I felt self-conscious about someone being next to me when I talked to Nancy. I know, it makes me sound shy, but that's how I am about some things. Plus, after a whole night of fake friendliness as Johnny, the real me wants to crawl back into myself. "Excuse me," I said to Frankie. I walked out to the nearly empty path in front of Unknown Pleasures.

Nancy picked up after a few rings. "Jing-nan?"

"Hey, Nancy, I'm going to be back a little later than I thought tonight. Frankie wants to take me somewhere."

She sniffed out my vague comment. "Hmm. Hopefully, he's not taking you to a whorehouse."

"Nancy, this is serious. I think he's going to take me to meet one of his gangster friends. Someone who might be able to help Tong-tong."

That sobered Nancy up. "Okay. I hope it works out."

"I also want to tell you that I met up with your former sugar daddy in jail." I paused. "He seems to be on the selfish side. He won't give me the chip design until I somehow get him a new trial."

"I don't think it's right to call it a selfish request. His original trial and sentencing didn't seem fair for a number of reasons."

"That may be true, but why didn't he just give me the chip design or tell me where it is? He's in jail but his life isn't in danger, either."

"It's the only thing he has left. Would you help him otherwise?"

"I may not even be able to help him now! Well, I sure can't before the deadline. Oh, wait, do you know someone named Liu Ju-lan? That's a friend of his who has some emails that could help."

"I do remember meeting *a* Ju-lan before," Nancy said thoughtfully. "It must be her. I wouldn't say I knew her well at all, though."

"Oh, there's one more thing, Nancy. They thought that Ah-tien might have given me the chip design so the prison guards searched me on the way out. They even grabbed my balls!"

"But you never hide anything back there!"

I told Nancy not to wait up, and in case I disappeared, she was to find Frankie. I joked that if worse came to worst, she could have my record collection including the first printing of Joy Division's *Unknown Pleasures* LP with the incredibly rare matte cover. I got a good price on it but the outsized shipping cost from the UK had been a known displeasure.

"Don't say you're giving me your records," said Nancy. "It's bad luck to talk like that. Frankie's going to make sure you're safe. You'll be all right."

"I'm only kidding around," I assured her. "Nothing bad could possibly happen. I'm actually going to come out of this healthier than when I went in."

After I hung up, I began to feel apprehensive. In all the gangster films, it was never the worst enemy the main guy had to worry about. It was the old pal, the best buddy, the most trusted guy in the world who stuck the knife in your neck or cut the rope while you were climbing it.

But, hell, if Frankie wanted to take my life, there wasn't any way I could prevent it. Anyway, what workers wanted to kill their bosses? They would lose their jobs *and* go to jail.

I went back to Frankie and told him I was ready. We let Dwayne handle the final closing matters, and the two of us walked down a darkened alley where the stalls had already closed. As we drew closer to the street, Frankie let out a quick high whistle. Two headlights flashed at us.

We came up to a four-door Nissan that was tucked under a tree.

"Take a seat in the back, Jing-nan," said Frankie.

The door locks clicked as we drew closer. I waited for him to climb into the front passenger seat before I popped open the rear door. I eased my way into the car and nodded to the eyes in the rearview mirror. Frankie slammed his door shut and then I did the same.

The interior lights were off and I wasn't able to get a good look at the driver. Based on the driver's wrinkles around the eyes and white eyebrows, I would guess that he was up in Frankie's territory, in his seventies. I would also guess that he had a taste for being discreet. A baseball cap with a curved brim essentially hid his entire face from any observers on the street.

The driver hunched up his right shoulder and the car started. He stared at me through the mirror and I shivered involuntarily. The eyes were large and indifferent but they weren't mean. He was an unblinking squid observing a fish haplessly struggling against the suckers of its arms.

Frankie adjusted himself in the front passenger seat as the car pulled away. Where were we going? Forward.

Frankie didn't seem concerned about our destination. I shouldn't be either. He tipped his head to a paper doll taped to the dash. "That's very nice," said Frankie.

The driver snorted in a lungful of breath. "My grand-daughter made it." The driver's voice was earthy and gave a profane charm to everything he said.

"Granddaughter, uh?" said Frankie. I don't think I've ever heard him speak with such tenderness.

Frankie gently stretched out the arms of the genderless figure. It was about three inches long and seemed stricken with severe scoliosis. The crooked smile was bigger than the face.

"Very pretty," said Frankie. "Right, Jing-nan?"

"Yes," I said. "It's very cute. Children are amazing."

"Jing-nan, this is my old friend Fu-xiang."

"Nice to meet you," I said. I stretched my hand forward and he pressed two fingers against my palm.

He was missing all the other fingers!

I jerked my hand back. His face split open and he burst out laughing. Frankie snickered.

"Jing-nan, you're worse than my little granddaughter!" Fu-xiang turned over his left hand and showed the other fingers tucked away. He laughed like a rusty gate in the wind and brought the car to a stop at a light. "I thought people who worked in the night market were supposed to be sharp!" A rhombus of white light from a streetlamp hovered on the dashboard and cut across my knees as we pulled away.

Not to stereotype, but older mainlanders in general have more disdain for their younger generations than *benshengren* do. After seven decades, they still haven't fully bought into the island mentality that each person, young or old, is important and deserves respect.

Frankie swung down the shade even though it was night, and cupped his right hand against the side of his face. Maybe I should hide my face since the two um, experienced, guys were.

"Why are you guys trying to avoid being seen?" I asked. They both seemed a little surprised. Societal norms dictated that I, as the "child," remain quiet and only speak when spoken to. However, that went out the window once Fu-xiang pranked me.

"Who's hiding?" asked Fu-xiang as he laughed some more. "I'm just trying to keep the glare out of my eyes."

"We're not supposed to be together," said Frankie.

Fu-xiang noisily blew air out of his mouth before speaking again. "Jing-nan, let's put it this way. There's never a reason to be seen. Why would you want someone to know where you are, where you go, who you're with and what you do? I'll bet your parents don't know where you are right now. You didn't tell them, right?"

My back suddenly felt itchy and I pressed myself against my seat. "Both my parents are dead," I said.

"Oh, shit, I'm sorry to hear that, Jing-nan. Yeah, I think I remember Frankie saying something like that."

"You think you remember because I did tell you," said Frankie in a measured monotone.

We came to another stop and Fu-xiang tilted his head. "Well, you know what? Since they're dead, they actually might know where you are. They're probably happy because there's no safer place to be in Taipei than when you're with me and Frankie, trust me."

Trust him? We hadn't even been together long enough to go two stops on the MRT. I was in the car of a man I didn't know going who knew where. Now, I could trust Frankie with my business and my life. In Taiwan, they were probably equally important, if not the same. One was no good without the other.

My thoughts turned to Ah-tien. He had to be planning a personal and professional comeback because the shame of the public trial hadn't destroyed his ego.

We headed south and soon we were on a bridge over Tam-sui River. I saw the Taipei 101 skyscraper to the east, a white jade pendant hanging from heaven in the night.

Fu-xiang snorted and then cleared his throat. "Jing-nan,

there's something else Frankie told me that I remember quite well," he said. "You want to know who could be behind this Tong-tong thing."

"Yes."

"Well, let me tell you something, Jing-nan. Kidnapping and abductions are so nineties. Nobody does it anymore. Low-profile crimes are much more profitable in the long run. You could make more money selling fake iPhones in the countryside than abducting a businessman."

"The kidnappers don't want money," I said.

His rusty laugh came at me hard. I was going to need a tetanus shot after. "Ah, they don't even want money! What does that tell you, Jing-nan?"

"That it's not about money?"

Fu-xiang joyously tapped the roof of the car hard. God, these old mainlanders are so excitable! "You know what, Jing-nan? You see the obvious. Seriously, that's a skill. It's something Chiang Kai-shek could never do. He never realized that he had lost China for good. Retake the mainland, my ass."

I thought I saw Frankie flinch. Fu-xiang continued.

"Anyway, of course it's not just about money. But what else is important? Chinese people aren't always good about passing down money through the generations, but what do they always give their children? Oh, never mind, I don't have enough gas in my tank to wait for you to guess right. Revenge! We love revenge! You don't get it, you *benshengren*. The Japanese perverted you in the colonial era. They bred a submissive streak in you to make you bend to the divine emperor!"

Shortly after crossing the bridge, we slowed and pulled close to the outside curb.

"I don't think we're allowed to stop here," I said.

"Who's stopping?" spat Fu-xiang. I looked through the windshield and saw that we were drawing nearer to a small exit partially hidden by the flowering branches of a weeping willow. The tree lightly raked the roof of the car as we took the exit. We found ourselves on a dirt road that tilted down and took us to the edge of the river. Reflected lights sparkled and quivered across the water's surface.

Fu-xiang parked and killed the lights.

"It's nice to come here at night and relax a little with old friends and hammer out business." He eased back the seat and exhaled with extreme satisfaction.

Frankie popped open the glove compartment, brought out a bottle and shook out two cups from a plastic sleeve. Fu-xiang took note and touched Frankie's arm.

"Old friend, we need a cup for Jing-nan, too."

Frankie turned to me and shook his head. "He's not drinking this stuff."

"Well, let him say so." Fu-xiang lifted the liquor in his hands and as soon as I saw the white ceramic bottle, I knew what it was. "Maotai," he declared. "Aw, Frankie's right. You have to have full Chinese blood to drink it."

"A lot of Taiwanese drink it, too," I offered.

"Sure, anybody can pour it down their throat, but you people don't really taste it because you've forgotten the graves of your ancestors back on the mainland. You don't remember them on your altars." He danced his fingernails against the bottle. "You want to drink some, anyway, kid?"

"No. I don't like the taste."

"He doesn't like the taste," grumbled Fu-xiang as he twisted off the cap and poured. "If it were a boba tea, he'd drink it." He handed a cup to Frankie. The smell alone stung my eyes.

"The younger generation doesn't go for alcohol like we did," said Frankie.

"We took to it like fucking fish," said Fu-xiang. They scraped the ribbed plastic of their cups together and swigged. Fu-xiang swallowed and gasped. "If it weren't for this, we wouldn't have made it through Green Island."

"You had booze in prison?" I asked.

"Anybody can be bribed, and anything can be done as long as the bribe is big enough," said Fu-xiang. "Right, Frankie?"

Frankie the Cat raised his eyebrow in a manner that could be an expression of surprise or a warning.

Fu-xiang cleared his throat and moved on quickly. "So, Jing-nan, let's talk about Tong-tong. This is a revenge situation. It's not even about the chip design, really. The whole streaming on the Internet thing is meant to humiliate him and his family." Fu-xiang unbuckled his seat belt and it whipped back into place as he turned to look at me.

I saw his entire face in full by the lights coming off the river. It was round and fleshy with big cheeks, fat lips and a double chin. It looked like Fu-xiang's face had been roasted to become dark brown at the higher points.

"That video was certainly embarrassing for Tong-tong," I said.

"It was effective," said Fu-xiang with a measure of admiration. "You have to find someone who lost face because of Tong-tong. Did he cross a business partner or bail out on a big project that left other people holding the bag? Maybe even his wife?" He scratched the bridge of his nose. "You know what? Actually, think about this. We're probably looking at a grudge that's a generation or two old, judging by the severity of this act. Take a look at what Tong-tong's father or grandfather did."

"You don't think the chip plans figure into this at all? People seem to think they're valuable."

Frankie brandished the bottle and Fu-xiang raised his cup to meet it. "I don't know anything about technology," he said. "But why would you abduct someone from a public event, which is harder than snatching him off the street? And why make your demands public, which increases the chances that you'll get caught? They're taking on extra risk because making all these details adds to the public embarrassment."

I heard a vehicle coming in through the weeds. A Toyota pulled alongside us, stopped and killed its lights. Fu-xiang raised his hat to take in a full view of the second car.

"Well, that's all I can offer, really," said Fu-xiang in dismissing me.

"Thank you for all your help, Fu-xiang." Two men who looked like they were in their forties exited the Toyota and approached.

"Say, you're Big Eye's kid?" asked Fu-xiang

"He's my uncle."

"Oh, that's right. He's got a daughter. What a shame. It's up to you to carry on the family line, Jing-nan. Make sure you have boys."

I felt my ears heat up but I decided not to check his chauvinist comments. He was probably proud of them. "Are you friends with Big Eye?" I asked.

"I know him," said Fu-xiang. Such faint acknowledgement in a society built upon exaggerated intimacy implied the subtext, *And I don't like him.*

Frankie and Fu-xiang wordlessly grasped all four hands briefly and released.

"Let's go, Jing-nan," Frankie said to me as he popped open his door.

I wasn't sure if I should shake hands with Fu-xiang but he reached back and touched my shoulder.

"I hope I helped."

"You did, thank you." Tong-tong probably screwed a lot of people over, but what had his father or grandfather done? World War II and the Chinese Civil War caused a lot of mainlander families to make some tough, selfish and inhuman choices. I know that families chose what kids to bring over to Taiwan and which to leave in China. Spouses split up, thinking the war would be over at some point and they'd see each other again soon. I seriously doubted that the cops explored this part of the Lee family's history.

First, though, I needed Frankie to get me home.

The two new guys and Frankie were all smiling big and sharing enthusiastic hellos in the way that people do in passing when they forget each other's names. How ya doing, guy! So good to see ya, man!

They were both dressed in thin sweat jackets and, ignoring the context in which I was seeing them, they could have been friends meeting up for the first time after becoming new dads. For their part, the new dads themselves each gave me a knowing once-over. They were slightly shorter than Frankie.

"*Lai le!*" Fu-xiang called out as the men climbed into his car and they responded in kind. It means, "You're here!" in Mandarin and it seemed to be a rather trite way to begin what was obviously a clandestine meeting.

The men had left the keys in their car. Frankie hopped in and tilted his head at me. I went around the Toyota's rear to the front passenger seat.

When our doors were shut, Frankie said, "It wasn't much, but maybe you found it useful."

"It was, thank you. I hope you didn't have to go through much trouble."

"Not much at all. Of course he doesn't know who's behind the kidnapping. He is right—this sort of crime itself is dated and probably has its roots deep in the past. I think Fu-xiang's sort of amused by it. I'm sure a lot of the brothers are. Well, you've tried visiting the guy in jail and that didn't help. I've done the best I could for you, considering the circumstances."

"If only you could just tell me who the kidnappers are or rescue Tong-tong yourself."

"I would if I could," he said. "It's usually good to take some action, but sometimes the best thing to do is wait for a decent opportunity."

We pulled back on to the road and I watched bars of light and shadow pass over head and body like scanning rays.

"They might kill Tong-tong," I said.

"They might," he concurred.

"Where do you think they're keeping him?"

"I don't know, but one thing is for sure. These kidnappers will slip up, sooner or later. For now, I'm going to take you home. Get some rest and tomorrow we'll see if there's something more we can do."

"I appreciate the ride, Frankie. I hope this isn't going out of your way."

"When I'm done with you, I have to dispose of the body in the trunk, huh huh." The Cheshire Cat smile stretched across his face.

"You're joking, right? Tell me you're joking, Frankie."

"Shh. Don't talk to me while I drive."

CHAPTER 8

Frankie dropped me off in front of my apartment and left without ever coming to a complete stop.

I was six steps away from my building entrance when my ear caught the sound of car-door locks firing. I turned and stood my ground. Now what?

A rear door of a parked car opened and a fatigued Peggy Lee swayed out.

"Where have you been? Nancy didn't know where you were and I've tried calling you for hours!" When she got close enough she slapped my shoulder hard.

"Ow!" I cried out. "I had my phone off because I was having a secret meeting."

Peggy stuck her face into mine. She was reviving herself more by the second and now anger enlarged all her skin pores. "You promised to help me!" she said. "You have to be ready at all times!"

I held up my hands. "I *am* helping you. In fact, I just learned from this guy—"

She shoved her phone into my chest. I scrambled to catch

it. The display was opened to an email with a video attached and ready to play.

"Peggy, I need some headphones."

"There's no sound," she said. "Just play it."

I hit the button.

It started with a familiar scene, the two men in dog cages. The camera wobbled and then a thin stream, probably urine, looped out and spilled through the bars onto both men. The cages rattled as the men thrashed.

The video was eight seconds long. There was no text in the video but the subject line of the email was *24 hours left*.

"Disturbing," I told Peggy as she snatched the phone back.

"That's all you can say? Did you know that my dad's a neat freak? He never even changed any of his kids' diapers. Left it all up to Mom and the nannies. I can't imagine how he feels being pissed on."

"Peggy, as I was trying to tell you, I met up tonight with someone who tells me the kidnapping is all about personal humiliation, not money. This is someone with a, uh, master's degree in criminality. The chip design itself might just be a distraction. They're going through lengths to make his ordeal a public display and probably want to torture him for as long as possible. Who knows. The chip design might not even exist, and Ah-tien might just be bullshitting."

She crossed her arms.

Kung stepped out of the car and slammed the door. "Hey, Jing-nan, where can I get something to eat around here?" she called.

I pointed over Peggy's shoulder. "There's a Family Mart two blocks that way, to the left."

"Thanks!" Kung stretched her back before walking away.

"Kung!" yelled Peggy.

"Yes?"

"Get me a beef bowl and heat it up in the microwave for a minute or two. I'll pay you back and I'll even give you a tip if you're quick enough."

Peggy didn't seem to take notice of the murderous look on Kung's face before the woman tore away. Peggy absently patted her stomach.

"Kung is probably going to spit in your food," I said.

"She wouldn't dare," said Peggy as she rocked back on her heels. "Where was I? Ah, yes, the chip design. I know for a fact it does exist and it could work."

I hooked my thumbs into my pants pockets. "How do you know for sure, Peggy?"

"I remember seeing them, Jing-nan. I was there at the meeting when my dad brought in an engineering buddy to look over Ah-tien's plans in his office to see if they were legit. My dad's friend tried to be very low-key about it, with Ah-tien looking as eager as a realtor to close his first sale. My dad's buddy kept saying to himself, 'Now, I'm not so sure, but, yes, maybe . . .' After Ah-tien left, the engineering guy really flipped out and told my father that the chip was a slam dunk and could be worth billions of dollars, not millions."

"Why didn't your father go into business with Ah-tien?"

Peggy played with the cuffs of her sleeves. "He's risk-averse. In general, he doesn't like investing in tech. He likes to invest in things he can see and touch. Intellectual property that can be licensed doesn't excite him.

"Despite that, he did go to China to meet with the Taiwanese companies that had chip-fabrication plants there. They all told him they couldn't produce such a chip yet. They wanted something that was a half-step up instead of a giant leap."

"Your father made a copy of the chip architecture?"

"Not a good one. A sort of blurry one lifted from the security camera in his office. It's useless but it's handy for demonstration purposes. Anyway, my father went back to Ah-tien to ask for something that was dumbed-down and the guy stopped talking to him."

I squared my feet with my shoulders. "Maybe your father's engineering friend, the guy who checked out the design, is the one who's behind the kidnapping."

"I had thought about it, but he's dead," said Peggy. "He's been dead a year now."

"Dead? How did he die?"

"Heart attack. He was obese and he smoked. You can only take that act so far."

"How about this, then. Think about people your grandfather or great-grandfather might have pissed off."

"The only viable enemies that I know of are other mainlander families and even those rivalries are on hold because we're all in business together."

"Do you want to ask your father's father who could have pulled this off?"

"I can't ask him anything because he doesn't know what the fuck is going on anymore. And my grandmother won't talk to me."

"Why not?"

"Because she's an asshole."

"What about the previous generation on your mom's side?"

Peggy shook her head. "No way. This is something on my father's side. My mother's family was working class until she became famous."

"What about people who work in your family's business? Maybe there's some mainlander executive who's been there for thirty years and never got what he thought he had coming to him."

"They're not all mainlanders, and anyway, they're one hundred percent loyal." She twisted her mouth and said thoughtfully, "The only company officers who are disgruntled at all are my three brothers."

I took a step back. Of course! A member of the family could be more resentful against the Lees than any outsider.

Out of Peggy's brothers, all of them older, two were on the flashy side, but only Da-ming, the oldest, was tabloid-worthy. His name literally meant "Big Bright." "Tommy," as he was known, had first made headlines by gathering his high-school pals for after-school sessions at love hotels with prostitutes. He was never charged by the vice cops but one of the most-viewed videos of all time is of him sitting in the back of a car, his schoolboy face unblinking in the face of camera flashes as his father picked him up at the police station yet again. Now Tommy ran two penthouse-floor nightclubs.

Peggy's youngest brother, Xiao-dong, or "Shawn," had a business in China that imported luxury cars from Germany. He spent more time there than in Taiwan, and his two American-born kids were attending a private school in New England.

The middle brother, Er-ming, was the quiet one, relatively. He was a pediatrician, I think. Some kind of doctor. He had such a low profile he didn't even have an English name. Er-ming was best-known for being seen with famous actresses, although he always called them "friends."

"Peggy," I asked. "Do you think Tommy had something to do with this?"

A pensive look came over Peggy's face as she cracked her knuckles. "Naw. He couldn't. None of them could. If they had that much drive, they'd already be heading their own divisions of the Lee family business. Their alibis checked out, too. In any case, they all hate me more than my father."

"How could anybody hate you?"

She smiled. "I outmaneuvered them all even though I was the youngest and a girl. They're all vice presidents but I'm an executive VP."

I nodded. That would really only matter in terms of succession, but if it really came down to it, the board of directors would likely appoint one of the sons as Tong-tong's successor because that's the kind of men they were.

"Well, you showed 'em," I said. Her brothers faded as potential suspects as quickly as they had presented themselves. The disappointment hit me like a sugar crash. "Say, Peggy, it's getting late. I should probably hit the sack. I don't think it will do much good, but maybe you should get your lawyer to go visit Ah-tien in jail. Maybe a carrot or a stick from a professional will loosen him up."

Peggy examined her knuckles. "I agree that it would be useless for you to go see Ah-tien again, especially since we aren't anywhere near getting him a new trial. But sending our lawyer there could make the news. You know, tabloids pay sources at prisons and hospitals to tip 'em off about famous people. Anyway, for that prisoner to tie his own fate to my father's is insulting, I've decided. It's pathetic. His wife isn't even clamoring for a retrial and he wants us to?"

"Did you find that friend of his, Liu Ju-lan, yet?"

"She left the chip industry more than a year ago and kind of dropped out of society."

"Ju-lan has copies of emails that supposedly can prove Ah-tien innocent."

Peggy shrugged. "I'm not sure she's that important. Anyway, we already have the best corporate lawyers looking at his case. If anybody can find something before the kidnappers' deadline, they can."

I still couldn't get that piss video out of my mind. Could anybody?

"What do you think is going to happen tomorrow night?" I asked.

"The cops think that the fact that they sent me this video and not a finger in a box means they're not serious about hurting my father."

"What do you think yourself?"

She sighed. It was a rare showing of uncertainty from Peggy. "I don't know. I just hope that somehow this is one big stupid joke."

I heard something rattle. It was Kung bearing a plastic bag of groceries with her left hand while her right hand held the hot entrees in plastic netting. The cop smiled slightly but it didn't dilute the overall defeat in her face. All the initial resentment and anger Kung had when Peggy tasked her with delivering the food was gone. Peggy was right. Kung didn't have it in her to fight back.

NANCY WAS ASLEEP WHEN I came in so I conducted my nighttime bathroom routine as quietly as possible. Calibrating the sink faucet to a minimal water flow reminded me of growing up in a house crowded with people on different sleeping schedules.

I crawled into bed and didn't wake up until I heard Nancy's toast spring. In that early morning fugue state of reacquainting myself with the world, an image came to me: a knife scraping a paste of jujubes across a piece of toast.

Damn, I'd forgotten about the last container of jujubes on the counter at Unknown Pleasures last night. I had to hope that Dwayne had stuck them in the fridge. I hate wasting food, mainly because that was lost money.

I was getting too caught up in the drama around Peggy's father, but then again it was becoming a national obsession.

I came out to the living room. Nancy was sitting on the couch, her feet up on the coffee table on either side of her toast, which glistened with oily peanut butter. She raised her hands to me in disbelief.

"Can you believe this shit, Jing-nan?"

The news station was doing a story about a rumored video of the kidnapper smearing feces across the faces of Tong-tong and the other executive. I had arrived in time to catch the beginning of the animated rendering of the supposed act. A man joyously defecated on a silver platter and carried it out to the prisoners like a high-class waiter. The cartoon must have been fun to make. I hunched my shoulders.

"It wasn't shit, Nancy." I told her how my night had gone, my trip with Frankie's pal and the piss video I had seen on Peggy's phone.

"You should've forwarded the video to your email so you would have a copy, too!"

"I don't want a copy of that! Besides, the cops are monitoring her phone—they would see me forwarding it. You know what this news report means, though? Someone in the police department is leaking information about the case."

Nancy reached out for her toast, but instead of picking it up, she turned the plate fifteen minutes counterclockwise. "That forty-eight-hour deadline ends tonight," she said. "Do you think one of them will end up shot?"

"I hope not. I actually asked Peggy if she wanted to send a lawyer to visit Ah-tien again, but she figured it would be useless. Her people don't need to see him in person to figure out if they can get him a retrial, and if there's no retrial, Ah-tien is not going to lift one finger to help Tong-tong."

Nancy's knees twitched. "I agree. Ah-tien doesn't change his mind about anything. If he wants a new trial, he's not going to hand over the chip design until he gets it." The animated cartoon began to repeat once again and she hit the mute on the remote. "Have they found Liu Ju-lan yet?"

"No, they haven't, but Peggy doesn't think they need to find her to get a new trial." Nancy sucked in her lips and looked up and to the right. "What are you thinking of?"

"Well, I told you before that I did meet Ah-tien's friend Ju-lan. Years ago, of course. Ran into her once in a restaurant and once at a movie theater." Nancy lifted her chin and rubbed her throat. "She knew Ah-tien was married. I think she even knew his wife. She was never mean to me, but she gave Ah-tien looks that could crush his soul. Ju-lan gave me some career advice. She said the corporate world wasn't fair to women and that I would have a better career as a researcher rather than someone who tries to climb the corporate ladder."

"The corporate world sucks for everybody, not just women," I said as I reached for Nancy's toast. She slapped my hand. "Ouch! Hey, if you're not going to eat it . . ."

"I'll eat it when I'm ready. Go make your own. Are you saying that it's just as hard for men as it is for women to get ahead? Look at Unknown Pleasures. You only hire people with dicks."

"That's not true. I didn't hire anybody. My grandfather brought in Frankie and my father gave Dwayne his job. I'm practically the intern there."

"Still, you don't have any women working there, Jing-nan."

"I promise—the next person we hire will be a woman. It might even be you."

She rolled her eyes. "I'm not working for you. I would put on so much weight."

"I manage to keep it off."

"Yeah, because you're so busy flirting with the tourists."

"That's just a guy who looks like me. The real me is trying to rescue Tong-tong."

I was heading to the kitchen to make my own peanut butter toast when I heard Nancy call me. I thought she was going to offer me her toast after all. Instead she wanted me to get her a glass of guava juice, with ice.

WHEN I GOT TO Unknown Pleasures, Dwayne accosted me.

"Jing-nan, what's going on with Tong-tong?"

"I don't think they learned anything else."

He folded his arms and leaned in to me. "I saw that news report with the shit-smearing."

"You want to know the truth? The video they sent Peggy showed a guy pissing on them. There was no shit involved."

Dwayne unconsciously tugged at the crotch in his jeans. "In a lot of ways, that's even worse. Where's Peggy?"

"At work, I guess."

Dwayne grabbed my shoulder. "Don't you think you should be with your friend? Just in case the worst happens?"

I coughed twice. "What? No, she's with her family and the two cops are going to be with her."

To drive his point home, he grabbed my other shoulder as well. "She's not close with her family and the cops don't really know her."

"She's not that close with me, either, and maybe I know her too well."

Dwayne saved his trump card for last. "You might not think you're close, but she considers you her closest friend. Think about it. She called you first when the kidnapping went down."

That was true. She probably hadn't called anyone else.

"Just go see her," Dwayne urged. "Hang out with her a few hours. Make sure she's all right."

I checked my phone. "I guess I could head over to her office for a little bit. You know, Dwayne, I always thought you liked Peggy."

He backed off and tilted his head. "What's not to like, uh? You have to admit that while she is crazy, she is cute. Hey, don't roll your eyes!"

I put my hands in my pockets. "I'm not going to be gone the whole night," I warned him. I called out to Frankie. "Do you think it's a good idea for me to see Peggy?"

"It's not going to hurt for you to go."

I turned to Dwayne. "You saved the jujubes, right?"

He gave me a sheepish look. "There were so few left last night, I just took 'em home."

"Aw, shit."

"There couldn't have been more than a dozen. It wouldn't have made sense to tell people we had jujube skewers, anyway. We would've just run out of them early and that would have pissed people off."

"Well, I hope you enjoy eating them, Dwayne."

"Honestly, they're starting to go bad. Mushy spots and all. It's going to be a struggle, but I'll figure something out with them. Maybe I'll make protein shakes."

I paused for a second to consider what they should be blended with before Peggy resurfaced in my thoughts. If I was going to see her, I should go now. "I'll call you if something goes horribly wrong," I told Dwayne.

"Yeah, you do that."

I left and walked quickly to the MRT. Damn, it was almost rush hour. Thank god I didn't have to make any transfers.

I slowed as I drew closer to the train station. Maybe it would make more sense for Peggy to come to Unknown Pleasures with Huang and Kung. After all, the first thing people do when they get together is eat. It might as well be my food.

I turned around and started walking back. I called Peggy and asked her if she wanted to hang out and eat at Unknown

Pleasures with the cops. She jumped at the invitation. Maybe I really was her best friend.

As I approached Unknown Pleasures, I saw Dwayne standing on a ladder. *Ma de!* Had one of those stupid ceiling bulbs burned out again?

When I got closer, the lighting seemed fine. In fact, Dwayne wasn't even near any lights and he seemed to be placing a camera behind an idol on our altar.

He saw me, hopped off the ladder and gave me the biggest smile he could muster. I saw the little boy in him.

"What the fuck are you doing, Dwayne?" I asked.

The smile faltered. "Nothing."

"It looks like you're installing a camera at my stand. Actually, it looks like you're hiding a camera."

Dwayne shoved the camera in his jeans pocket and crept down the ladder. "Damn you, Cat, you were supposed to tell me if you saw Jing-nan!"

Frankie pointed at me. "Hey, I see him."

Dwayne stood in front of me and bowed his head until we were the same height.

"Dwayne," I said, "what's the deal with the camera?"

"Well, you know, I got friends who work security. They've been telling me to get cameras in here for our own protection for quite a while. People know that you're Peggy's friend . . ."

"Best friend," I said.

"Well, yeah, best friend, so there might be some unwanted spillover from the kidnapping. What if someone abducted you?"

"Don't worry about me, man."

Dwayne raised his head. "What if someone abducted Nancy?"

I took in a deep breath. "Why would they do that?"

"Who knows? There are crazy people out there."

"Okay, there are crazy people out there, but why didn't you just ask me instead of going behind my back?"

"Well, Frankie was okay with it."

Frankie didn't even look up from his work. "I'm not involved."

"Frankie," I said, "is this a good idea?"

"Maybe."

"Well, I'm for it, and you're right, Dwayne. I mean, I've been shot at before, so this isn't a bad idea."

Dwayne brimmed with vindication and scrambled back up the ladder.

"Do we have to put up a sign telling people they're on camera?" I asked.

"Nah," said Frankie.

"Maybe any footage we get isn't legally admissible, but we're not going to need the law in order to get justice," Dwayne called down.

"So we go after people with baseball bats?" I asked.

"There are three of us," Dwayne reasoned. "And we've got knives."

The camera recorded to a wireless hard drive hidden in an empty box of aluminum foil. Dwayne had borrowed the ladder from Uncle Bing at Beefy King so I brought it back.

"Jing-nan," said Uncle Bing. "What are we going to do about tonight?" He gave me a knowing look.

"Same as we always do at the night market—sell as much food as we can."

"I mean, the thing." He formed a handgun's barrel and hammer with his right index finger and thumb. "Do you think I should turn on the television for that? Or maybe I should have it off?"

"Uncle Bing, I don't think it's going to happen."

He seemed disappointed. "Why are you saying this?"

"I think there's reason to believe that this is more a process of giving Tong-tong hell than actually killing him."

His eyes narrowed as he swept out his tablet from behind the cash register and placed it in my hands. "So this is bullshit, Jing-nan?"

The tablet was opened to a streaming site. An animated GIF scrolled three images—a picture of Tong-tong, the other kidnapped executive and a gun—with a text message: ONE WILL DIE TONIGHT: STREAMING AT 8PM.

My fingers tightened against the frame.

There was sure to be a commotion in the night market over this and Peggy was going to be here in the middle of it all.

Uncle Bing gingerly took the tablet and stashed it behind the register. "I guess you didn't know about that, Jing-nan. It looked pretty real to me, too. Two hours from now, huh? I guess it could still be a prank, but do you think I should turn to the channel? I should probably charge a minimum to everybody who gathers around the TV, right?"

I was still stunned. "I don't know, Uncle Bing," I said absently.

"I admire your prowess as a businessman, Jing-nan. You really turned around your business. Help me out here!"

"Just follow your heart," I muttered and walked away.

"What kind of advice is that?" I heard him say.

I called Peggy but she wasn't answering. No sense in leaving a voicemail. I tried to send her a text: ON SECOND THOUGHT HOW ABOUT I GO TO WHERE YOU ARE?

But the text wouldn't go through. You suck, MobileTone!

I was bagging up chicken gizzards for a sullen teenaged boy when Peggy, Huang and Kung showed up about fifteen minutes later. I came from behind the counter and shoved the bag at the boy.

"Hey, kid. Just take 'em." He broke into a smile and made his getaway. "Peggy, I tried calling you."

She punched my arm. "My battery died after I talked to you. You must be the grim reaper."

I tried to laugh it off.

Huang looked worn out. He stood there, rubbing his big nose like a molt was coming on. It must have been exhausting being with Peggy around the clock.

Kung looked worse. She had dark circles under her eyes and her body language said she couldn't pull the plow anymore. Peggy must have the worst slumber parties.

"I'm glad you're here, officers. Please sit down. I want to talk to my good friend here. Dwayne, how about you get these two nice officers a plate of skewers?"

Dwayne bowed. "Yes, my Han Chinese master!"

I grunted and threw an imaginary dagger at him. "Peggy, I think the kidnappers are going to stream a shooting tonight."

She squared her stance. "I know. I saw the GIF. Isn't that why you called me?"

"No. I found out later. If I knew about it, I wouldn't want you here, basically surrounded by a gaggle of people watching it. Some of these losers might even film you."

Peggy flared her nostrils. "I don't fucking care. I'm already living my life in public, thanks to the kidnapping." She narrowed her eyes. "It's not like I'm going to be sobbing. No matter what happens."

At seven o'clock, there was a noticeable slowdown in people going by. There weren't fewer people—they were just moving slower because their eyeballs were pressed against their phones. I went back and forth between drumming up business and telling Peggy stories about food. For example, armies were responsible for many of China's traditional foods. Skewers were originally cuts of meat cooked on swords after a battle.

At 7:30, word seemed to get around that Beefy King would show the stream across all three of its widescreen monitors. Viewers were expected to make a minimum purchase of an entree and drink in order to hold a spot.

At 7:45, Uncle Bing came to Unknown Pleasures to personally ask Peggy if she and the officers wanted to watch the stream on his monitors. He reasoned that the cops could get a better look at the environs on his big screens. Maybe they could find clues.

Kung put a hand on Peggy's shoulder. "We don't want to put you on public display. It could invite a copycat."

I think it was Kung's patronizing touch rather than what she said that compelled Peggy to tell Uncle Bing yes.

UNCLE BING HAD ROPED off a small area in the front for us. Dwayne came along since business was probably going to be dead, anyway.

Peggy scoffed at the barrier posts and unhooked the retractable belts. "We don't need this," she said.

A Beefy King flunky moved the posts aside. Huang reached across my chest to touch Dwayne's arm. "Hey, tough guy. I need you to stand behind Peggy. And you, Jing-nan, stay on her left side."

I moved without questioning my orders. Dwayne puffed out his chest and pointed at his own nose. "I have a name, you know?"

"Everyone does," said Huang as he plugged in an earpiece. Dwayne grumbled as he moved into position. I looked around for Kung and saw her standing in the back, just outside the periphery of the crowd and also wearing an earpiece.

I looked up at the three monitors. They were all pointed at the streaming account, which displayed a large number 10.

I looked over the crowd. There were probably three hundred people here. I doubted if all of them could see the monitors clearly. I looked at Peggy. My old classmate stood somberly, arms at her sides.

"Peggy, maybe we should get out of here."

She shrugged. "And go where? I'd only be thinking about this." Peggy looked at me sideways. "It's not like I'm going to be the center of attention. Nobody's going to be looking at me."

I turned around and found that assessment true. Everybody's eyes were up. I noticed that Kung was now standing on top of an overturned bucket to get a better view of the crowd.

People suddenly let out a collective gasp. I turned around and saw that the "10" had become a "9". The countdown was on. At "5," Peggy grabbed my hand and held on. I closed my fingers around hers to reassure her.

She had nice hands.

At "1," Dwayne clamped a hand on my left shoulder.

There was no "0" count. The monitor displays flipped to the dog cages in triplicate. The kidnappers had set up rudimentary lights so that the shiny fear in the gagged faces of Tong-tong and the executive came through. Beefy King's PA system amplified the sounds of fingernails scraping metal cage bars as the men wallowed.

The kidnapper didn't make any speech before the gun came into view, clutched in his right hand.

"Which one will it be, huh?" the off-camera voice asked casually as the thumb caressed the side of the gun.

He began to sing "Two Tigers," a nursery song in Mandarin set to the tune of "*Frere Jacques*," and playfully swung the barrel of the gun from one cage to the other with each beat.

Two tigers
Two tigers
Run so fast
Run so fast
One of them has no eyes
One of them has no tail
Very strange
Very strange

The song ended with the gun pointed at Tong-tong.

"Let's give it one more beat," said the kidnapper. He turned to the executive's cage, pushed the barrel of the gun through the bars and fired three times. The shots were so loud that each one caused the sound to cut out momentarily.

People in the crowd cried out. Peggy's hand was hot and sticky like melted cake icing. Dwayne dug his fingernails lightly into my skin.

The echoes of the shell casings bouncing on the floor died away. Agonized moans came from Tong-tong. The gunman's free hand, which was gloved, stroked the cage bars.

"Oh what's wrong there, little tiger? Don't worry. Now you get to have twice as much food!"

The impact of the shots had carried the executive to the back of the cage. Only his bare feet were visible.

The kidnapper retreated and the camera view wiggled slightly before shutting off. All three monitors went black.

I pulled Peggy to me and I hugged her. I never thought she could feel so soft.

Ten tactless seconds later, the monitors switched to Beefy King menus. Callous to his core, Uncle Bing called out to the crowd, which had been stunned to silence.

"Well, the show's over, but combos are ten percent off for the rest of the night!"

CHAPTER 9

Now that there was a confirmed death in a public execution, the police ratcheted up their response level. Huang and Kung's radios squawked with commands for the rank-and-file beat cops and street patrols.

After the crowd melted away, about thirty people remained. I wouldn't have expected so many people to respond to Uncle Bing's discounted food offer, but then again, a shouted bargain on good food will never fall upon deaf ears.

The five of us walked in silence back to Unknown Pleasures. We instinctively formed a protective ring with Peggy in the center.

We reached the stand where I found Nancy sitting in a booth. She stood up and I patted her shoulders.

"Did you see it?" I asked.

"On my phone," she said, her face somber. "I got here a while ago. Frankie said you guys were at Beefy King but it looked too crowded for me to get up front and join you." Nancy reached out and touched Peggy's arm. "I'm sorry about the situation."

Peggy rubbed the back of Nancy's hand. "Thank you, thank

you," said Peggy, sounding tired. "I hope this nightmare ends soon."

Kung leaned in with her shoulder and broke the physical bond between the two women. "Nancy, it's nice to meet you in person. I'm Kung. I called you on the speaker from the lobby last night." They shook hands before Kung turned to Peggy. "I have some not-so-great news. I've just heard from our commanding officer. We have to move you to a safe house."

Nancy cautiously held up a hand and turned to Peggy. "I want you to know that I've found Liu Ju-lan, Ah-tien's friend with the emails that prove he's innocent. Maybe now your lawyer can use them to help get Ah-tien a new trial."

Peggy smirked. Confused, Nancy looked to the cops and then turned back to Peggy, who now raised an admonishing finger. "Why should I help that bastard get a new trial? Because of him and his selfish stubbornness, a man is dead. Maybe Ah-tien deserves to die in jail."

Nancy's face turned completely neutral, which indicates that an Asian is at her angriest. "Your father is still alive," she said evenly. "You can probably keep him that way if you contact this woman."

Huang stepped in next to Kung. "We have to go right now," he said. "The car's here." The crowds parted as a sedan rolled to Unknown Pleasure's storefront.

"Hey!" I yelled at the car. "You're not allowed to drive up here! It's for pedestrians only!" I went around Huang to confront the driver.

A man of aboriginal descent in a suit stepped out of the car and looked through me. He glanced at Dwayne before nodding at Huang and Kung.

"Ready," he said.

"Let's go," said Kung. She didn't grab Peggy, but her raised arms blocked any escape from the car.

"We have to go back to my place so I can pack a bag," Peggy protested.

Kung nodded. "We'll make a list later and I'll go get what you need." Peggy must've been worried for her own safety; otherwise she would have never tucked herself into the back of the car so readily. Kung followed her in.

"We'll help you out," said Huang as he shut the door. He went around and dropped himself into the driver's seat. The aboriginal officer looked around, smelled the air and then sat in the front passenger seat. The car was gone a few seconds later.

"She didn't intend to sound so mean," I told Nancy. "She's under a lot of stress right now."

Nancy nodded. "I understand that, but that doesn't make this any less urgent. They're still going to need the chip plans from Ah-tien."

"I'll send the information to the cops."

Nancy pushed her mouth to the side. "Actually, I should be sure it's the right person. If Peggy had given me a minute I would've explained that I was only ninety percent sure it was the right Ju-lan."

Dwayne picked this moment to give me his assessment of the aboriginal officer. "That brother has killed before," he said. "I can tell."

I put my arms to my sides. "Hey, let's not talk about killing people, all right, Dwayne? I still can't believe what we saw tonight."

Dwayne and Nancy nodded. Frankie turned down the heat on the grill and approached us. "I just happened to notice something," he said in his understated way. "Look." He showed us a screen shot of the dog cages on his phone and pointed at a shadow on the wall that looked like a thick line. "Keep your eye there." He slid to the next image, which was a video capture, and pressed play. It looked like the shadow was wiping a corner of the wall over and over.

"That shadow's moving back and forth," I said. "That's weird."

"It looks like it's repeating, but it's not," said Frankie. "It's not even the same shadow." He spread out his fingers and moved them over his phone display. "I think they're spokes of a big wheel. The dog cages aren't in a basement. They're holding Tong-tong in a warehouse with windows high up."

"Do you mean that could be a wind turbine," said Nancy. "Do you think the warehouse is by a coastline?"

"That's not a wind turbine," said Frankie. "Turbine blades aren't that big. I think we're talking about a Ferris wheel."

I spoke up. "The only Ferris wheel I've seen in Taipei is from the MRT when it crosses over the Tamsui River."

"That's Miramar Park," said Dawyne.

"Miramar Entertainment Park," said Frankie. "Have any of you been there?" All of us shook our heads. "It's this giant, high-end shopping complex, topped off with that Ferris wheel. Guess who owns a big chunk of the commercial real estate around there?"

"That couldn't be Tong-tong, could it?" asked Nancy.

"You bet it is!" said Frankie.

Dwayne whistled. "Man, that would be so fucked up if he were being held in one of his own buildings! Frankie, can you tell from the video where he's being held?"

Frankie shrugged. He pocketed his phone and rubbed his nose. "If it were daylight, I probably could. I'm not familiar enough with the area at night."

I touched Frankie's arm. "You should tell Huang and Kung!" I said.

He tapped out a cigarette from his pack and stepped away

to smoke it. "They'll find out soon enough. I've already sent a message to a guy I know on the force."

Nancy decided to stay with me at Unknown Pleasures because she was freaked out by the shooting. We all were.

It was a weird night for me. It's always strange acting out my Johnny persona in front of my girlfriend. I'm normally not conscious about what I do and say, but with Nancy right there, I felt like a fake. A cheery fucking fool. She wasn't even actively watching me. Her eyes were on her phone and she looked grim as hell.

About an hour later, Nancy called us all over. Frankie's guy had come through. The police were going to hold an emergency press conference to announce they had rescued Tong-tong.

None of us felt like walking back to Beefy King so in order to see it on a bigger screen, Dwayne fired up the tablet that he liked to charge at work, at my expense.

The cops said that Tong-tong was safe, in relatively good health, but the perpetrators were still at large.

While they declined to say where they found Peggy's dad, they noted that after a night of medical observation and rest, Tong-tong would hold his own press conference tomorrow. The cops didn't take any questions.

"They didn't even mention the murdered executive," said Nancy.

"Nobody needs an update on a dead man," I said.

Dwayne put his tablet to sleep and zipped up the carrying case. "Somebody had to care about him," he said. "He had to have a family."

Nancy sighed. "If he did, he probably never got to see them," she said. "If you're working for Tong-tong, you're probably doing eighty-hour workweeks at a minimum."

I shuddered. "The guy worked like a dog and then he took

a bullet for his boss," I said. "I would never ask you guys to be like that for me."

Dwayne stashed his tablet up on a shelf for safekeeping. "I wouldn't do it," he said.

"Nope," said Frankie.

If the televised shooting cut the crowd in half, the press conference convinced the remaining people to head home. Pretty soon all of Shilin Night Market was a ghost town. We packed it in before 10:30 P.M., possibly the earliest we have ever closed.

TONG-TONG WAS ONE OF these guys who lived to work and worked to live. In other words, a typical Taipei person. Even after a few days in captivity in a dog cage, that maniac had called a press conference at 7:30 in the morning at his office in the Taipei 101 building.

Nancy and I sat on the edge of the couch to watch and she held me tightly. Peggy had texted me beforehand to make sure we wouldn't miss it.

You'd never know Tong-tong had been away from showers, clean clothes and a bed. He mainly looked as he always had. Tall, unattractive and wearing an expression that said he was somewhat dissatisfied with his life.

His mouth was different, though. It was tense, like it was a size or two too small. His words were different, too. As ruthless as a businessman he was, he had never come off as mean before.

"The past few days have been the most harrowing ones my family has had to endure since the civil war in China," he declared. "In the depths of the pit, however, I have found new clarity. I know for sure now that there are people who hate me and my family and our money. I know those people need to be eliminated from our society.

"I am offering a reward of one million NT to whoever finds these bastards! I don't care if you have to beat them up! I don't care if you have to carry them to the police station in bags! And to celebrate our most vigilant and steadfast citizens for the Double-Ninth holiday, I am offering a bonus of one thousand NT for each year a claimant is over sixty!"

A thousand NT? That was like nothing, especially compared with the million NT reward. Well, people will just focus on the word "bonus."

Tong-tong raised a fist. "Let us all unite and find these lowlifes. Mainlanders, *benshengren*, Hakka, aborigines, and even you people from Southeast Asia who snuck in here illegally. I promise that if you snuck into this country and you catch my kidnappers, I will get you citizenship or at least delay your deportation!

"I have already given the police all the exhaustive details of my captors, but I'm going to give you the most relevant ones." Tong-tong took a swig of water, unfolded a piece of paper and adjusted his gold-rimmed glasses. "There are at least three of them. One is in his mid-thirties, average height with a deep voice. You'd recognize it because he was the man in the video with the gun. He killed my friend Associate Vice President Peng Wan-chang, who had been by my side over the last thirty years. I have spent more time with him than any of my kids. If we were gay, I couldn't have loved him more.

"The police kept Peng's identity secret to protect his family, but we weren't able save his life. I'll be personally visiting his relatives and passing on my condolences.

"Anyway, the second suspect is in his twenties, average height. He was the driver of the van that was used to transport us. I don't know what his voice sounds like.

"The third suspect is also in his twenties, average height, but on the fat side. He is the one who set up the camera and

Internet streaming. He has a high-pitched voice, as if he was a girl.

"One thing you should know about these men, actually, is that they all spoke Mandarin a little funny. Like they were native speakers of Thai or Indonesian. Is Indonesian a language? What language do they speak there?" He threw his hands up to show he didn't much care what the answer was. "Well, whatever it is, it isn't Mandarin. That I can tell you."

Tong-tong stepped away from the podium, muttered something and then returned with sheets of paper.

"I made these myself," he declared as he held up sketches of the three men. I didn't know if they were accurate, but they were surprisingly good for a businessman. Maybe he learned how to draw people by making self-portraits. In fact, the three suspects, as rendered, all seemed to resemble Tong-tong, particularly in the nostril end of the nose and in the eyebrows.

"My art is downloadable on my Facebook page," said Tong-tong as he set down the sketches. "Print them out and tape them everywhere. While I'm driving around Taipei, if I see you holding them up in the street, I'll give you a hundred-NT note! Any business I come across that has them in the window, I'll give a five-hundred-NT note to whoever's behind the counter!

"I'm ready to pay, Taiwan! Now let's make these criminals pay with their lives!" He stepped back and rubbed his cufflinks before approaching the microphone again. "Any questions?"

A reporter from Taiwan's least-scrupulous newspaper, *The Daily Pineapple*, raised her hand. "Yes, sweetheart, you have a question?"

She was in her early twenties and seemed inappropriately happy. "Tong-tong, I'm glad you're safe."

He saluted her. "Thank you! You are lovely, aren't you?"

"You're welcome. I just want to make sure I understand you. You want the suspects—"

"Criminals! They are not 'suspects' because they are definitely guilty!"

"All right, the criminals, you want people to go out and physically assault them?"

"Of course! I want people to do what I would if I saw them. Don't worry about any harm you cause—I will cover any legal fees you incur! Did any of them show Associate Vice President Peng Wan-chang one iota of mercy? No! Do they deserve any leniency themselves? No!" Tong-tong then pointed to a grey-haired man I recognized from the conservative right-wing-leaning TV China, a cable station based in Taiwan, despite its name.

"Tong-tong, do you think it was a good idea for you to sketch the suspects?"

"It was a great idea! I'm the only one who knows exactly what they look like!"

"You're not a very good artist, though. The three men all look the same."

"No, they don't!"

"And they even look like you a little bit."

"Sit down and shut up. I'm not talking to you anymore. Maybe it's time for you to leave."

"I'm going to have to point out the shortcomings on my show tonight."

"So what? Your ratings are lousy because no one watches anymore. Your show is weak. I'm done with you." Tong-tong flicked his wrists. "I'm going to take one more question. Yes, you, sweetheart." He made a groping motion in the direction of a wide-eyed and underdressed young woman, a species native to cable channels desperate for viewers. She blinked and brushed her hair back over her ears.

"Tong-tong, what would you say to the kidnappers if they're listening right now?"

He smiled, tilted his head and looked straight into the camera. "You put me in a dog cage, you bastards. You humiliated me in front of the whole country." He leaned forward. "Now the dog is out and I'm coming for your balls."

Gasps arose from the assembled journalists. Realizing that he had delivered a hell of an exit line he couldn't possibly top, Tong-tong stomped off in triumph.

The highest-ranking policeman present, a hapless hippo in plain clothes, rushed to the microphone. "Of course, Tong-tong is very excited right now and he's exaggerating a little bit. We urge the public at large not to take the law into their own hands. Do not confront people you think match the descriptions. Call the police immediately and you will still definitely get your reward."

By early afternoon, bands of retirees were walking the streets, clutching broken-off broom handles. At dusk, schoolboys sported baseball bats bungee-cabled to their backpacks for immediate access. At pedestrian crossings, traffic cops fondled their radios and nodded approvingly at both groups. "Be careful," they offered to the few female bounty hunters.

The suspect sketches were everywhere. The sound of them fluttering was like an invasive avian species. On my way to the night market, I saw that our nation's most industrious parents had already laminated them to the vests of their toddlers.

STALLS AT THE NIGHT market were wallpapered with the sketches as if they were talismans to ward off evil. Some poor kids who were forced to work at their family-owned stalls entertained themselves by wearing masks of the sketches, tearing eyeholes in the appropriate places.

I arrived at Unknown Pleasures in time to catch Dwayne putting up the final touches to the stall—he had covered all available vertical space with the damned things.

"Have you lost your goddamned mind?" I asked him gently. "What the hell are you doing?"

He stood up and hid a roll of packing tape behind his back. "What does it look like? I'm making sure that we continue to conform to community standards." He lifted his chin. "Those standards change from time to time."

"We don't have to mummify the place. One of each sketch would've been fine."

Dwayne raised an eyebrow at me. "Do I have to remind you, Jing-nan, that Tong-tong is our landlord?"

"Landlord, not overlord," I said. I turned to Frankie, always the most reasonable person among us. "Three is enough, isn't it?" I asked.

Frankie wiped his hands with a ragged blue towel. "Peggy is your friend. Tong-tong is her father. She'll probably be here somewhat frequently, now that she's no longer sequestered. She'll see these flyers as a sign of support." He stuck a cigarette in his mouth and paused before lighting it. "It's all right to look stupid for the sake of a friend."

"She's free to roam around again?" I asked. "I missed that."

"Of course you did," said Frankie. "Say, why don't you invite her and her father to come by? That'll drive up business because he's a bigger celebrity now than he ever was."

My money muscle, located on the right side of the back of my neck, began to twitch. It gets a workout when I assume my Johnny personality. When it's sore, I know it's been a good night for the register.

"That would be a good idea, wouldn't it?" I said to myself out loud.

I texted Peggy to congratulate her on her new freedom and asked if she and her dad wanted to make an appearance at my stand at nine-ish tomorrow night. It would be good publicity for both of us. She said sure. I quickly wrote up announcements on social media to say that the Lees would be at Unknown Pleasures at eight. I could use the hour in advance to process all the anticipated food sales. No vegan special could compete with the star power of Taiwan's most famous crime victim.

I didn't tell her that it was probably Frankie's tip that led to Tong-tong's rescue. Honestly, if she were on the fence about her dad coming, I might have pulled it out.

NANCY ASKED ME TO meet her at her apartment at the end of the night. That meant she was either angry or busy. Turns out she was both.

"So, it's true," she spat. "You're doing a publicity stunt with Tong-tong."

I wobbled on one foot as I took off my shoes. What had I walked into? Maybe I should put my shoes back on and retreat right now. "It's not really a stunt, it's more like an event. What's wrong with it? You know I'm friends with Peggy, and I hope you agree that it's a good thing her father's been found."

Nancy admonished me by wagging her phone at my heart. "Do you know what happened tonight?"

"What happened? Did they catch the kidnappers?"

"No, Jing-nan. It hasn't been picked up by the mainstream media, but the Southeast Asian student group on campus is sending this around." She thrust her phone at me.

I took Nancy's phone. It was opened to a group email about Southeast Asian people who had been targeted and beaten. The formatting was a little broken up because a few recipients added subsequent stories of more incidents. One claimed that three Vietnamese men had gone to a police station in Taoyuan to report they were assaulted and were given a second round of beatings by some officers at the precinct. Another told of an Indonesian woman who had been pushed to the ground and had her hijab torn off by a group of five teens.

I scrolled casually through the rest. In all, there seemed to be about a dozen victims. I couldn't recognize my modern and tolerant country in the incidents. It was like reading about past human-rights abuses during the martial-law era. These things couldn't possibly happen here anymore, could they?

"Tong-tong is to blame for all this!" declared Nancy. "He put all those racist goons in the street!"

"Could some of these things be made up?" I asked tentatively. "I mean, stupid guys are always going around and getting in trouble, right? It doesn't mean it was a racist thing."

I quickly discovered that *I* was in trouble.

"Unarmed men were beaten by people with sticks," said Nancy as she snatched her phone back. "And people were yelling at them to get out of Taiwan!"

"I hope these are just isolated incidents," I said. "I'm sure Tong-tong disavows them all."

THINGS ONLY GOT WORSE and were bad enough that by morning, cable news channels had to cover stories about Southeast Asian men and women being targeted in the streets. The number of victims was up to fifty.

The Dynasty Network had phone-video footage of a beating shot by a bystander. One man had another in a chokehold while a third man was swinging a broken-off broom handle into the choked man's stomach. With each swing he yelled, "Get out, monkey!"

All three faces were blurred out.

The network tried unsuccessfully to get in touch with the victim. The stone-faced female anchor stated that although they couldn't show viewers the victim, the man didn't resemble any of the three sketches. She added that police had already arrested two suspects connected with the assault, and that they were unemployed construction workers.

After a commercial break, a young male correspondent did manage to track down Tong-tong's cell-phone number. The station put up a still shot of Peggy's father announcing some building project, captured in mid-speech with his lips pursed, as if ready for a kiss. The reporter, a teen heartthrob in a sports jacket, stood in sharp contrast next to the still of the unattractive Tong-tong, as he called Tong-tong live on the air.

There was a click, a scraping sound, and then a, "Hello?" It was Tong-tong and he seemed wary.

"Good morning, Tong-tong!" The reporter beamed, his eyes shining. "This is Alan Qiao of The Dynasty Network. You're live on television right now."

"How did you get this number?"

"You own twenty-five percent of our company and we had someone dig through our internal paperwork to find your information."

"Oh, I guess I still own a part of you. It's slipped my mind because you haven't grown much in value."

"We are all so glad that you're safe."

"Yes, thank you."

"We wanted to know if you're aware that some, very few, of your supporters have allegedly been assaulting immigrants. I say 'allegedly' because no official police reports have been filed."

Tong-tong scoffed. "You know why there's no police reports?"

"Why?"

"Because those people are all here illegally. They should expect to be beaten, if not deported."

Qiao's pupils dilated. High-definition television didn't miss anything.

Tong-tong carried on. "I'm grateful for all the people out there trying to hunt down these scum of the earth. The cops are doing what they can, and frankly, Alan, the media should be doing their part in finding these guys. Get out there on the streets and put your cameras to work. Y'know what I'm saying?"

"Tong-tong, don't you feel responsible for these acts of violence?"

"I'm not responsible, Alan. Remember, I'm the victim in all this! I was locked in a dog cage for three days and saw Associate Vice President Peng Wan-chang, one of my top guys, murdered right in front of my face. I. Am. The. Victim."

The victim was doing a hell of a job acting like a petulant child. I squirmed in my seat. I had made a mistake by inviting him to come to my place of business. Maybe I should text Peggy and call the whole thing off.

"I should mention something," said Tong-tong, as if reading my mind. "I'm doing an event tonight. I'm going to say a few words of gratitude to my supporters and offer more encouragement to people taking up the mantle of enforcing the law. It's going to be at the Shilin Night Market inside of a very excellent food stand run by a friend of my daughter. What's the name of the place, sweetheart? 'No Pleasure'? Sounds dirty. Oh, 'Unknown Pleasures.' Still sounds dirty. It's run by the guy that gangster tried to shoot, but he defended himself with a cooking pot. Just like how we all need to defend ourselves against this wave of lawlessness in Taiwan that was brought by illegal immigrants. What we have going on is a lot worse than China, believe me."

"I was thinking," the anchor interjected, "that maybe you want to apologize to the immigrant community, the great majority of whom are—"

"Apologize? You want me to apologize? Do I have to state the obvious again, Alan? I'm the victim! They should apologize to me and my family for not keeping their own people in line."

"That might sound a little racist," suggested the anchor.

Scuffling sounds indicated that Tong-tong was switching his phone to the other ear and stronger hand. "Alan, if you want to call me racist, think about this. How many Southeast Asians do you have on your network? I'd say zero. You know how many of those people I employ? Hundreds, through my construction subsidiaries and in my hotels. I have everybody of every species working for me. I discriminate against nobody."

"What do you have to say to the woman who had her hijab pulled off?"

"I say that's a terrible thing and that I'm sorry she had to experience it. At the same time, though, why is she wearing a hijab in Taiwan? I mean, we don't have a problem with that, but when you think of Taiwan, you don't think about women wearing hijabs is all I'm saying. When they have the big Islamic holidays, have you seen Taipei Main Station, Alan? Have you?"

The reporter turned his head slightly and raised his perfectly trimmed right eyebrow. "I'm honestly not sure what you're talking about, Tong-tong."

"Well look at the pictures online, Alan! All the Muslims are gathered there, squatting in their hijabs and maybe some are waiting for buses or trains, but it looks like a marketplace in the Middle East!

"We either have a country or we don't. If you're going to come here, even if you come here illegally, you have to love our people, our way of life, our customs. You have to love Taiwan." Tong-tong cupped the phone but some intense whispering still came through his end before he spoke into the phone again. "Listen, Alan, I have to run now, but everybody come out to Unknown Pleasures tonight and we're going to have a great time."

As the phone clicked, the reporter put on a furious smile and handed off to another reporter, who was standing by to do a live report on a dancing troupe of people older than seventy.

I think I exhaled for the first time since the interview started.

"I never knew what a fucking asshole he was," I said. Nancy slapped the back of my right hand. *"Gan!"* I yelped. She pointed her finger at my nose, menacing me.

"You need to cancel that appearance of that racist jerk tonight. I will lose all respect for you if you let him onto your property." She muted the television and tore open the latest issue of her trusty biomedical journal.

These actions were meant to convey to me that hers were the final words on the subject. I just needed to point out how she was technically wrong.

"Nancy, he owns the land the night market is on, so, really, Unknown Pleasures is on his property, not mine."

"Excellent point," she said not looking at me. "You've really changed my mind about Tong-tong."

"I'm not trying to change your mind."

"So then you're canceling his appearance, right?"

My money muscle tensed. "All publicity is good publicity," I started. She rolled up her magazine and swatted my head in energy-efficient swats that have surely killed many flying insects. "Seriously, Nancy, I'm a businessman. I can't say no to the number of people he will bring in."

"You're a businessman? Like how Tong-tong is a business-man? That is, without a moral conscience?" She unrolled the magazine and resumed ignoring me.

"Look, Nancy, before he goes on, I'm going to speak and set the tone for the entire event. I will make it clear that we do not support prejudice in any form and that Tong-tong is only calling out for justice. How does that sound?"

Nancy rolled up her magazine again and tapped it against her chin. She looked thoughtful. "That is acceptable to me. This is your business, your livelihood." She sighed. "But you have to be in control. Tong-tong steamrolled that journalist. I can see where Peggy gets her drive from."

The mention of Peggy lit up a dim memory in my head. What was Nancy trying to say to Peggy?

"That woman," I said to Nancy. "Liu Ju-lan, Ah-tien's friend. You said you found her."

"Oh. Yes, I think I did. But Peggy didn't seem too inter-ested in tracking her down. Or helping Ah-tien."

"Well, we should go see her. If she has the goods, then Ah-tien really should get a retrial."

"That's a good idea, Jing-nan. Very selfless of you."

Only a minute ago she was beating me and now I've man-aged to turn it around. Maybe I should be in public relations. I went to the kitchen, plated two pineapple cakes and grabbed two cans of Mr. Brown from the fridge.

"Where is Ju-lan?" I asked as I handed breakfast to Nancy.

"I think she's running a bed and breakfast in Ximending."

We shook our canned coffees before popping them open.

"Yuck. I could never run one of those. You have to cater to all these annoying tourists in order to get their money."

She raised her eyebrows at me. "Don't you depend on tourists for your business?"

I bit my lip. "Yeah, but everybody who comes to Unknown Pleasures is a cool tourist."

"If only Tong-tong were as smooth as you." She touched my face. "Actually, you're not that smooth. You need to shave."

CHAPTER 10

Nancy and I took the train to the B&B. We decided not to call beforehand just in case Ju-lan didn't want to talk and pulled a runner. Nancy didn't really know her, after all.

A few groups walking through the MRT stations looked like cleanup crews with their brooms and standing dustpans. The fliers taped to the front and back of their shirts made their true identities clear. Tong-tong supporters. They weren't technically carrying weapons, but those handles could be twisted off and wielded in two seconds. Cops on the platform watched them carefully.

We walked into the lobby of the building that housed Ju-lan's business. The middle-aged guard at the front desk was playing an erhu. He put down his bow to try to hand us some Tong-tong fliers but we shook our heads. He grimaced, showing off red-stained teeth from years of chewing betelnut. He might have served in the military for decades.

"Where are you come from?" he asked in English.

"We're on vacation from the United States," I declared, doing my best Southern-accented American English. He nodded and waved us through.

I know, it's not cool for us to pretend to be other people, but I had to save us from what would undoubtedly be a long-ish lecture in Mandarin about how we needed to help catch Tong-tong's kidnappers with maybe an anti-foreigner segment thrown in for good measure.

As we waited forever for the elevator, I noticed the guard shaking his head. All day, every day, all he saw were tourists. The guard picked up his bow and scraped it across the erhu's two strings. We entered the elevator and I pressed the "close" button repeatedly. I wasn't sure what section of the military our guard had served in, but it sure wasn't in the band.

DURING THE RIDE UP, I suddenly became a little apprehensive about meeting Ju-lan. My mind called up an image of a middle-aged woman pulling out a baseball bat and swinging it at us.

Our car jerked to a stop and the door lurched open. We stepped to a desk where a woman in her early thirties stood.

"Excuse me, miss," I asked. "Do you know where we can find someone named Ju-lan?"

She responded by standing up and wiggling her glasses. "There's no one here by that name," she said. "I'm Ling-yu." The woman seemed a little stiff. Damn, I thought, wrong place. Then she saw I was with somebody. "Nancy?" she asked. "Is that you?"

"Ju-lan! So good to see you." Nancy reached across the desk and the women awkwardly rubbed each other's arms. Ah-tien's friend was way younger than I had thought. She wore her hair short and maintained an expression of professional concern for what we'd say about her business online. Ju-lan glanced at me.

"You're married now, I see," said Ju-lan. "Good for you."

"We're not there, yet," I said as I reached out a hand to her. "My name is Chen Jing-nan."

"Hello, Mr. Chen," she said in a clear voice the tourists probably loved that was too loud for Taiwanese to talk to each other in. She petted the back of my hand. "Well, this is some coincidence seeing you, Nancy."

Nancy folded her hands and pressed them against the desk. "I was trying to find you."

"You were?" Ju-lan's voice was tinged with concern.

"Yes, it's about Ah-tien."

Ju-lan swallowed and cast an inquiring look at me.

"It's all right," I said. "I know all about them."

Jul-lan exhaled. "Okay. So, what can I do for you, Nancy?"

"I understand that you have a bunch of emails that Ah-tien sent to you for safekeeping. Just in case he ended up in jail." Nancy unstuck her hands and placed them flat on the desktop. "Actually, I think you were supposed to release the emails after he was arrested."

Ju-lan's face shrank five percent and she nodded. "I was supposed to, you're right." She sank back into her seat and swiveled slightly away from both of us. "I didn't, though."

Now was not the time to push.

"Yes," said Nancy.

Ju-lan still couldn't face either of us. "Do you know why I didn't? I could have been swept up in the corruption probe, as well. Ah-tien's company wasn't the only one bribing officials. Pretty much the entire industry was. Of course, the ones who paid the biggest bribes were the most successful, like Ah-tien's company. Then they decided to cut back on the outlay. That was a big mistake. When the investigators closed in, Ah-tien took the blame for his company and the entire industry, as well."

"Ju-lan," I asked, "how were you in danger?"

"The justice department had subpoenaed us for any emails regarding Ah-tien or his company. I showed the emails to my legal department. The top lawyer pulled me into a conference room. He told me that the government could use it to prove collusion between our companies and also between Ah-tien and me personally. I could have faced the same charges as him." Ju-lan pulled herself toward us and held up her hands. "I wasn't ready to go to jail, too. That wouldn't help Ah-tien at all. That's what the emails would've done. They would've ended up condemning both of us."

Nancy lowered her head. "That's really awful, Ju-lan."

"I'm sorry you had to face that choice, Ju-lan," I said. "You don't have copies of the emails, do you?"

She ran a finger along the rim of a pot bearing a chrysan-themum. She had a few of them on the counter. The tourists wouldn't get it, but "Ju-lan" means "chrysanthemum."

"No, I don't," she said. "I ended up quitting a few months later. The semiconductor business is no place for a woman. Not that we are unable to do the job. It's just not a female-friendly industry." She crossed her arms. "I had to make a clean break, so I changed my name to Ling-yu." Ju-lan looked at Nancy expectantly. "How did you find me?"

"I remember you mentioned that your dream was to open a B&B. That was how I tracked you down," said Nancy sheepishly. "I looked up B&Bs named Chrysanthemum."

"It's a very nice place you have here," I said, even though we didn't see anything beyond the lobby.

"It keeps me alive," she said. I wasn't sure if she was refer-ring to the money or the work itself. "Some foreigners are very nice and that's why it's so disappointing when people like Tong-tong say the things they say."

I could feel Nancy glaring at me but I couldn't meet her face. Instead I looked to Ju-lan. "Pardon me, but you wouldn't know anything about a chip design that Ah-tien had been trying to shop around."

She leaned on the counter and turned her eyes to the left. "He did have a chip, a low-power chip."

"Yes," I said. "That's the one."

She shrugged. "He told me he was working on it, but I honestly don't know much about it. My specialty was in graphics chips." Her phone rang and she glanced at the blinking light on her phone.

"It was nice meeting you," I said. This time she gave my hand a full shake. She and Nancy rubbed arms again.

Down in the lobby, the guard was giving two unfortunate people the full-on Tong-tong indoctrination. It was hyperventilated and spittle-punctuated, but still better than hearing him play music.

WE WERE WALKING BACK to the MRT station when Nancy checked her phone and told me there was a big rally planned at her university, Taida.

"For what?" I asked.

Her eyes flashed. "It's an anti-Tong-tong, anti-racism rally. They want the school to give back all his donation and scholarship money."

"I thought he didn't make that big donation yet."

"He didn't, but he's contributed in the past. A lot."

"That doesn't make any sense," I said. "If you don't like someone, wouldn't you want to take away their money?"

Nancy stopped in her tracks to take me to task. I stopped walking, as well, and someone rudely pushed past me. "Most people—not you, Jing-nan—don't want to be seen as being supported by someone they find disgusting."

I was jostled again as two men elbowed their way around me. I was annoyed but I kept my eyes on Nancy because I had to make a point. "Here's the thing, though," I said, raising a finger to show that I had exactly one point. "How do you really know what someone is like? How can you judge a person by only one aspect of their personality? If a customer's having a bad day and, oh, I don't know, they end up screaming at me or Dwayne, does that mean they're a bad person?"

Nancy bent her left arm and pushed the elbow into my chest. "If someone says racist things on live television, he is definitely a bad person. Tong-tong is a bad person, Jing-nan."

Someone shoved me so hard I nearly fell over. Luckily, Nancy caught me.

We heard shouting in the distance. On a level above us, two men were squared off, each holding a broken broom handle. Three MRT police were trying to keep the crowd at bay. One hardy officer, a woman in what looked like a bulletproof vest, was trying to separate the two combatants, but each would scamper around her back to take a toddler-like swing at the other.

"Avenge Tong-tong!" yelled one of the fighters. A part of the crowd obediently repeated it.

"Fight racism!" yelled the other. Jeers from the Tong-tong crew drowned out any audible support.

The woman, like all MRT officers, was unarmed, but also unafraid. The struggle hit a new low when the Tong-tong supporter grabbed her cap and tossed it into the crowd. Her freed ponytail whipped against her furious mouth as the officer swung her head around. The Tong-tong supporter had unwittingly unleashed a beast.

She kicked him in the stomach and he scuttled across the floor, flailing like a lobster trying to escape from a weighing scale. In a cinematic touch, she raised a fist over her head in victory. Nancy and I were amazed, along with the entire crowd, which had fallen silent.

The other fighter tried to bolt but the crowd pushed him back. Two of the male cops soon had him by the elbows while the third collected the broom handles. The woman picked up her cap and slid it back on.

"Get out of here, everybody! Or I'll arrest you!" she roared. The crowd slunk away.

Nancy spun her hand to circle the aftermath. "That's all because of Tong-tong," she said. "He's inciting people to attack each other. Do you still want him to speak at your business?"

"Shit," I said. "It's too late to cancel it, but I think I'm going to need some muscle."

I called Dwayne. I knew he was friends with a lot of bouncers and security guards. I asked if he could have a few of them show up and play defense for Tong-tong's appearance. He said it wouldn't be a problem because their usual work shifts didn't start until later in the night. I would have to pay them cash and maybe provide some food. I had no problem with that at all. If I had it my way, of course, I would want to hire that ass-kicking female cop from the MRT station.

IT TURNED OUT, THOUGH, that another female cop showed up at Unknown Pleasures a few hours ahead of Tong-tong's scheduled appearance. Kung, Peggy's erstwhile errand-girl, looked well-rested. She even had enough time to cover up the scar on her cheek.

"Are you here in an official capacity, officer?" I asked.

"Yeah, I am," she said. "I heard that you're hiring some bouncers to watch over the crowd."

"My main concern is that everyone is safe."

"I bet you'll probably move a lot of food tonight, Jing-nan."

Dwayne joined us, wiping his hands with a towel. "People

get hungry when they're mad," he said, "and Tong-tong's base is begging to get worked up."

I crossed my arms. "They're angry about a lot of things," I said. "I want to make it clear that I do not buy into most of Tong-tong's rhetoric, especially the anti-immigrant stuff."

"I'm glad to hear you say that," said Kung. "My mother's from Vietnam."

"You should tell him."

"I did. He looked over my body and said, 'I love Vietnamese women!'"

Dwayne touched her shoulder. "He said that? I would've broken his nose if he said shit like that to me!"

Kung shrugged. "At least he didn't say he hated Vietnamese women. He's been very good to the Taipei police. He's the biggest donor to our union. We honor him at our banquets every year."

"Ah," I said, nodding. "No wonder you guys went all out to try to find him when he was kidnapped."

Kung suddenly straightened up. "We might have a situation here."

I turned and observed two fairly tall guys in their early thirties approaching. Their mischievous expressions were a little unnerving. Did they come here to bust up my joint before Tong-tong even said a word? Dwayne walked up to them and the men all shared hearty embraces. I was relieved. Dwayne had some scary-looking friends.

"This is where you work, huh?" said one of them. He had looked lanky from ten feet out but up close his muscles became apparent. The man looked at me and stuck out a hand. "You must be the big boss man, Jing-nan!"

I took his hand and found his grip reassuring for my purposes. "Good to meet you," I said. "What's your name?"

"My name is Attun. I was named for the last holdout

soldier of imperial Japan. He was Amis, you know. Didn't surrender until 1974."

I took a step back. "Wow, I had no idea. I hope you're as tough as him. There could be some real troublemakers tonight."

He cracked his elbows. "I'm ready."

Dwayne brought over his other friend. "Jing-nan, this is my friend Show." Show was a bit aloof and merely nodded at me. I nodded back. It wasn't just an Amis thing. It was a Taiwan thing. Sometimes people are shy.

This would never fly in the US. You offend people if you don't shake hands or hug. Or act like someone's your best friend right away. If you merely nodded when you were introduced to an American, they'd think you had something against them.

I hoped Show had nothing against me. Unlike Attun, Show looked like he was muscular from a distance and downright intimidating up close. His aura of strength was somewhat dimmed when Dwayne muttered something and Show revealed a laugh that sounded like a pre-pubescent teen's homeroom giggle.

"Doesn't he?" asked Dwayne out loud, encouraging more yucks from Show. "Doesn't he, huh?" In all likelihood he was making fun of me.

"What's going on?" I asked.

Dwayne turned sheepish. "I was just telling Show that you looked like the type of guy who was into Joy Division. He's heard their songs before and he can't figure out who would like the band, either."

Show managed to stifle his laughter. "I'm sorry, Jing-nan, I don't mean to laugh at you," he said.

"It's fine with me," I said. "I'm just glad you're here. Please, let's all eat up before the rush." I cracked my knuckles and readied myself to carry a few trays of food. "Say, Frankie . . ." I called, but I stopped because he was already setting food down on a table. He looked at me and gave me one of his signature smiles that nearly curled up to his eyes.

I DIDN'T REALLY WORRY until five minutes to nine. Many people had a loose definition of time, but a guy like Tong-tong would be twenty minutes early for everything. I had a few texts from Peggy around eight-thirty, when she said traffic was bad but that she still expected to get to Unknown Pleasures on time.

I tossed some grilled meats into a glassine envelope once again and rang up the sale. We were running low on wooden skewers, but we were also probably having the best night ever.

I looked around and ignored the next customers, who were yelling something at me. A survey of the assembled crowd showed that it was eighty percent male. Men ate more, so good for me. I glanced to my left and right. Show and Attun stood on either side of the Unknown Pleasures' counters. Scowling with arms crossed, they were my brave temple-door guardians. If they had swords they wouldn't be any more intimidating.

WHERE ARE YOU GUYS? I texted Peggy.

HERE, she wrote back.

I scanned the sea of black hair and baseball caps but failed to see an entourage approaching. Then I saw Tong-tong's bare hand and suit sleeve cutting through the black-headed crowd like a shark fin. He was probably thirty feet away, but I could hear him even above the whoops of support.

"Excuse me! Pardon me! Thank you for being here!" It was just him with Peggy in tow. When they were close enough, I saw that he wasn't worse for the wear after pushing through the boisterous crowd. Tong-tong's suit was not even rumpled and his tie was still straight. Peggy was holding his briefcase. They both had big toothpaste-commercial smiles on.

As the two crossed the goal line and entered our dining area, Show and Attun closed in and blocked the entrance. Maybe I had been overcautious in hiring them. After all, there were already plain-clothed police in the crowd and the people were more concerned with solemnly recording the event on their phones.

Peggy grabbed my hands. "Jing-nan, thank you for doing this," she said. "People have been saying horrible things about my dad that just aren't true. I'm glad you're giving him a forum where he can clear the air." She pulled at the armpits of her pantsuit with anxiety.

"You're my friend, so he's practically my dad, too," I said as I tried hard to stitch sincerity into my voice.

Tong-tong came up and clasped each of my shoulders with a powerful hand. He gave me a big smile, which I was forced to return. The guy had charisma.

"You're going to introduce me, kid?"

"Yes, Mr. Lee."

He released me and patted my right arm. "Call me Tong-tong—everybody does!" He turned and waved to the crowd. "Whenever you're ready," he said to me out the side of his mouth.

I flipped on the kitchen boom box and patted my hand against the karaoke microphone plugged into it. A light thumping sound came from the speakers. I cleared my throat and did my best to sublimate myself into my public persona. Johnny wouldn't be nervous addressing a few hundred people.

"Thank you all so much for coming out to Unknown Pleasures. We welcome everybody here. That is the spirit of Taiwan. Over the centuries, how many immigrants and refugees has our island taken in?"

I heard Dwayne sarcastically grumble, "Too many." Well, as an indigenous person, he did have a point.

"We must remember the original inhabitants of Taiwan," I said. "They shared their land, often by force, and we recognize their sacrifice. Everybody who's here now simply wants to be at home here.

"I'm sure that many of you have heard bad things about Tong-tong in the media." A chorus of boos rose up. It was my first reaction from the crowd and it was loud enough for me to feel the vibrations in the air. "You've heard that he's a racist, that he's against immigrants, that he has hate in his heart. None of that is true. He is a victim of crime and is only looking for justice. Anybody who supports justice must support Tong-tong. Thank you."

I bowed slightly to the crowd and was nearly carried away by the applause. It was addictive and I allowed myself two selfish seconds of it before handing the mic to Tong-tong.

"That was a very nice introduction, Jing-nan. Very nice. Yes, you're right. Nobody loves immigrants more than me. I'm an immigrant myself. My family was torn apart by the Chinese civil war and some of us managed to escape to this beautiful island. I'll tell you something, my grandparents grabbed what valuables they had and they shoved them in their, ah, orifices. You know what I mean? So when people say that the Lee family shits gold, it's not because we are particularly rich, but because that's where we hid the jewelry."

The crowd erupted in laughter and applause.

"You're all good people. It means so much for me to see you all here. Now, it's true. You heard it. I am the victim here. You've all seen me humiliated. I'm passionate about finding these criminals and punishing them. Anybody else here witness their friend killed right in front of them? A part of me died, too, when I saw Associate Vice President Peng Wan-chang shot to death. It was horrible." He paused and reached out an arm. Peggy immediately placed an opened bottle of water in it. He took a swig and passed it back before continuing.

"Don't you think, though, that while we search for the particular guys who abducted me, we should also weed out other criminals, a lot of whom are in our country illegally? Shouldn't we stop them before they commit crimes? Am I wrong?"

Enthusiastic cheers let him know that he wasn't.

One voice yelled out, "Boo!"

Tong-tong shaded his eyes and searched the faces.

"Hey, who said that?" he said in a voice thickly sweet with venom. "Over there, was that you?"

About ten people deep on the right side, an arm rose up and extended a middle finger. Men pounced on the heckler and dragged him off to the side in a four-person tangle to even louder cheers.

Tong-tong dropped his hands and shook his head. "Man, I would love to punch that guy right in the face." The crowd laughed. "But we are a peaceful people. I would never do that. I know for a fact that nobody here would ever commit an unwarranted violent act. Then again, we don't back off when someone raises a fist at us, right?

"So, let's give the police department of Taipei a big round of applause, they deserve it." The crowd dutifully clapped. "And let's do our part by continuing to flush out these, ah, problem neighborhoods. Let's nail these guys, huh?" He was about to hand the mic over to me but he decided to add, "Hey, buy food here at Unknown Pleasures and support Chen Jing-nan, a really great guy who makes a mean skewer. I don't want any food left over whatsoever."

We sold out that night, in more ways than one, Nancy later told me.

"ANYBODY WHO SUPPORTS JUSTICE must support Tong-tong."

My words came back to haunt me. Another night, another incident of men from Southeast Asia being beaten by a crowd of Tong-tong supporters.

There was phone-filled footage of him in the lobby of the Taipei 101 skyscraper shrugging off the episode. "What's everyone complaining about? They knew how to fight back. They're no angels."

News coverage was rather wide—every channel I switched to, in fact. Even the Taiwan Indigenous Television station found the time to condemn Tong-tong's anti-immigrant rhetoric. The report ended with a clip of me, as they all did, because they needed positive quotes for balance.

"YOU NEED TO DO something soon, Jing-nan," Nancy told me at lunch at a B-list noodle shop on Xinyi Boulevard that catered to tourists, who were in the dark on current events and wouldn't recognize me.

We usually went someplace around her campus but she told me it was too dangerous for me to set foot at Taida. Apparently Tong-tong was as toxic as the legacy of Chiang Kai-shek, and I was being identified as a Tong-tong supporter.

After taking our English orders for "beef noodle soup," our waiter looked at me and did a double-take before he left.

"Shit," I said. "What should I do, Nancy?"

"You should hold a rally for immigrants. I don't know, call it 'Justice for Immigrants' or something. If you don't, people are going to boycott Unknown Pleasures."

"Luckily for me, I've always got my tourists. It's all right if the locals turn their backs on me."

She straightened up. "What if the tour guides start telling them to skip your stand? What if the English-language travel blogs single you out as a hatemonger?"

I straightened up. *Ma de*, those travel blogs have been pretty damned good to me. They post almost every picture I ever send, along with my written caption, as long as each shot I send to rival blogs is slightly different. I've been interviewed by email more times than I have fingers. I'm always complimented on how great my English is and I return the kind comments on their Chinese-character phrases pasted-in from Google Translate.

They've always been on my side, and hundreds of Americans have told me they've only found Unknown Pleasures through these blogs. If they stopped covering me, I would miss out on some of the most ardent eaters. I saw American dollars fluttering in the wind.

"Jing-nan!"

"Urgh?" I said.

Nancy glared at me. "You were spacing out!"

"No, I wasn't. I was thinking. You're right. Let's hold that rally for immigrants tomorrow night."

AFTER LUNCH, I GOT on my phone and posted about the rally on Unknown Pleasures' social media accounts. I declared that I needed to clarify that I and my business were pro-immigrants, and that Tong-tong was not voicing my sentiments. I promised there would be a diversity of speakers and encouraged people of Southeast Asian descent to speak.

I felt good. It was the right thing to do.

But later I arrived at Unknown Pleasures to find a furious Peggy, backed up by the cops Huang and Kung, who both looked sheepish. My old classmate screwed up her face and pointed at my nose.

"Jing-nan! Is this some kind of joke? Are you really hosting an event tomorrow that disparages my father?"

"It's a pro-justice event," I said coolly. "So it's really in support of what your father's looking for."

"We were so good to you, Jing-nan! He didn't charge you anything to show up here and Frankie told me you sold out of food for the first time ever!"

Frankie shrugged. "That is a fact."

"Dwayne told me his friends had a great time with my dad."

Now it was Dwayne's turn to shrug. "Tong-tong stuffed thousand NT bills into their hands and called them indigenous hero warriors. They love him now."

Exasperated, I said, "I thought you people didn't care about money!"

Dwayne raised an eyebrow. "We didn't used to, but we've been corrupted by the ways of the Han Chinese."

Peggy waved a hand in my face. "Listen, Jing-nan. This little anarchist rally of yours is not going to happen. Consider it canceled!"

"Who's canceling it?"

"Me! Your fucking landlord, that's who!"

"It doesn't say in my lease that I can't hold gatherings. In fact, now that I think about it, I don't actually have a written lease with you. It's all on the honor system."

"That's funny because you've been acting dishonorably. You and Nancy! This was all her idea, right? You wouldn't have been able to come up with this yourself. Your cute little moral compass put you up to this."

I felt needles sticking into my neck. "I wanted to do this because I want to give everyone a chance to express themselves. I even did your father the courtesy of letting his event happen first."

Peggy shook her head and snapped her fingers. "I've heard enough! Huang and Kung, shut down this rickety old stand now!"

Huang wiped the side of his nose with his left thumb. "We've explained this to you already, Peggy. This is outside our jurisdiction. If you want to close his business, you have to bring it to the court and let a judge decide. If he's been paying rent, it will be really hard to close his business, even if you don't have a formal written lease."

"I've been paying," I said. "I pay good money for rent!"

Peggy tossed her hands to the ground. "Fine! I don't need your help, I'll shut this thing down myself!" For some reason, she thought the first step in this process was to give me a shove and stand with her arms crossed. Peggy was smaller, but her center of gravity was lower than mine, and she actually caused me to stumble. Dwayne grabbed my arm to help me recover my balance. I crouched slightly to make my words more menacing.

"Listen, Peggy, if you really do manage to close down Unknown Pleasures, do you have any idea what sort of backlash you'll face? Students, who have nothing better to do, are going to raise hell against all the Lee family businesses. How would you like them to move their rally to the lobby of Taipei 101?"

Peggy snorted and jammed the toes of her right foot into the ground. I knew from experience that that was a common sign of indecision. If she were a potential customer, I'd offer her both of the things she was considering at a discount. But she didn't need a value meal. She needed one more push to force her decision.

"If the rally is here," I said, "there won't be any media

coverage. If they go to Taipei 101, it's going to be on every cable station." I touched her shoulder. "You don't realize it now, but I'm actually helping you by having it here."

I felt her body quiver. She sighed and nodded. "What you're saying makes sense. This is like a controlled demolition instead of letting a wrecking ball run loose."

I tried not to nod too hard. "You see?"

"Okay, Jing-nan. But if anything goes wrong, you're completely responsible!" She added a final dig. "You and Nancy!"

"She had nothing to do with it!"

Peggy whipped out her phone with an exaggerated flourish. "Nothing, huh? What do you call this?" She pushed the display in my face. It was an email chain, and it started with an original post from Nancy that read, *Hey guys, I've convinced Jing-nan to hold a rally for justice at Unknown Pleasures.*

After my face fell, Peggy withdrew her phone and raised her chin in triumph.

"Where did you get that from?" I asked her.

She got a distant look in her eyes and smiled faintly. "I've got paid informants in the student movements who let me know what's up. It's insurance that our businesses won't suffer from any misguided notions that could pick up steam." Peggy looked me in the eyes. "I might even have Dwayne and Frankie on the payroll to keep tabs on you!" I looked over. Both men shook their heads vigorously. Peggy snapped her fingers to get my attention. "You tell Nancy to watch her step!"

"I never tell her what to do."

Peggy stalked off. Huang rolled his eyes and slinked after her.

"Sorry," said Kung. She put her hands in her pockets and followed Huang.

CHAPTER 11

The crowd was smaller than Tong-tong's event, but the hundred people who showed up were younger, louder and rowdier.

One held up a sign that I think went too far. It featured Tong-tong's face with a big bone glued across his mouth. PUT HIM BACK IN THE DOG CAGE! it read.

Nancy stood next to me and patted my back. "I'm so glad you're doing this."

"We're doing this," I said. Nancy tilted her head away slightly to acknowledge that she was pleased that I included her. She handed me her phone. "These are the speakers and short bios for them."

"I'm the MC?"

"You're so good at it!"

I shifted my feet. "I am, aren't I?" I glanced at the list. Whoa, the first one was Liu Ju-lan, the woman now running a B&B! "Ju-lan got in touch with you, Nancy?"

She shook her head. "Not directly. The signup sheet was online. Anybody could add their name."

"I hope this isn't some weird prank."

She tapped my shoulder. "You're the only one who does online tricks, writing reviews for your own business."

I held up a hand. "I don't do that anymore."

"And signing them with fake American names, too."

"Well, people had fun reading them, judging by the marks my reviews got."

I looked at the front counter with concern. These students and lefties didn't seem to be into eating or at least spending money on food. A lot of them looked like vegans. It's too bad those jujubes were all gone. At least I got my money's worth out of them before Dwayne absconded with the last of them.

It was now about fifteen minutes after the rally was supposed to start, so it was the time to get things rolling. Everyone who was going to show up was already here. I approached the mic stand.

"Hello, people! How are you doing tonight?" Enthusiastic applause rained down on me. "I'm sure a lot of you have seen me on television. I want you to know that my comments were taken out of context—never trust the media!" More applause.

"Well, just to let you know, I'm offering a special sale tonight, ten percent off all our items because I support an inclusive society. Look at our stand. Unknown Pleasures employs a mainlander, a *benshengren* and an aborigine!" Dwayne clasped his hands and waved them over his head. "We all work together!"

Someone yelled out, "How come you don't have any women workers?"

This was a direct challenge. Years of thinking on my feet have taught me to address skeptics quickly and directly but with humor.

"Women are too smart to do this kind of work for the low wages I pay." The crowd liked what they heard and the potential heckler was defused. I should write a book about street-level marketing.

"Speaking of smart," I continued, "I'd like to bring up our first speaker tonight. She's Liu Ju-lan, a proud small-business owner and a recovering corporate employee. Please give her a round of applause."

I backed away from the mic as Ju-lan emerged from the crowd. She waved a dog collar in the air. "Tong-tong should be wearing one of these, not a tie!" The crowd roared.

As she continued to slam the guy, my eyes strayed to the counter. Only about five people were lined up. This sucked. Not only were they not buying food in a material sort of way, they were blocking traffic from potential hungry customers. I knew there were many rich liberals in America, but there didn't seem to be any in Taiwan. People with money here were like Tong-tong. Why couldn't we have a fun billionaire like Oprah Winfrey or Bill Gates who goes around buying stuff for people?

I was daydreaming a bit about making more money when Nancy nudged me. I looked at her and she pointed to her bare wrist. She'd stopped wearing a watch but I knew she meant the time. Shoot, this Ju-lan was over her five-minute limit!

She was going full-throttle about how men had taken away opportunities her whole life. Now would be a bad time for me to grab back the mic. I pulled a stunt I saw on a Japanese show. I walked out and stood just within her peripheral vision and bowed deeply to her. She gave me a puzzled look. I pointed to my own bare wrist where a watch would be. Ju-lan covered her mouth, instantly embarrassed.

"Oh, my gosh, I'm over my time limit! Thank you for listening, everybody." She waved before crouching down and slinking away.

I started clapping before I reached the mic.

"Let's give Ju-lan a big hand, everybody. It takes a lot of courage to go first." I waited a few seconds for the applause to fade. "I want to tell you something really important. Unknown Pleasures wasn't always the best establishment at the Shilin Night Market. It has very humble beginnings as a food stand that my grandfather set up in the heart of the martial-law era. He struggled to provide for his family. Some of you will recall that it was illegal to speak Taiwanese then. He struggled along in Mandarin, a foreign language to him, and worked hard to provide for his family. He always believed that justice would prevail someday. I'm glad that he lived to see Taiwan bloom into a full democracy."

Clearly obligatory applause arose. I glanced at Frankie, whom my grandfather actually hired, and he looked over my shoulder while flashing one of his big smiles that seemed to stretch past the boundaries of his face. He knew that while I was being factually correct about my grandfather, I was leaving out details including that the old man had been an extreme misogynist, a racist and had a terrible gambling problem that created enough debt to fuck over the next two generations of his family. He would mouth off about the mainlanders this, the mainlanders that. I don't know how Frankie took it. Did he stay out of a sense of obligation? Or did Frankie need the money that badly? Which part of his life experience had Frankie tapped into to get himself through, his tenure as a dutiful teenage soldier or his ordeal as a political prisoner?

"I'm asking you to try some of our skewers, or if you're hungrier, one of our stews. We haven't changed my grandfather's recipes because that would dishonor his memory." I cleared my throat. "Okay, the commercial's over. Now, we're on to our next speaker."

The story of my grandfather seemed to have worked. Or maybe people naturally became more hungry as the evening wore on. There was enough business that Dwayne was starting to break a sweat. Mr. Tough Guy whistled at me to give him a hand between introducing people at the mic. Each time, I handed Nancy's phone back to her so I'd have both hands free to work.

None of the speakers seemed to have timed themselves or stuck to a prepared statement. I had to cut all of them off when their time was up.

As I walked off the stage, I handed the phone to Nancy with some finality.

"That's the last person up there," I told her. "After her, I'm going to wrap up and thank the crowd for coming, blah blah."

"You did a great job, Jing-nan!"

"Well, your pals finally did a good job on my food!" I ladled out a spicy stew of pork, cabbage, innards and congealed blood. That last component actually has a consistency of tofu and, like tofu, hasn't much flavor on its own. The pot was bottoming out so I told the young woman ordering the stew that it would probably be more peppery than usual, due to the higher ratio of peppercorn slurry in the soup, but she said it was all right.

By then I had developed a keen sense of how long five minutes was and when it felt right, I made my way back to the mic. Nancy tried to hand me her phone.

"Hey, Nancy, what are you doing? I don't need your phone again."

"One more person just signed up. Please let him speak. I promised that nobody would be turned away."

What were five minutes to me if it meant one more person buying food? I glanced down at the name. Erwin Lee. All right, Erwin. Close the show with some style.

"Hello, my good friends, I was going to tell you that the

event had come to an end, but one more person has signed up. We said we wouldn't turn anyone away, but our next person is definitely the last." I glanced down at her phone to read the bio of the speaker. "Erwin Lee," I said into the mic. "Erwin is a sports-medicine doctor and has treated some of the country's best-known sports figures. Let's hear it for Erwin!"

A thirty-something man wearing a red polo approached. Erwin looked familiar. He had a bit of a halting style to his speech, as if he were used to being interrupted.

"Yes, hello. I am Erwin Lee. I understand that a lot of you are angry at Tong-tong. I understand your anger because I have disagreed with many of his values for most of my life. I am his second son, Er-ming." A buzz arose in the audience and then applause broke out.

Whoa! So Er-ming had taken an English name, after all! The quiet and studious brother who went to medical school was now making a public appearance.

"Maybe you don't recognize me. I have managed to live a relatively private life. The last time I was in a newspaper was when I was dating the singer Rangsit. I denied it at the time, but I'll admit now that we were in love.

"We married in secret a number of years ago. We're expecting a baby boy soon." He raised a finger. "But I would be ashamed to introduce this boy to his grandfather. I will not allow Tong-tong to see him until he apologizes to the people of Taiwan for his hurtful words. Because you know what? When you speak words of hate against strangers, you hurt your own family. Thank you."

He received the longest and loudest applause of the night. He nodded, embarrassed by the reception but also emboldened by what he had just done—take a public stand against his own father. He was going to be all over the news tomorrow, if not tonight. More than a few people were going to sell their phone-camera footage to cable stations. Erwin Lee was going to be famous.

I hastily moved to the mic to close out the event. Formalities should always be observed. Not to do so was sloppy.

"Thank you all so much for coming," I said heartily. "Have a great night, everybody." Then I chased after Erwin in order to get him to pose for a few pictures at my stand with the signage clearly in view.

"Erwin!" I said as I steered him like a loaded wheelbarrow. "Hey, how are you? I met you years ago. I'm a good friend of your sister, Peggy!"

He sucked in his lips as he evaluated my face and processed the information I had just provided. "Yes," he said. "Of course I remember you." He extended a hand and his grip was soft but reassuring. If I were being told that I would never walk again, I'd want the conversation to start with a humanizing touch like that. His hands retreated to the pockets in his jacket in an accustomed manner. "I think the last time I saw you, you were wearing one of those big overcoats and your hair was short and spiky."

My hair had never been spiky, but I nodded along.

"Yes, that was me," I said cheerily. "It was so great to hear what you had to say."

"Are you going to see your family tomorrow?"

What an odd question. "No, what made you think of that?"

He let out a laugh that shook his whole body. "Tomorrow's Double Ninth! We're going to go on a hike with my mother and my grandmother." He shrugged. "I don't like mountains, but it's a tradition."

Man, I had completely lost track of the holiday. "I'm going to be too busy," I said. "The work just never ends here." Why should I bother to tell him my family was gone? It would just be a bummer on a good night. "Are you hungry at all, Erwin? Can I fix something for you?"

"I wish I could, but no thank you. I've got to get back home—as I told everyone tonight, my wife's pregnant!"

"Let me bag something up for you and get a few pictures." Dwayne and Frankie already saw what I was up to and moved into position behind us. I fumbled with my phone to position a selfie when Nancy stepped in.

"Let me take the pictures!" I handed her my phone. After a few snaps, Erwin waved his arms.

"Hold on, please. You have a photo with four men here. Let's have a woman join us. Miss?"

"Yes?" asked Nancy.

"Please join us. You're the organizer of the event, after all. Oh, and you, too!" Erwin gestured behind me to Ju-lan, whom I had completely forgotten about.

Ju-lan stood in the center next to Erwin as Nancy scuttled in next to me and deftly set up a few selfies.

"I thought you were wonderful," Erwin said to Ju-lan. "I only came to observe and see how people were feeling. But when you spoke, I felt something inside me and it inspired me to find the courage to eventually get up and speak."

Ju-lan looked embarrassed, the socially acceptable response to compliments. "Oh, it was wonderful to hear you talk, Er-ming," she said. "No one has ever said that I inspired them before."

Erwin turned to Nancy. "Can you send me some of those pictures? Use the same email that I signed up with."

"Yes, absolutely. You were the last speaker, but certainly not the least."

"I had to let everyone know that not everybody in the family was behind Tong-tong."

"I'm glad you spoke, too," interjected Dwayne. "You know, Rangsit is from my tribe."

A sheepish look came over Erwin's face as he tucked his chin. "I am really ashamed to admit that I don't really know how to speak Amis."

Dwayne maneuvered closer and they shook hands. "That's okay."

"She is part Thai, too, and I've learned some of that language. I have no excuse, however, for not knowing any Amis. I will try to better myself."

Dwayne nodded. "So is Rangsit working on a new album?"

"Oh, she's written some songs but she will announce a tour first. She'll probably sing the new songs at the live dates and then record them after they've all been tested in front of an audience. It drives the record company crazy because they want to release the CD before the tour, but nobody tells her what to do. Certainly not me." He took a step away from us all. "I really have to go."

Frankie saluted him. "Thank you for speaking for all of us," he said.

Erwin smiled and waved. Was he walking to the train? No fancy car? Even though some excited activists kept pace with him, Erwin didn't break and run. He seemed open to talking to them.

"I think I'm going to be going, as well," said Ju-lan. "Thank you, Nancy, for organizing this. You're a leader of your generation. And thank you, Mr. Chen, for letting this happen in your space."

"Please call me Jing-nan," I said. "I didn't do much, certainly not as much as you. It was actually very selfish of me to have it at my business. Um, speaking of business . . ." I pressed a stack of Unknown Pleasures cards into her hands. "Tell your guests to come eat here and they'll get ten percent off."

She flexed the cards in her hands. "Is it true that you're a close friend of Tong-tong's family?"

"I'm close with Peggy," I said. "Maybe too close. We are old classmates." A thoughtful look came over Ju-lan's face. Was she going to chuck my cards into the trash? "I wouldn't say that I'm friends with Tong-tong himself," I quickly added.

"But didn't you let him speak here? You said that if you supported justice, you had to support Tong-tong."

"That was taken completely out of context," I said. She didn't look like she bought it.

Erwin Lee was indeed featured on the news, but he wasn't the lead story.

What was getting most attention was a video that had been uploaded by Tong-tong's kidnappers. It featured Tong-tong in the cage talking to one of his abductors who was off-screen. It seemed that Tong-tong had been crying for some time.

"I just shit my pants," he wailed.

"Why didn't you take your pants off?"

"I don't know!" wailed Tong-tong.

It was only a five-second clip, but the tiny video destroyed Tong-tong's nascent strongman image. Support for him evaporated. Everybody was going to remember this Double Ninth. "I just shit my pants" was sure to be a meme to remember.

The last time I heard from Peggy was when she tried to shut down my stand. Right now she probably had her hands full trying to prevent her father from spontaneously exploding.

I was a little relieved, honestly. The video clip took heat off of me for staging the rally for him. It was probably even more effective at that than wider coverage of the pro-immigrants rally would have been. Funny as it was, though, the new upload showed that the kidnappers were still at large and not impaired in their ability to use technology. In other words, they weren't afraid they would be caught.

The hot news story now was tracking down former Tong-tong supporters and making them recant on camera. Quite a few did. I had two voicemails asking me to do the same, but I ignored them. I didn't need to resurface in the media again.

In the afternoon, Tong-tong lashed out with a simple, furious post on his company's official blog: *Find the criminals at any cost!*

What did "any cost" mean? His few remaining supporters took his words to mean that they should stand outside the dormitories of overseas workers and hoot at people going in and out. It wasn't worse because of the presence of security guards—whose usual duty was monitoring the workers and accepting bribes when they missed curfews.

The dorms were mostly situated along commercial districts, not far from the construction sites, plants, or health-care facilities where people worked.

The Tong-tong faithful dished out equal anti-foreigner hate to workers from the Philippines, Vietnam, Thailand or Indonesia. "Get out and go back!" the lowlifes chanted at the indifferent people, who didn't seem shocked by the brazen display of hate.

Some of the overseas workers figured the best defense was a strong offense. Four Thai factory workers carried metal rods back to the dorms and beat the crap out of some hooligans, one of whom turned out to be an off-duty cop.

Speaking of the police, they didn't seem any closer to finding Tong-tong's kidnappers. The more I thought about it, there was one thing I knew that hadn't been publicly disclosed, if it were true. Frankie had had a hunch Tong-tong had been held captive near the Miramar Entertainment Park, close to the Ferris wheel.

"Frankie?" I asked him the next night. "Were you right about the Ferris wheel? Did the police find Tong-tong in a warehouse near Miramar?"

He arched one eyebrow and looked cautiously side to side. "I won't hold you in suspense," Frankie said quietly, "but it was just like I thought." He took a deep breath, exhaled slowly and seemed relieved he got to tell someone. "Now, I don't know exactly where it was, but it was either north or south of the wheel, based on the shadow, because the wheel's axis is north-south."

"Why didn't the police publicize where he was found?"

"Keeping some details nonpublic ensures that interlopers don't show up and contaminate the crime scene. Did you ever hear about the guy in Kaohsiung who wanted to prove that he could pull off the perfect murder?"

I rubbed my hands. "No."

"He killed someone at random in a park, cleaned up the scene, disposed of the weapon and then waited. The police couldn't solve it. It made him so angry that he went into a police station to tell them how stupid they were and provided every detail of what he did."

"That's weird."

Frankie blinked slowly. He picked up his phone and tapped something into it while speaking to me. "It was a weird crime, and that sort of criminal behavior is of the mental-illness type. Not the revenge type, which is what Tong-tong's case is." Finished with typing, he pocketed the phone and brushed his palms against his pants.

I had an idea. "Frankie, maybe they're waiting to see if the kidnappers return to the scene of the crime."

"Are you a detective, now, Jing-nan?"

I shifted my feet. "No."

"Have you ever committed a crime?" Did Frankie have something on me?

"I don't think so," I said slowly.

"Let me tell you something, since you've never been on either side of breaking the law—real criminals never come back. Only the amateurs do. These guys were not amateurs." He raised his eyebrows at me and casually drew out his phone again. "The police didn't release where Tong-tong was found by special request."

"By the government?"

His eyes narrowed. "By Tong-tong himself."

CHAPTER 12

"Jing-nan?" Peggy's voice through the door was muffled somewhat but the surprise was audible.

"Hi, Peggy, yes, it's me. Sorry to drop in on you like this, but I happened to be back early from the night market. Nancy and I were sitting in her apartment; we were thinking that you and I needed to patch up our friendship a bit. I thought you might still be at work but Nancy said she saw you go up the elevator."

"She did see me," Peggy replied stiffly.

"Well, I hope you didn't eat yet because I've got some great food that I just heated up. It's ready to serve." I glanced at Nancy. "And Nancy has picked out a really good wine." I heard a soft click and the door opened. Peggy was dressed in pinstripe pajamas and wingtip slippers. It was 8:30 P.M.

"Not to put you down or anything, Nancy, but I think my liquor closet has you beat by a little bit." Peggy hooked a thumb into her gold chain necklace and made the fish-shaped jade pendant dance against her throat. "But I know Jing-nan's food is great. I'd hire him to be my chef but my money's no good with him."

She stepped back and swung the door wide open. We stepped out of our slippers and stood in our socks.

Peggy let go of the door. It swung shut and two magnetic bolts rang dull and metallic. "Jing-nan," she said, "we're old friends, so there's no bad feelings between us when you fail to see reason."

"I feel exactly the same way about you," I said.

She reached and touched Nancy's wrists. "Nancy, I wanted to hold the elevator but you were much too far away and I didn't want to hold up all the people waiting with me."

Nancy gave a big smile. "It's all right, Peggy. I caught one that was less crowded."

Peggy smiled back and stomped down the hall to the kitchen. Under her breath, Nancy said to me, "Her elevator car was empty."

We followed Peggy down the hall. Neither of us had been inside her apartment before. The track lighting on the ceiling slashed to the left and right to highlight art. The walls had built-in niches to display things such as a pristine example of a glazed Tang Dynasty camel sculpture. It was thousands of years old but it glistened like a hot donut. In another was an ancient ceremonial jade axe blade. The iron seam running diagonally to the sharpened edge had oxidized over the millennia to dark brown, and looked like dried blood. As a kid, I remembered seeing one at the National Palace Museum on a field trip. That one was much smaller.

Passing by nearly priceless treasures unnerved us. Nancy and I couldn't even talk. As we neared the end, Peggy had to double back to check on us.

"Christ, are you guys sleepwalking or something? We're hungry!" She turned to the kitchen and yelled, "Hey, Jing-nan and his girlfriend brought food!"

We stepped into the kitchen and found Huang and Kung

sitting at an oak table that could seat a dozen. They were hunched over plastic bowls that contained prepared entrees from 7-Eleven.

Peggy pointed at the bottle in Nancy's right hand. "Lemme see that." Nancy tried to hand over the wine but Peggy scanned the label without even touching the bottle and shook her head. "Not in my house," was her assessment.

I was glad the mock label looked real enough to disgust Peggy.

Nancy set down the fake bottle on the smaller marble counter.

"Stop eating that right now," I ordered the cops.

Kung slapped her disposable chopsticks flat against the table and said, "Thank Mazu."

Huang, who hadn't even started eating, pushed away his container of what was probably upscale dog food. "Can you believe that one of the richest people in the world doesn't even have anything to eat in the refrigerator?"

Peggy leaned against one of the kitchen's three marble counters. "I told you both right off the bat that my ungrateful chef quit two months ago. I fed her way more than she ever fed me, that's for sure!" She pointed her right elbow at me. "And you thought I was joking about hiring you as a chef."

I set my two bags on the table. "Maybe you'd like my cooking, Peggy, but I assure you that my lack of manners would really irk you." I helped serve Peggy's two guests, who were too hungry to talk or listen.

She suppressed a burp before speaking. "Confucius said that it was better to be without clothes than manners."

"Confucius didn't think women should be educated," said Nancy. "I'm sure he wouldn't like me being in graduate school." Dryly, she added, "Actually, many of the male professors don't like me being in graduate school."

Peggy jerked open her refrigerator and smirked at Nancy over her shoulder. "I'm sure Jing-nan doesn't like you being in grad school. He's probably the sort of guy who wants his woman working by his side at the night market." Peggy leaned in and came up with two wine bottles tucked in her arms like rescued twin babies. She allowed the fridge door to shut on its own. Her hands cut away the bottle foil in such an accustomed way that Peggy didn't even watch what she was doing. She kept her eyes on me. "Jing-nan didn't finish college himself, so he probably has a dim view of highly edu-cated people." She winced as she worked out the cork. "Isn't that right, Jing-nan?"

I put up a restrained smile in defense. You need to watch out when someone gives you one of those in Taiwan. A small smile means, "You're pushing things far enough to make me think of killing you in front of all these witnesses. Stop now." In general, any smile unaccompanied with genuine laughter is like a snake's rattle going off.

I would have finished my degree at UCLA if I could have stayed in America. If my father hadn't gotten cancer. If my mother hadn't died in a car accident on the way to pick me up at the airport. If my family hadn't owed a shitload of money to our landlord/crime boss.

It had been a very iffy time. Well, tonight certainly was an iffy time. A few of those ifs have already broken my and Nancy's way, though.

If Peggy had allowed Nancy's "wine" to be served, we would have had to tell her it was a joke and that the bottle was empty. It was leftover from a prank at Dwayne's birthday, when a fake snake sprang out and bounced off his chest. Nancy would have had to palm her old phone, which was now inside the bottle recording everything that was being said.

If the two cops hadn't been there, there likely wouldn't

have been anything worth recording. Peggy probably didn't know exactly where her dad had been found but if she really did, I couldn't trust what she said.

If Peggy were serving wine from her own supply, she'd probably err on the side of pouring out too much. I already knew she had gotten Huang and Kung blotto at least once, so I knew they didn't have much of a tolerance. Well, not as much as our host.

I hoped to be able to swing around the conversation to where, exactly, Tong-tong had been found, but only at an appropriate time when the cops were in shape to yield information. Being fed good food would put them at ease and good booze would drape a nice warm shawl over their chests.

If I were capable of remembering to do so with a few drinks in me, all the insults from my good friend Peggy would be worth it.

"We are good friends, aren't we, Peggy?" I asked. "I mean, anyone listening to you speak like that to me would think you had something against me."

She had been pouring wine into glasses big enough to eat soup out of but her hand lifted the neck of the bottle abruptly. Drops of wine shimmered in the air briefly like a necklace of fake garnets.

"Who's listening to us?" she asked.

I breathed in and pumped a few fake laughs from my mouth. "I'm listening to you now, and so is Nancy, and the fine members of our police department."

Peggy grunted and resumed pouring.

"We're off-duty from official business," Kung said. She was joylessly eating prime selections from the finest grill of the night markets. How could anybody be so glum while eating my food? It wasn't what I usually served, but still.

I had altered the recipe a little bit when I was cooking. Wary that food might slow the flow of alcohol to the bloodstream, I gave the skewers a few coats of brandy, to Dwayne's chagrin. Frankie had warned me to clean the grill thoroughly after, lest it ruin the flavor profile of all our food.

"You're off duty?" said Nancy. "I'm sure that calls for drinks. You've had a really rough week, I'm sure!" She picked up two full glasses and set them down, taking a seat next to Kung.

"Hey, Nancy, don't forget about you and Jing-nan!" called Peggy. She looked at me suspiciously. Or maybe I was feeling too self-conscious.

"Oh, we'd never pass on a chance to drink with one of my oldest friends," I said as I picked up two more glasses. I took a seat next to Huang, across from Nancy.

"We are old friends, aren't we? Shit, I remember you in second grade, Jing-nan. No, first grade! Someone put a bug down the back of your shirt and you reached in to grab it and smashed it in his face!" She picked up her glass and sat next to me.

Why was she talking about bugs? My eyes went to our fake wine bottle. Did she know I had tucked a digital recording device in it? Man, I was getting really paranoid.

"You like it, huh?" asked Peggy.

I hid my hands under my legs. "Like what?"

"My dad's painting!" She went over and swiped the portrait off the wall with such glee she nearly knocked over the bugged wine bottle. She held it a foot from my face and the image danced in her unsteady hands. "Check it out!"

I hadn't noticed it before because I have only contempt for mass-produced goods and had thought it was a store-bought reproduction of an original in some Paris museum. The painting was that good. It featured a somber man and woman observing some event behind the viewer. They were old, in their forties, and seemed somewhat well-off but unaccustomed to whatever strife they were witnessing. They were pictured only from the waist up but the positioning of their arms suggested that they were holding baggage.

"Ya like it, don't you?" asked Peggy as she nodded slightly.

"It's very realistic," said Nancy.

"Do you really think so?" Peggy squealed.

"It's almost like a photo," I said. "The expressions that the people have look real."

She smiled and lifted the painting in triumph and carried it over to the table. We all scrambled to lift our glasses out of the way. "Painting is my dad's real passion," Peggy said. She set down the artwork and sloshed back into her seat, briefly grabbing my thigh for balance. "He went to art school in France for a few years before my grandfather forced him to come back and work for the family." Peggy dragged a chicken gizzard skewer onto a plate and licked her fingers.

"Let me guess," I said. "Your grandfather cut off Tong-tong's allowance and your dad came running home?"

"Hah. You don't know my father." She filled half her mouth with food and continued talking out the other half, quite articulately, as she chewed. It was a feat of multitasking she must have learned by watching her father eat. "Tong-tong was holding out fine without the allowance. He had fallen in love with a French girl and he wasn't going to come back. My grandfather had lots of friends in the military. They sent in rangers and abducted Tong-tong. Drugged him, flew him out." She closed her mouth for the final chews before swallowing. Her eyes opened wide to make sure I knew how serious Tong-tong's situation had been.

As a follow-up to the story of her father's return trip, I'd be curious as to her family's role during the martial-law years, when the military was called upon to handle many extra-judicial tasks. But now was not the time to explore that area.

I noticed that the cops had emptied their glasses and were nearly done eating. I sought to bring Huang and Kung into the conversation, one that I was going to steer firmly but gently.

"Your father seems to get abducted a lot," I said. "Only that time it wasn't really a crime because it was a family thing. This latest thing, I can't believe it hasn't been fully cracked yet." I held out one hand each to Kung and Huang. In my pitchman body language, reaching out was always rewarded with some reaction from the target, usually positive. Kung sighed.

"We're doing everything we can to find the kidnappers." She shot a glance at Huang. "Well, everything we're permitted to do."

Huang's face had taken on that of a stonefish—frowning, ugly and venomous.

"What do you mean by 'permitted'?" asked Nancy.

The stonefish rolled its eyes to Nancy and then to Kung.

"Yeah, what do you mean, Kung?" said Peggy. She was either needling or truly oblivious. It was a fifty-fifty proposition.

"Your father . . ." Kung started.

Huang pounded the table.

"Whoa!" I said in genuine surprise. "What's the problem?"

He licked his lips and made a kissing sound. "I don't want to talk about it!" Huang said. But clearly he did. How could I get him going?

I pulled my chair closer to the table and lay my hands flat on the surface. "I've told you before that I've had a lot of interactions with the police," I said, feeling my feet dance under the table. "I feel that as individuals they've all tried to do a good job, but they have all these restrictions placed on them. When they manage to accomplish something, they get zero credit from the public."

Huang narrowed his eyes. I was worried he would slip back into fish mode. Instead, he took a deep breath.

"That's the story, pretty much. You know what the worst thing is? It's when the supposed victim of a crime stops you from solving it."

I waited two seconds to see if he needed nudging or not. "Has that happened a lot?"

"Five years ago—this was before you were up here in Taipei, Kung—I was investigating a knifepoint bank robbery. I won't mention the name of the bank, but if you look it up, it should be pretty obvious. Anyway, I caught the goddamned robber. There had been a torrential rain shower right before and he left a wet footprint that was incredibly complete on the sidewalk. It was under the bank's awning, so the shadow kept it from drying in the sun.

"I caught the goddamned guy. The footprint matched another next to a moped tire tread in a dirt lot at the end of the block. The tread ran down a sandy alleyway and to the moped itself. The guy lived with his mother two blocks away from the bank in an illegal house. You know the kind, built with PVC piping and metal sheets.

"So it turned out that the bank had illegally evicted him and his mother from their home. They demolished the building and sold the land in less than a week. The bank figured it would be bad publicity if it came out, so they actually paid the robber some more and said they wouldn't press charges if he didn't say anything to the press." He tipped his glass slightly and rolled the bottom's round edge against the table. "You'll never believe who bought that property."

"Who?" asked Peggy. "I'm almost jealous."

"Well, don't be, because it was your dad. Through a sub-sidiary company." Huang righted the cup. "Don't worry, Tong-tong's completely in the clear about that. He could deny he knew how the bank had made the land available. It would stand up in court."

I stood up and poured Huang another glass. The first bottle was long gone and the second bottle wouldn't last long. He didn't try to stop me so I went a little more than halfway.

"When you think about it," said Peggy, "my father was also a victim in that transaction. He was getting bad karma."

Huang took a long pull on his glass in silence, then exhaled loudly, clearing his blowhole.

"Talk about karma," said Kung.

I filled her glass and she tried to wave me off a quarter of the way through but I brought her glass up to where Huang's had been. "What about karma?" I asked her.

"You know what's really preventing us from apprehending the kidnappers? Tong-tong himself."

The skin on Peggy's face nearly audibly tightened. "How dare you accuse my father like that, you fucking bitch!" Kung made two fists and put them on the table. After all the grief she had taken from Peggy, she had finally snapped. Kung wasn't going to hold back now no matter what look Huang gave her. I could see booster rockets firing in her eyes.

"Tong-tong won't let us investigate the warehouse where he was found or any of the properties around it. He's a fucking idiot for barring us and our boss is a fucking idiot for standing down."

Peggy picked up her glass and defiantly swirled the wine. "That's our land, our property," she declared. "Our security people know those blocks better than anybody. They've got it covered, believe me."

"You own Miramar Entertainment Park, Peggy?" I asked.

Peggy's eyes narrowed as she considered the real-estate portfolio. "Not the park and the mall itself, just a bunch of the commercial property around it. Some of the residential. It's a good thing we own only parts because the value of the properties has tanked. Some of our tenants went bust and the buildings are empty, like the warehouse my dad was held captive in."

"Your dad told the cops to stay out?"

"My dad's lawyer, to be specific, told them. You can see why. They would only fuck up the place and hurt the value. Don't forget, there are active construction sites there. It was a very unselfish and principled stand. My dad was thinking about the workers, who need the jobs and money."

I squirmed in my seat. "Peggy, do you know which building your dad was rescued from?"

She shook her head. "Naw, but he said it wasn't familiar to him."

Huang couldn't contain a scoff. "It should've been familiar. He owned the damned thing."

This was my opportunity. "Which was it?" I asked gently.

Huang curled his right hand into a fist and brought the knuckles up to his chin. "And why do you wanna know? Are you some sort of demented thrill seeker? Do you want to go there and jerk off?"

Nancy came to my rescue. "Jing-nan has an interest in crime and how the law works because he was almost a victim in an attempted shooting."

"I knew that," Huang said defensively. "Here's something else I know, sweetheart. His uncle is a major underworld figure."

"He's never been convicted of a crime," I interjected. Which is different from being innocent, I know.

Kung pushed aside her now-empty glass and pointed at me. "I'm sure he's a legitimate businessman, right, Jing-nan?

Maybe you're involved in criminal activity yourself, huh? Maybe if we had a stakeout of Unknown Pleasures, we'd dig up some shit about you."

Surprisingly, Peggy now stuck up for me. "You see this, Jing-nan? This is why you can't trust the cops, not completely. They suspect everybody of doing something."

Huang and Kung settled back in their chairs.

"All I did was bring them food and now they accuse me of being a criminal," I said with as much humiliation as possible. I lowered my head slightly while still keeping their faces in view.

Kung threw her head back. "I was only kidding," she said.

I surveyed the table. Only one skewer was left. In Taiwan, everybody hated to eat the last of anything because taking it would indicate how selfish one was—a big no-no in pretty much every Asian culture. Someone had to force someone else to take it and after an excuses-as-filibuster struggle, somebody finally would.

Maybe I could use the cultural convention to my advantage.

"Huang," I said, "you should take that last skewer. I know it takes a lot of energy to hold in all those secrets that you have."

"I don't hold in secrets," he said, quickly stifling a belch.

"You have many, many secrets, things you won't tell anybody because you're very important. You're the highest-ranking person here." Kung shivered slightly as I slid the container over to Huang. "Please take it."

Huang's fingers lay in wait like a sea-floor predator, and he licked his lips. "Okay. I get it. You want to know where the building is." He glanced at Peggy. "You don't even know, right?"

She straightened up and blinked. "Not specifically, no."

He nodded and grabbed the skewer. Huang had literally

taken the bait. He twirled it in his fingers as he spoke. "It was a factory for textiles. Tong-tong is going to knock it down to build another shopping mall."

"Where's the building?"

Huang cracked his fingers. "Now, I wasn't there myself. I only had a picture from a friend who was on the scene." He leaned to the side to take his phone out of a pants pocket and fiddled with it a little bit. "There it is." He held out the display to us. "It's on a street corner."

The building was made of hastily poured concrete. It seemed to be slightly lopsided. There weren't many windows and they were all near the roof.

"Where is this relative to the Ferris wheel?" I asked.

"I don't know. Maybe to the back of the photographer."

Peggy reached in and grabbed the phone. "You shouldn't have this image. It's a private property."

"Hey!" said Huang but he watched her delete the image. "I wasn't going to post it online," he said as she handed it back.

"I can't have you leaking it to the press for money."

"How much do they pay?"

"A lot."

Huang looked in wonderment at his phone.

"Do you have a copy on your computer?" Peggy asked him.

"No," he said, his voice hollow.

"Did you see the building in person?" I asked him.

"I picked up my friend there because even though we had just rescued Tong-tong, the guy ordered everybody out."

"Do you remember the street corners?" asked Nancy.

Huang crossed his arms and his face showed he was remembering a time of light pain. "If I think about it . . ."

Peggy slapped her thighs and stood up. "Hey, anybody feel like seeing a movie? I feel like we should watch something."

I could tell the next move was for the living room with the

projection television bolted to the ceiling. "Maybe we can talk a little bit more here," I said. "Huang's in the middle of something."

"We can talk during the movie!" she grunted. Peggy turned on the living room light and flicked another switch that plunged the rest of us into darkness. "Let's go!"

Six two-seater couches were laid out like rib bones. Peggy thumbed through the menus on the universal remote.

"When I left my husband, I only regretted leaving all those DVDs, but now everything streams, so I get the last laugh." She called up a black-and-white film. "I love the old Italian films. They're so fast. Taiwanese films are too slow and nobody ever says what they really want to."

"Personally," I interjected, "I don't like movies where people talk too much." But I really liked when people who were being recorded talked too much. Speaking of which, it would be really great to get that bottle into the living room and press Huang some more.

Kung looked like she was a lightweight drinker. I guess Huang was, as well. He had seemed fairly sober while seated at the table, but now he was crawling on the sofas on his elbows and knees. Kung had to give him a hand so that he wouldn't drop on the floor. He nodded to thank her.

Did he have anything else that was useful? How trustworthy was his memory at this point?

I glanced at Peggy. She was kneading the universal remote with both hands in frustration.

"Can someone help me here?" she asked God. I looked at Nancy with anticipation.

"I'm pretty good at this," said Nancy. Peggy handed over the remote but hovered. I sidled up to Huang who was now in a sitting position but looked dazed.

"Would you mind unlocking your phone?" I asked. I

wanted to see if maybe I could find the text or email that had the image of the building.

He must've been more gone than I had thought because he shrugged, punched something into his phone and eagerly handed it to me.

I almost handed it right back when I saw the screen because at first I thought he had entered his code incorrectly. Then I read the notification again: *Are you sure you want to delete this image?*

I pressed NO and grabbed at my own phone. The first thing I did was take a picture of the picture. Then I opened the information window on Huang's phone. Luck was with me—it had the GPS coordinates for the photo. I took a picture of that, as well. I clicked my phone off just in time to hear Peggy make a declaration.

"Well, I could have figured that out, Nancy!" The remote was back in Peggy's hands.

"You mean after I showed you how to do it?" asked Nancy as she coiled up on the couch.

Peggy put on her cultivated hurt look, almost on par with any B-grade actress playing a character with no last name. "How dare you!" That was her opening. "How dare you insult me after I opened the door of my home for you!" She winged the remote into a couch cushion and stomped to the kitchen.

No, I thought. Please, whatever you do, don't grab our wine bottle. She reentered the room brandishing exactly that.

"And this is what you brought? This is what you had to offer? This joke-ass wine?" Peggy was brandishing the bottle as if she were about to launch a ship. The plastic looked like a dark glass, but it sure didn't feel real. Peggy couldn't be so wasted that she didn't notice. She slammed the bottle twice against the wall, under a framed film poster signed by Ang Lee.

Splinters of plastic broke off and flitted through the air. Nancy's old phone, which had been concealed inside, came hurtling at Kung's face. She lazily reached out and caught it.

I stood up and put my hands on my hips. "I've been looking everywhere for that phone!" I declared, not even convincing myself. "I can't believe I left it there!"

"My old classmate," said Peggy, tonelessly. "My old friend was spying on me."

"I wasn't spying on you, Peggy. I was spying on the cops. I'm trying to help you and your father find his kidnappers."

"The Lees don't need your help!" She waved an arm to encompass the entire room. "We don't need help from any of you!"

Kung raised a hand. "I swear, after the way you've been treating me, I wasn't going to help you one bit."

"I think I've reached that point, as well," said Huang.

"Good!" declared Peggy.

Huang wasn't quite through. "And, I'd like to repeat, your father is preventing the police from doing their jobs."

"All the evidence has already been removed from our property and delivered to you. It doesn't make any sense to have people trample through the building over and over when there's nothing left to see."

"Peggy," I said, "how do you know the warehouse's been searched thoroughly?"

"My father told me it was! Considering that he was a prisoner there himself, I think he would know best."

"I think we should let Kung and Huang check it out on their own."

"No," said Kung.

"Absolutely not," said Huang. "We've already been warned by our superiors to stay the hell away from there."

Peggy beamed with triumph. "There you have it, Jing-nan. It's over."

"Why don't we go there?" asked Nancy. We all turned to her. She pointed at Peggy. "Me, you and Jing-nan. We'll just have a look around. But if we find something that may be interesting, you have to agree to allow the cops in to evaluate it."

Peggy assumed a defensive stance by sitting down and crossing her legs and arms. "What if we don't find anything? How are you going to compensate me for my lost time and wasted effort?"

"Jing-nan won't circulate the picture of the warehouse that he's taken from Huang's phone."

Peggy swung her accusing eyes at me. I shoved my phone in my front pants pocket to keep it safe. "Don't you hate it when you have to click twice to delete something?"

CHAPTER 13

Peggy agreed as long as we went to the warehouse right then. I think she was counting on Nancy and me nixing the whole thing because of the lateness of the hour and our own fatigue.

She didn't know the resilient nature and infinite patience of *benshengren*.

Didn't we wait out the Dutch occupation of Taiwan until the pirate Kochinga drove them out? Didn't we wait fifty years for the Japanese colonial masters to leave? Aren't we now waiting for the mainlanders to go back to their beloved homeland? Well, the bad ones, anyway.

Actually, here's one thing I don't understand about mainlanders. How come when they came over in 1949, they were all about "Kill the Commies," but now they love the People's Republic?

What could have changed the minds of the mainlanders, who are, in general, incredibly stubborn?

As we entered the empty warehouse, I decided to put the question to Peggy.

"Pardon me, I was wondering something about your family."

Peggy unlocked the main door with a card swipe, then pressed a button on her fob, causing her sports car to chirp. "Yeah, what, Jing-nan?"

We walked into the lobby, which was only partially lit. It smelled like the floor had been mopped recently.

"Your family, you guys were all Nationalists back in China. Why do you love the Communists now?"

Peggy laughed to herself as she jerked open a drawer where a security guard had once sat. "You people are ridiculous," said Peggy as she handed flashlights to Nancy and me. "You have no idea what it was like in China. During World War II, you were lounging around in your kimonos like a bunch of Nip-lovers. Meanwhile, we were fighting the Japanese twenty-four seven. Then after that, thanks to Mao's treachery, the Chinese turned their guns on each other. My family was lucky to get out, but not all the Lees were so lucky."

I turned on my flashlight to test it and shone the light in her face. "Wasn't Chiang treacherous, as well?"

She pushed my arm down and trained her light on my face. "You would have been the same way. If you didn't fuck over someone when you had the chance, they'd end up getting you."

"What an awful way to live," said Nancy. She turned on her flashlight and flipped through the logbook on the desk. "I can't believe the kidnappers didn't have the courtesy to sign in and out."

I walked away from Peggy's flashlight beam but she continued to talk. "My family did what they had to in order to survive and ensure that their descendants prospered. They didn't love the Nationalists. I can say that now."

"Peggy," said Nancy, "you said that some of your family didn't make it out of China?"

"I think some stayed," said Peggy. "Some made it out to some other countries. We were one of the big landlord families, so all of those peasants wanted a piece of our ass. But enough with the family history—let's try to find something to catch those kidnappers or else we're just wasting time. If we come up empty then we pack it up and head home. The basement entrance should be around here." She began to walk, one hand extended in front of her.

"Why can't you turn on the lights?" asked Nancy.

"There are no lights to turn on. The building is basically offline." I heard a click and a metallic door groan as her flashlight beam swung in the dark. "I found it! Let's go already!"

We followed her to the stairwell entrance. She stomped down the grated steel steps.

"Are you sure you can do that in heels?" Nancy called after her.

"I got this," Peggy yelled back. Nancy shrugged and followed. I went last because I had remembered that a man had been killed here on a live-streamed video, and it had begun to creep me out.

On the basement level, we all noticed that the rear was fairly well lit. The signs from the gigantic shopping mall caused the Ferris wheel's spokes to cast shadows along the walls. Some areas of the room were bright as day.

"Well, we're here," said Peggy. "Now what should we do, Captain Jing-nan?"

I swung my light around. The room was smaller than I had thought it would be and it appeared to be empty. Still, it was about half the size of a basketball court and there could be clues lurking somewhere.

"I think we should split up and search the floor thoroughly."

"I'm sure my father's people already did."

"Let's just make sure," I said. "Peggy, take the area along the left wall. Nancy, you take the right. I'll walk around the center. If you guys find something, don't touch it. Take a picture, mark it with GPS and we'll have the cops check it out. Let's meet up at the far wall." Peggy proceeded as directed. "Don't be scared, Nancy," I said.

She pushed me playfully. "Just for that, I should hide and jump out at you."

"No!"

"All right, Jing-nan. Seriously though, what should we look out for?"

"I'm not sure. I just feel like there's something about this place that everybody's missed."

Nancy touched my back. "I'll look carefully," she said as she left.

I stretched the oval of my flashlight beam along the floor from one side to the other. The three of us walked at the same measured pace. A foot of dust rose up to haunt me with each step. It seemed to clear up for a stretch, and then I found what looked like a comet spray of blood.

That executive had been shot right here and died. I swept my light around and found two lines in the blood pattern that must have been made by the dog cage. I pinned my flashlight to my waist with my elbow and tried to focus my camera on the stains. My fingers twitched as I snapped a few pictures, most of them focused.

I've had my hands covered in blood up to my elbows, but that was animal blood, not human. The sight of the stains made me sick. I hoped Tong-tong's people had allowed the cops to come in and record all this. I mean, the cops must've when they took the body out. My pictures were only going to supplement what the cops had.

There wasn't much else I encountered on my walk to the wall. Some old cardboard apparel tags, piles of plastic hangers and collapsed ghosts of plastic bags.

I noticed Nancy had paused at some point near the end of her walk.

"Did you find something?" I asked her.

She made a gross-out face. "I found a plastic bag of clothes," she said. "I didn't touch it, but it smelled like shit and it was covered in ants."

Peggy charged over to us. "Were those my father's pants?"

"I don't know. I saw the fabric. It looked like a suit."

Peggy stalked off in the darkness, retracing Nancy's steps. "I am not going to let the cops get a hold of it!"

"Peggy," I said, "don't mess with evidence!"

"Like hell it's evidence! It's just one more thing that could embarrass my father!"

We heard footsteps doing double-time on the metal stairs. Whoever was making the racket had much better flashlights than ours. They were practically car lamps.

"Who's here?" a gruff voice demanded.

"It's Peggy Lee," she threw back. "I'm the owner of this building."

The footsteps slowed to a stop. "Oh, Ms. Lee, I'm so sorry." The outline of a uniformed security guard began to define itself as he approached. "It is you, isn't it?"

Peggy put her hands on her hips. "Yeah, we're not neighborhood kids playing hide and seek, are we? And what's up with the gun, pal?"

I hadn't noticed that he had a gun drawn. He mumbled something and holstered it.

"Since when do we authorize our people to carry weapons?" asked Principal Peggy.

"It's a precaution," said the guard. "Because of your father." He pushed back his snapback cap and wiped sweat away from his forehead. I caught a dopey look in his eyes before he pulled his hat back down. LEE ENTERPRISES it read on the front.

A slightly shorter security guard trudged up next to him.

"Are you carrying a gun, too?" accused Peggy.

"Uh, one gun between us is good enough. We saw some lights in here and we had no idea what to expect."

Peggy pointed at the taller guard. "You. What's your name?"

"Lee. Like yours."

"Your name just happens to be the same character, but it's not like ours. Anyway, there's a bag of shit-stained pants near the wall over there. I need you to pick it up and get rid of it. Throw it in the incinerator, if there is one around here."

He swallowed. "A bag of shit?"

"You have a problem with that?"

"I'm a guard, not a garbage man. I'm not even a low-level security guard." He stammered a little. Clearly he didn't think carrying shit was in his job description. "I'm stationed at the dormitory across the street."

The shorter guard couldn't suppress a giggle.

"Hey, shorty," said Peggy, "what do you do?"

"I'm . . . I'm a footpost guard."

"Go pick up that bag of shit!"

WE WALKED TO THE dormitory guardhouse, a small concrete bunker next to the rolldown steel gate. It was the place where migrant workers had to check in before entering and being locked in for the night.

It was meant to be a one-man security post, and Lee was justifiably surprised to find another guard sitting in the seat with his back to us.

The guest was a big man and his ill-fitting uniform shirt didn't reach his waist. The hat was on backwards and an opened beer bottle was clutched in his right hand.

"*Ma de!*" declared the returning guard. "That's *my* booth, asshole!"

Dwayne turned around in the seat.

"I would have to say, sir, that your time really is up."

Lee drew his weapon. Nancy pressed herself against me. I shifted until I was between her and the gun. Peggy sauntered behind the guardhouse.

"Hey, what the fuck are you doing here?" I heard her say. Then I heard a muffled clicking sound. Frankie appeared, his hands clasped at his chest level as he took measured steps toward Lee.

"Would you happen to be a gambling man?" he asked Lee.

"What?" He was confused why his drawn gun wasn't acting as a deterrent.

"Do you like to gamble? Shit, you were in the army, weren't you? Don't tell me you don't like to toss dice in a bowl."

"I could arrest you right now," said Lee. "Both of you! What are you, homeless foreigners?"

"Us? Foreigners?" said Dwayne. "My people are as old as the soil and my children are going to live to see everybody else leave."

"Mr. Security Guard," said Frankie. "There's already been enough maligning of foreigners lately. Let's just stop." The shorter one began to back away and Frankie whistled at him. "You. Stay here with us. I'll give you good odds. I'll give you three-to-one odds that your friend here is going to put down his gun when I show him what's in my hands. Are you in?"

"No!"

"I'm in for one hundred NT!" declared Nancy. I tensed up but she whispered in my ear. "I asked Frankie and Dwayne to come just in case we needed backup." That calmed me immediately.

"I'm in for a hundred NT also," I said.

Frankie raised his hands over his head and shook them. "Sorry guys, I don't take bets from anyone I know. Anybody else? Betting closes in three, two . . . one!" Frankie stared at Lee. "Ready?" Frankie opened his hands and several bullet cartridges flew out and twinkled in the air as they fell to the asphalt. "Drop it, Lee. An unloaded gun is only good for hammering nails."

Lee pounced on a bullet. I wish I had my phone camera ready. I could've created a slo-mo video recording of Frankie flying through the air and kicking the gun out of Lee's hands. It would have gone viral on Unknown Pleasures' Facebook page.

Lee spun to the ground, landing on his left shoulder. He lay there and massaged his right wrist.

"Looks like you brought a gun to a fistfight," said Frankie.

"Get fucked, old man," said Lee as he remained prone.

I walked up to the guardhouse and pointed at Dwayne's face. "You look ridiculous in that uniform. I think you should wear it to work every day."

Dwayne lazily folded his arms behind his head. "This is my real job. Saving your ass."

"I'm glad you and Frankie came," said Nancy.

"No sweat at all. It was an easy MRT ride." Dwayne glanced over his shoulder. "You know what, though? I do want to ride that Ferris wheel at some point. But not tonight."

Lee dusted off his hands and legs. Before he stood fully erect, he pointed at Dwayne. "My employer will have your head!"

Dwayne leapt out of the guardhouse and smashed his fist into Lee's face, just below the left cheekbone. I'd be surprised if fewer than two teeth had been knocked out. Lee hit the ground like a skydiver without a parachute.

"I do the headhunting around here," Dwayne spat at Lee, who was splayed out like the fossil of a flying dinosaur. The other security guard tried to break into a run, but Frankie already had him by the sleeve.

"Don't worry, we know you're just a low-level chickenshit fuckup. They'll go easy on you, assuming you're not up to anything else."

Peggy, sensing that any threat was over, came out and stood next to Dwayne.

"I'm calling the cops now because I don't know what the hell is going on!"

"Huang and Kung are already on their way," said Nancy. "Along with other interested parties."

"Jing-nan better have a good lawyer for you two," said Peggy, pointing at Dwayne and Frankie.

"You oughta put in a call to your lawyer, Peggy," Frankie parried.

"For what?"

"For throwing the book at your guard Lee. He abandoned his post, for starters."

"He deserved to get punched out for that?"

Frankie idly rolled his right foot on a loose bullet. "No, not for that," admitted Frankie. "But for kidnapping your father and killing that executive, yeah, he deserves it." He turned to the guard in his custody. "You, what's your name?"

The guy cleared his throat. "Chen."

"You know how the old fairy tales always have some generic guy named Chen who gets killed by page two? In any case, are you related to Jing-nan here?"

"No. I don't know him."

"Does this guy look familiar to you, Nancy?"

She leaned in slightly and narrowed her eyes. "I don't think I've ever seen him before. Should I know him from somewhere?"

Frankie tilted his head back. "Oh, this is my fault. We're

playing this game with the wrong pair of people. Peggy, take a good look at that poor bastard on the ground. Dwayne, roll him on his back. There. Does he look like anyone you know?"

Peggy cracked her knuckles and approached Lee until her toes were inches away from his head.

"I don't think I've seen him before. It's weird, he sort of looks like one of my uncles, a little." She brought her hands together in a sudden clap and raised an eyebrow. "Is it my uncle, after plastic surgery?"

"I don't know about the plastic surgery part, but if you were on better terms, you'd be eating at the same extended-family banquets. He's apparently the grandson of your grandfather's oldest brother."

Peggy squared her feet with her shoulders. "What? My great uncle's family went to Thailand after the war. We never heard from him again."

Frankie flashed a smile. "His family's been keeping track of you."

"If you don't mind, Peggy," I said, "I think it's time to invite the police to enter this zone and help get this all straightened out."

Nancy danced in place. "First things first, Peggy! You have to thank me for texting Dwayne and Frankie. If they weren't here, this guy would never have been caught. Who knows, maybe he would've killed us."

Peggy looked at Frankie and then at Nancy. "He wasn't going to kill us, was he?" She walked over to Lee and nudged his face with her shoe. "Hey you, were you going to shoot us? Even me, your own blood?" The man was completely out and a small trickle of blood came from his lips.

Peggy glared at Nancy. "I don't believe in gratuitous appreciation, but you did go above and beyond. I even told you not to tell anyone but you still told Frankie and Dwayne. Thank you." She punched a number into her phone and put it to her ear. "But I wouldn't promote you because you disobeyed orders."

"I wish she were my boss," I muttered to Nancy.

"I heard that," Peggy stated.

PEGGY HADN'T CALLED THE Taipei police. She got in touch with a family friend at the Republic of China Air Force.

When three unmarked SUVs rolled up I thought they were some of Frankie's underworld friends, but the men who emerged were dressed in jumpsuits and jackboots. A single man hoisted up Lee by the armpits and pulled him into the back of an SUV. It spoke to how efficient they would be in retrieving injured comrades. They shoved the shitbag in with Lee, and strong-armed the other guard, Chen, into the middle of the back-row seat. Another man entered the security booth and remained standing at attention.

The air force guys were under orders to take custody of the lot of us. I didn't feel unsafe, however, as I got into what turned out to be the second car in the convoy. Nancy sat next to me and Dwayne sat behind us with a man who was as upright and alert as a dog show Doberman pinscher.

We rolled west toward the general headquarters of the air force. The man left in the guardhouse saluted us.

During the ride, Dwayne told us in a hushed voice that after he and Frankie had gotten Nancy's message, they took a taxi to the warehouse and walked the perimeter of it. Dwayne noticed that a guard on duty had fallen asleep, and snuck up on him, ready to scare him as a prank. Then he saw the man had a holstered gun.

Frankie managed to pry open a window and get a hold of the gun. After he removed the bullets and replaced it, Frankie called a friend to trace the weapon's serial number. Dwayne and Frankie were debating what to do when the other security guard came strolling in and they quickly decided to hide. Chen woke up Lee and the two were joking around when they noticed lights were flashing around the warehouse windows.

Chen and Lee took off for the building. When it was clear they weren't coming back soon, Frankie searched the booth and found a number of incriminating papers, documents from the Chinese government and names of Chinese spies in Taipei. Lee had figured that his booth would be the most secure place to stash such things, but it became a convenient place to find everything in one spot.

I interrupted the story. "Dwayne, where is Frankie right now?"

He cleared his throat. "He's in the general's car behind us. They're going through the papers right now. A bunch of people are gonna be in deep shit."

Nancy raised her hand. "What about the gun? How did Lee get one?"

Dwayne glanced at the rearview mirror of the SUV. "It's a military issue, of course. Frankie thinks the gun was sold by a gang that operates within the army. These air force guys are going to look up the serial number, see what the deal is and then make it disappear. You watch."

I turned to the tinted window and watched the edge of the dark road wriggle through the night. I thought about my parents and my grandparents and the choices we all made so that I would be right here, right now.

Nancy said something just as I had the same thought. "I wish Peggy had called the cops instead."

Dwayne made a disapproving sound in his throat. "I don't. If the cops showed up, they'd probably let Lee go to meet with his attorney or whatever. I say to hell with his civil rights."

I glanced at the Doberman-faced guard. If he were listening, he showed no sign of it.

Nancy tried to wrap her arms around herself and crossed her legs. "I don't see why they had to take us with them," she said.

"All of us have to corroborate Peggy's story. And Nancy, you'll have to explain that you brought in me and Frankie. It will help in case there are charges for trespassing on private property."

"I'm glad we were with Peggy," I said. "We couldn't very well be trespassing with a member of the owner's family. Huh, Nancy?"

One corner of Nancy's mouth twisted into a line chart projecting lower revenue for the next fiscal year. "Does the air force really have the personnel and the time to interrogate us?" she asked.

Dwayne propped up his elbows on either side of my headrest. "It's not the air force that's gonna be demanding answers, Nancy!"

CHAPTER 14

Tong-tong was in an agitated and yet dreamlike state. The man wiped both sides of his face and raked his fingers through his scalp to the back of his neck. The continuous action appeared to simultaneously soothe and enrage him.

He paced the stage with big and slow strides. "I just can't believe this," he said into the wireless mic. "How could this be?"

We were sitting in stadium seats in a below-ground-level auditorium. The first row was occupied by five of Tong-tong's personal bodyguards. Lee, who was sporting a black eye but seemed alert, was handcuffed to a chair on the stage. Seated on either side of him were two unamused air force officers.

We had already passed the mic around the room once. Peggy went first with her account of the night. Nancy said that she knew that a police presence would rouse suspicion from the bystanders and the kidnappers alike, so she had called the two most-competent "agents" she knew, Frankie and Dwayne.

Frankie could have talked about the shadow in the video

and how he tipped off the police that the place had to be near the entertainment park. Instead, his story started with how he and Dwayne snuck up to the guard booth. Dwayne added that he had punched Lee in the face out of anger and apologized for it.

I didn't know what to say to account for myself, especially when I saw a throbbing vein on Tong-tong's forehead. I decided to offer him my condolences. "Tong-tong, I hope that now we've found the guy, you find some solace."

With that, I handed the mic to an air force officer who looked about my age. She opened a manila envelope, withdrew a sheet of paper and read aloud from it.

"Our preliminary investigation of the papers found in the guardhouse show that the documents appear to be genuine. We have already apprehended Chinese agents, identified by the paper work, who were working in the National Immigration Agency to aid in this plot.

"The guard has been identified as Lee Wei-yin, also known as Lee Shui-long, a grandson of Lee Shih-chao, who was the older brother of Lee Shih-yao, who is the father of Tong-tong. Lee Shih-chao, who is now deceased, was not able to escape from China until the Korean War began in 1950. Shih-chao boarded a ship bound for Bangkok, Thailand. Shih-chao tried to get in touch with Shih-yao by phone and letters, demanding his share of the family fortune that Shih-yao had managed to bring to Taiwan years earlier. Shih-yao apparently never replied.

"Shih-chao started a business in import-export that did well for years but collapsed in the financial crisis of 1997. The entire family was plunged into debt and shame. In 1999, when Wei-yin was thirty, he went to China to work for a rival's company and complained frequently that Tong-tong's father stole the family fortune.

"The Chinese government had been interested in a chip that Tong-tong had been shopping around several years ago. Taiwanese manufacturers were successful in lobbying Tong-tong to not make the chip, which would disrupt too many operations within the semiconductor industry. That interest became more pronounced earlier this year after Taiwanese company SMC relocated wafer-fabrication plants to Malaysia from China after attempts were made to steal its intellectual property.

"The Chinese Ministry of State Security contacted Wei-yin about a year ago, after determining that he was indeed related to the well-known Lee family of Taipei. They had wanted Wei-yin to ingratiate himself to Tong-tong and steal the chip design. Wei-yin went along with it but he had his own plan.

"With two other as-yet unidentified members of his family, Wei-yin entered Taiwan in January with a migrant worker program. Because he held a college degree, he was eligible for higher-placement positions, which is how he was appointed a security guard.

"Wei-yin was supposed to approach Tong-tong only in a friendly manner but instead plotted the kidnapping. He planned to sell the chip design to the highest bidder, not necessarily China. The unavailability of the design thwarted the plan. We are interrogating agents from the immigration department about the other two kidnappers, who may have left the country already."

The officer finished reading and slid the paper back into the envelope. She carried the microphone to Tong-tong along with the envelope.

"Is this the only copy of this report?" asked Tong-tong. The officer nodded. He folded up the envelope and stuck it inside his suit jacket. It was the last thing he said clearly.

TONG-TONG CONTINUED TO SLOWLY walk along the edge of the stage and at times he walked dangerously close along the edge. I saw Nancy and then Dwayne stifle yawns. I wish I hadn't seen them. I remember hearing a theory that yawning was a vestigial remnant of a group-howling activity that our primate ancestors practiced. Its contagiousness is bred in our bones. I yawned so hard I teared up.

When I regained control of my face, I found that Tong-tong was staring right at me.

"Am I boring you, Jing-nan?" the room's speakers thundered. "This man almost killed me and you're so unconcerned that you're falling asleep?"

I propped myself up and tried to look alert. This was embedded in my muscle memory from years of school and cram school. "Mr. Lee," I said to be respectful, "I'm really sorry, but I'm usually asleep by this time." The acoustics in the room were good enough that a mic wasn't necessary, but I wasn't going to tell Tong-tong that. Not while he was in this state.

"I'm usually fucking asleep by now, too, Jing-nan! It's one thirty in the fucking morning!"

"I know you're tired, too. Maybe we should take a break for the night, have the authorities take custody of Mr. Lee and let them figure out what to do."

Tong-tong wrung the mic with both hands, probably imagining that it was my neck. "Don't you know what an embarrassment this is for me? For my family, including Peggy, your friend and classmate? How can we hold our heads up when people find out that I am related to the piece of shit who kidnapped me?" He paused briefly to prowl the stage some more. "No way am I handing this guy over to the police."

"Why don't you just kill me?"

We all turned to Wei-yin. He had his head down.

"I would love to oblige you," said Tong-tong. "But I can't. My conscience won't allow me to kill one of my own." He breathed heavily into the mic. "I think you felt it, too. When you were supposed to shoot me, you shot Associate Vice President Peng Wan-chang instead."

Wei-yin nodded slightly without lifting his head.

Tong-tong continued, his voice strained. "Why didn't you write to me? Or call me? Of course I would have helped you and your family. I could have even brought you all here to Tai-wan."

Wei-yin sat up with his neck deferentially bent. "Your father didn't help my father." Lee's voice was heavy with resignation. "Your father never answered any of my father's letters. Why would you be any different?"

Tong-tong stamped his right foot twice. "I would've been! I am not my father! I've always wondered what happened to the family that got separated."

"Sure you did."

"He never told me he got those letters. Maybe they never reached him."

Lee reached over to scratch his knees, causing his hand-cuffs to clink. "We got one letter back from his secretary telling us that your father didn't know us and to never write again." Lee's face was somber as he pointed his free hand at Tong-tong. "Your father denied knowing his older brother."

"How is your father doing now?"

With some incredulity, Wei-yin said, "He's dead."

"Oh yeah, the report said so. Well, my father's dead, too." Tong-tong said it again, to himself: "My father's dead."

I looked at Peggy. I don't know what I expected to see. Dismay? Mild amusement? She had also reverted to school behavior and was doodling, detached but still aware.

Frankie had his eyes on Wei-yin. Maybe he was recalling

what it was like being a prisoner. Dwayne was pinching himself to stay awake.

Nancy was staring at me. I wished she were close enough for me to give her shoulder a reassuring touch. All I could do was nod and she returned the gesture.

I wished we didn't have to spend so much time in strained situations like this. I wished we were zoned out on the couch watching big, mushy American shows on Netflix.

That was not our lot. She knew that.

A sobbing sound came over the speakers. Nancy and I broke away from our shared reverie to see Tong-tong, who was, remarkably, hunched over embracing his former captor.

"I'm going to take care of you," he said through tears. "This is what family does for each other."

"Dad," said Peggy as she continued to draw, "are we seriously going to put him up in one of our apartments? The guy who put you in a dog cage."

Tong-tong sniffed hard. "Oh, no," he said. "Actually, we can't even have him in this country, at this point. No, he has to go back to Thailand. We'll provide for him, though. Give him money to start a company."

Peggy gave a resigned sigh. "He killed someone, though."

"Well, I've already provided for Mr. Peng's family. They have no cause to complain."

Wei-yin turned in his chair. Maybe my thinking was impaired but the black eye made him look like a stuffed toy. "Do I really have to go back to Thailand?" the toy asked.

Tong-tong slapped his shoulder, hard enough to prove he was straight. "Oh, yes," said Tong-tong as he signaled his bodyguards sitting in the front row of the audience. "You're leaving tonight and never coming back."

Tong-tong's two guys got up and stood at the front of the stage. Three air force officers, including the one who had read the letter, approached and all five of them conferred together.

Frankie stood up, stretched and headed for the left exit of the auditorium.

"Hey, Frankie," called Tong-tong. "Who said you could go?"

Frankie's arms hung loosely at his sides in a casually menacing manner. "Who said I couldn't?" Without waiting for Tong-tong to answer, he called to us, "This way." Nancy, Dwayne and I followed.

As I was about to pass Peggy, who was still doodling, a thought crossed my mind.

"Hey, Peggy, have you thought about that chip that the Chinese want?"

She was shading stitches on the face of Frankenstein's monster. "A little."

"Maybe you want to reconsider getting Ah-tien a new trial?"

"Fuck that guy. He didn't help us in our time of need."

I paused and looked around. Wei-yin looked resigned to whatever fate had in store. Peggy, too.

Nancy was waiting for me in the doorway. Dwayne stood behind her, frowning and making vaguely threatening gestures at me. It was time to go.

On my way out, I realized that the other guard, Chen, was nowhere to be seen. I wondered what they did with him.

I HAD THE HARDEST time sleeping. For some reason, all my senses were heightened. Maybe we had been exposed to radiation as we walked by a secret weapons lab at the air force headquarters. Maybe my mind was a battleground as my subconscious tried to work out a way to help Nancy's former sugar daddy while my id was torching the drawing board.

Or maybe my life was in danger without me being fully conscious of it.

I was able to hear every slightest sound. Nancy's breathing was deep and its slow cycle became universal in stature in the dark. There was no beginning or end, there was only in and out. Only a few hours ago, we were in danger and now here we were, safe in bed.

Man, I had to piss. I slipped out to go to the bathroom. After, I went to the kitchen to drink some tap water that tasted salty and perfumed.

I sat in the dark of the living room, which wasn't actually dark at all. The cable box, the television and DVD player all watched me with angry, unblinking red eyes.

There was a soft knocking sound at the door. I wasn't that surprised to hear it and maybe I had been expecting it, considering that I was up.

I moved through the apartment and glanced through the peephole. I was satisfied with what I saw and undid the locks.

"Hello, Ju-lan," I whispered as I opened the door.

"Hello, Jing-nan," she whispered back. "I hope I'm not disturbing you."

"I was awake, anyway, but Nancy is still sleeping."

"I'm glad I didn't disturb her. I just wanted to talk with you." She entered cautiously and I closed the door behind her. She walked stiffly to keep quiet, which I appreciated on Nancy's behalf.

"Can I get you a glass of water? I'd offer you ice cubes in it, but I think it would make too much noise."

For some reason, she chose to ignore my question. "There's nobody else here, is there, Jing-nan?"

I rubbed my hands. "Just me, you and Nancy. If you want to say something you want to keep private, you're not going to have a problem here."

Her face twitched as if she were about to sneeze. Ju-lan opened her pocketbook, I assumed to grab a handkerchief.

Instead, she came up with a gun.

"Whoa," I whispered. "What's this for?"

The fingernails of her grip gleamed. "Stay quiet and come with me."

"Tell me what this is about."

"Shut up, or I'll make Nancy come with us. You want that?"

"No, I don't. Can I at least put on slippers?"

"Just be quick."

I glanced at the double rack of footwear by the door. Could I possibly leave a clue of what happened to me?

Ju-lan read my mind. "Jing-nan!" she hissed. "Hurry!"

I walked into a pair of rip-off Crocs. I hoped they managed to hold up, wherever I was headed.

"What did I ever do to you, Ju-lan?" I whined. "I know you've been screwed over by men many times, but not by me! I even let you speak at my open mic."

"I have nothing against you, Jing-nan, and I have even less against Nancy. This is just business."

She made me leave first and closed the apartment door behind us.

A CAR WAS WAITING by the curb. The rear passenger door opened and a large man wearing shades stepped out. He gestured for me to get in. I ducked and sat in the middle seat, next to a man wearing a fedora pulled over his face. The large man heaved himself back into the car. He leaned over and crushed my right side as he shut the door.

"Pardon me for that," he rasped as he eased his body away from me. "Little tight back here."

"Maybe you should let me out," I said. "I'll take the bus instead."

He laughed through his nostrils.

Ju-lan climbed into the front passenger seat and lifted something to her face. I smelled coffee. She sucked her teeth and said, "I think it's time for lights out on this one."

I turned my head to try to avoid the blow and the last thing I remembered was my body jerking back in my seat.

CHAPTER 15

I became aware of a great field of flowers basking in the sun, gently swaying in the wind, left to right, front and back.

A dim salty taste.

Ugh, snot collecting in my throat. I tried to move it away with my tongue and accidentally swallowed.

"I think he's coming out of it," said a voice to my right. I realized that my eyes were closed and that now was probably not a good time to open them. I went as limp as I could. "Never mind, false alarm," said the man.

"You clocked him good," said Ju-lan. Her voice was prickly. "When I said 'lights out,' I meant for you to tie the blindfold around his head."

"Blindfold? Naw, that doesn't do the job. He could count the turns and figure out where he was going."

"Even so, put the blindfold on him now."

"All right, all right," said the man. Under his breath he added, "Fuckin' bitch." He twisted and exhaled heavily with effort. He'd recently been eating spicy rice crackers. The man wound fabric around my head, sometimes pulling a hair or two. I managed to not cry out. He tied it tight enough for me to feel it in my eyeballs. Is it possible for the head to go numb?

The car turned to the left and I allowed myself to slump on the man's shoulder. Thanks for not putting on my seatbelt, guys.

Ju-lan wasn't done with chewing the man out. "Do you understand that he's no good to us if he looks injured?"

The man stretched his legs, propped me back into my seat and held up my chin. "There's not a mark on him. Well, not much anyway."

"That doesn't matter. Do what I tell you to do. Understand, Li-min?"

The man tapped the door handle. "Fine. I will obey you."

We slowed into a turn. I heard a siren nearby and a loud scraping sound. It must be a parking garage door opening. We eased our way forward and the car tilted down.

Shit, where were they taking me? I slumped against the man to my left. He felt oddly bony and seemed to know where exactly to place his elbow to force my body to fold in half. I eased myself away from him as naturally as I could pretend.

I don't know how many levels we went down. At certain points I could hear our car engine amplified due to proximity to a wall. Other times loud echoes clanked back from the other side of a space that must be as big as the warehouse Tong-tong had been held in.

At a certain point, the car slowed to a stop and I heard something big slither by. Was that a dinosaur? We eased forward and the dinosaur retraced its steps behind us.

We stopped again. I heard Ju-lan swing her door open and step out. "Has Jing-nan rejoined us?" she asked Li-min.

"Lemme see," he said and pinched me inside my right thigh, right next to my balls. I hadn't been expecting it so I couldn't stop my legs from jolting. I might have cried out a little bit, too. Li-min laughed through his nose again. "He's up."

"Let's get him out. We don't have any time to waste."

"Should I get the equipment out, too?"

"Of course. Let's set it up and get something on the Internet soon." Li-min creaked his door open, put his feet on the ground and grabbed my arm. "You think you can walk on your own, kid? I'm going to have my hands full."

I took my first full breath of air in ages. "Can I take off this thing so I can see?"

"Sure. Take a good look around you."

I fingered the knot tied behind my left ear and pulled one of the loops until I felt it loosen. Soon I managed to untwirl the entire thing from my head. I blinked in the clinical light of fluorescent bulbs and rubbed a sore spot under my right cheek.

"Sorry about that, but I had to," said Li-min as he stepped out from the car. The shades had been pocketed, revealing a flabby, boyish face marked with a faintly apologetic smile that *heidaoren* have perfected. I'm a criminal, the smile says, but that doesn't mean I'm not a fun guy.

Li-min backed up, allowing me to ease my way out of the car. I stood and tried to stretch. Gravity feels strong when you're recovering from being knocked out.

"Excuse me, Jing-nan," said Li-min. "I gotta get that stuff in the back." I stepped out of the way and he leaned in and reached for the other man in the back seat. Only it wasn't a man. It was a tripod and some other equipment covered with a tarp. Li-min stuck the fedora on his head.

He saw me staring at him. I was still shocked it wasn't a man I had been sitting next to the entire ride. Li-min dipped the brim of his hat at me and winked.

"A gentleman never wears a hat in a car," he said, kicking the door shut behind him. Both of his arms were full.

I nodded and looked around. If I had seen an open door, I would've bolted. We seemed to be in an unfinished private parking spot connected to a garage. Apart from that sliding concrete barrier, there were no doors or windows. Linear fluorescent light bulbs dashed across the encrusted spray-cement ceiling, which was about ten feet high. Electrical wires spilled out of the fixtures like flower filaments.

The entire space smelled moldy. I could see puddles of groundwater here and there. It was difficult keeping water out of underground developments because it required using a good sealant and following building codes. Both were pricey, too pricey, especially if the building was going to be knocked down again in a few years and rebuilt as something else.

I looked carefully along the lines where the walls met the ceiling. I heard Li-min laugh out of his nostrils again.

"What are you looking at? Are you going to dig your way out through there? Look, Jing-nan, you're gonna be here a while. You might as well settle in and make the best of it."

Ju-lan approached. "Well, if they're smart, he actually won't be here long at all." She slipped out her phone and tapped away. "Li-min, let's get him set up." She gave him a hard stare and just to make sure there was no misunderstanding, she added, "Let's cuff him to the wall and get that equipment set up. I'll be back in a few hours." She gestured to a wall through which passed a pipe wide enough to accommodate bowling balls.

Li-min nodded. "Right. Got it."

"Let's get him cuffed before I leave."

Li-min put everything down and rubbed his palms against each other. He opened a small sack and pulled out a pair of handcuffs and a chain leash with links thick enough to hold back a crocodile.

"Let's go, Jing-nan."

"Don't forget," said Ju-lan. "I still have my gun."

"I'm more scared of this guy," I said. It was true.

The driver, a slight and stooped man with a face worn featureless by regret, padlocked one end of the chain to a lag-eye bolt in the wall. He drew out the other end of the chain and handed it to Li-min, who looped one cuff through the last link and locked it. He shook the open cuff at me, the metallic claw swinging.

"Jing-nan, I need one of your wrists. You choose which one."

"He's right-handed," snapped Ju-lan. "Lock up his right hand."

Li-min gave her a withering look. "Why would you want the stronger arm to be in the cuffs? It's easier for him to break it!" He had caught her off-guard.

"Then . . . put the left hand in there."

"Why would you want to do that and leave the stronger hand free to pick the lock?"

Ju-lan chuckled in disgust. "All right, I see what you're doing. Just cuff him and be done with it, already."

Li-min turned to me. I lifted my left wrist to him as quickly as I could. He snapped the cuff around it and tightened it.

"Good choice," he said. "Are you really right-handed?"

"In reality," I said, "I was born left-handed. But my grandfather forced me to use my right hand and punished me when I used my left."

Now it was Li-min's turn to chuckle. "Don't you hate all our stupid superstitions?"

"Hey, no one hates them more than me. I don't even like praying."

Ju-lan threw her shoulders back and regarded me. "Honestly, a few prayers right now wouldn't hurt, Jing-nan."

The driver read her body language and scrambled away to

the car like a bug avoiding a slipper-swat. He had it started in seconds.

Ju-lan opened the passenger door. Her final warning was for Li-min, not me. "Like I said, have everything set up and ready to go by the time I get back. You shouldn't have a problem. The salesman said a high-school kid could figure out the camera."

The concrete wall began to slide open. It reminded me of those old Japanese monster movies with bad special effects. Small pieces fell off as it moved. Was the wall made cheaply? Or maybe the track it was running on was laid down by an underpaid and undocumented worker.

It wasn't pretty, but it worked. In any case, it wasn't built to meet public approval.

The car curved out and waited until the wall shut before driving off. Li-min bunched up the tarp in his arms and laid it down at my feet.

"It's not the most comfortable thing in the world, but it isn't bad."

I took a step to the side to look it over fully. It didn't seem booby-trapped. "What do you want me to do with it?"

"Well, you can sleep on it, if you want. It is four in the morning."

"I don't know if I can."

Li-min rubbed his earlobes. "I'll tell you what, I'm pretty sure I can. No funny business while I'm down."

"But isn't Ju-lan coming back soon?" I asked.

He rummaged through the pile of things he had unloaded. "She won't be back until the afternoon. She's just giving me a hard time." He pulled out a rolled-up inflatable mattress.

"Hey, can I get one of those?"

"Naw, naw, there's only one. I'm one of the captors, so I should definitely get the nicer bedding." He brought over a kid's plastic sand pail. "You can have this, though."

The object filled me with dread. "Do you have any toilet paper?"

He shrugged. "I'll tell you what. She'll definitely bring some. She's in hospitality, you know."

Li-min walked off to the other side of the cavernous room. We could see each other plainly and yet the distance gave some sense of privacy. I spread out the tarp and lay on it. We were underground and the insulation from the surrounding earth provided moderate warmth. I could feel every bump in the concrete floor through the tarp but that didn't stop me from falling asleep instantly.

I WOKE UP TO the same ceiling lights. Should I be awake? I didn't have my phone, so I had no idea what time it was. I saw Li-min still laid out on his nice air mattress, comfortable as a zoo bear. I could hear his hibernation snores clearly and I felt bad for anyone else who had been subjected to it. I rolled to face the opposite wall and felt the chain snake across my chest and back.

I think I knew part of what Ju-lan had in store for me. She was going to stream some video of me. Why? I wasn't sure, but the timing seemed to indicate it was a retaliatory action for Wei-yin being found out and deported.

How did Ju-lan even know about Mr. Lee? He hadn't made the news, and he wouldn't. Her association with a hired heavy such as Li-min, however, indicated that she was connected and knew a wide range of people.

She certainly knew how to find me.

I closed my eyes and tried to think her story through. Then it hit me. Ju-lan didn't hear about Wei-yin on the news. She found out about it because she was also a part of China's spy network.

I heard some distant rumbling, cars driving through the

parking lot. Maybe I should try screaming. No, that would only end with Li-min socking me in the jaw again. He might not want to, but he would to shut me up.

Li-min seemed to be a nice guy at the core. At some point in the night, he had left a paper cup filled with water within my reach. I felt parched as soon as I saw the cup, and drank all the water immediately. I had to piss right after, and made sure to aim at the side of the pail to minimize the sound and not disturb Li-min. When I was finished, I lay down again. Maybe if I managed to fall asleep again, I'd wake up and find this was all a dream.

Instead, I began to wonder what Li-min's story was. Not all gangsters were pricks like my uncle. A lot of these criminal types are people who have fallen through the cracks in Taiwan's hypercompetitive society. Maybe the parents had split up or lost their jobs and the kids couldn't afford cram school, hurting the chances of getting into the top high schools and colleges. Maybe the kids who weren't in cram school weren't so focused on professional development. Maybe they all went shoplifting together, got busted and tagged with a juvenile-delinquency record. Once that happened, most of the legitimate paths to upward mobility were cut off for good.

I'd seen that story unfold in a popular soap opera that was praised for its gritty realism. I can't remember exactly how it ended but there was definitely a scene where one of the gangsters was on his hands and knees before his parents, crying and begging for forgiveness. It made some valid points about society, but all the stars of the show were so light-skinned and thin, they were nearly transparent. The lead hood was played by an actor who had been a pre-med major at Taida, the same prestigious university that Nancy attended.

In our country, even the fuckups are portrayed by the overachievers.

In our country, I was a fuckup.

Never mind that I was a successful businessman. Any matchmaker who selected me would be banished from the profession, if there were a governing body that exercised oversight. I wasn't a doctor. Hell, I didn't even have a college degree.

But I had Nancy.

I rolled on to my back and heard my chains rattle. I wondered what she was doing now. Did she know that I was missing already? I would never leave the apartment without leaving a note or email. If she tried to text me, she'd be startled by my phone's chirp in the bedroom. Then she'd know something was seriously wrong. I never forget my phone. I don't always have it charged, but I don't forget it.

I wasn't so much worried about what was in store for me as I was concerned with how worried Nancy would be. I guessed she might try calling Dwayne and Frankie. Maybe Peggy at some point. Man, I really hoped she'd never be desperate enough to ring up my uncle Big Eye, because he was the nuclear option.

I wound the chain around both hands and tugged lightly. There was zero give. I looked over at Li-min. When I saw that he was still checked out, I stood up and pulled with all my weight, planting my feet in the tug-of-war against the wall.

Nothing happened. Not even a crumb of cement broke off.

I stopped and massaged my sore wrists. Even if I had managed to break away, how would I be able to leave the room, never mind avoid Li-min, whose fist had an undefeated record against my face?

I wondered about the guys, Dwayne and Frankie. Surely Nancy would get in touch with them before it was time to open Unknown Pleasures. Would they just go ahead and operate the stand without me, hoping I would turn up at some point?

I heard a dog bark and I jumped. Li-min rolled over, groaned and hit something on his phone, which made the barking stop. Ten minutes later the alarm went off again and Li-min repeated his actions. The next time the alarm sounded, he turned it off and got up on one knee.

"Jing-nan!" he called over.

"Yes."

"Let's get up."

"What time is it?"

"Eight."

I stretched and yawned as if I had just woken up while he rummaged through a small box. Then I yawned again, this time for real. I was usually up an hour or two before this, so I shouldn't be too tired. Then again, my sleep routine had been interrupted.

"Do I have to do anything?" I called out.

"Actually, you don't, unless you want to piss in the bucket." Li-min approached and set up the tripod about five feet away from me. It was close enough for me to see the threads of the height-adjustment knobs.

I could swing my legs around to snag the tripod. Then I could take it up in my hands as a weapon. No, that wouldn't end well. I was still chained to the wall. I decided to remain quiet and wait for a good opportunity.

Li-min unfolded a shaky fabric-and-wire chair next to the tripod and began to toy with a video camera. It had two flip-out control panels and several indicator lights that immediately signaled that Li-min didn't know what he was doing.

This was the initial setup stage. The user is expected to set parameters such as the date, time and WiFi connection. The more reputable brands allow you skip this step so you can start shooting right off the bat. This camera wasn't a Sony or Panasonic product, however. It wasn't even Samsung. The name on the strap was "Hatiss."

After a few minutes, Li-min heaved a sigh and set the camera on the tripod. He picked up the manual and flipped through the first few pages. Growing flustered, he went to his phone to read up on the camera.

A doorbell alert went off and Li-min read whatever text or email had just come in. It must have come from Ju-lan because he groaned. Then he put in his earbuds and turned the phone sideways to watch a video. That led to another video and another. Then I think he started playing a game, one that required the player to turn the phone in order to steer a tank through a battlefield or guide a marble through a maze.

It's not much fun watching a guy on his phone, whether or not he's playing a game. But he was more interesting than the floor, the walls or the ceiling, so I continued to observe him.

While he was distracted with the game, I contemplated pulling the tripod and camera over. Once I had the camera in my hands, I could threaten to destroy it if he didn't release me.

No, that wouldn't work. For one thing, even if I destroyed it, Ju-lan could get another camera in about 10 seconds in Taipei. Besides, Li-min might just beat the crap out of me before I could articulate my threat.

Think of something else, damn it!

Li-min had been acting like a nice guy. He just might be amenable to letting me help him set up the camera.

I couldn't snatch it right away. I should help set it up and hand it back to grow his trust in me. No funny business.

"Say, Li-min?"

He looked at me, slightly startled upon emerging from some virtual world. He fumbled to pause his game. "Yeah!"

"I couldn't help but notice that you were having trouble with the camera. I could give you a hand."

He did a slow blink and snapped his head back. "Why should I give you a chance to fuck up the camera?"

"I won't mess it up, I promise. After all, you guys are going to stream me on camera, right?"

His face turned to steel. "Yeah. Well, I guess that's pretty obvious."

"I need the camera to work so you guys get what you want and then you let me go, right?"

"How do you know what we want?"

"I don't. All I know is I want to get out of here, and that's only going to happen if the camera's working. So let me give it a shot."

Li-min pocketed his phone and locked his arms around his chest. A scowl ripped across his face as he thought. He was probably imagining how badly Ju-lan was going to chew him out for not being able to figure out the device. If I could do it for him, however, he would be in the clear.

Li-min stared hard at me.

I tried to make myself look as innocent and helpless as possible. Being chained to a wall helped quite a bit. I ran a hand through my greasy, unshowered hair and smiled.

"Okay," he said. "One thing, though. If you get this thing working, don't tell Ju-lan you set it up. For all she'll know, I did it all by myself."

"Of course," I said. "Anything."

He leaned over to pick up the camera and brought it over to me in both hands. "Don't mess with this thing," he warned me. "Don't drop it or break off any pieces. Anything you do to that camera, I'm going to do to you. Got it?"

I immediately thought of the wise answer, *You mean you're going to turn me on?* Of course I didn't say it. At some point in the future, my thoughts might return to this very moment and I could laugh out loud at what could have been. Right now, though, my job was to get to that future and in as healthy a state as possible.

"Don't worry about a thing, Li-min," I said. "I will handle everything."

He didn't believe me at first, as he kept his hands underneath the camera, at the ready, like a new dad allowing someone else to hold his baby for the first time.

"Don't do that," I told him. "You're making me nervous. It's bad enough that I have one hand cuffed."

"I don't want you to drop the camera on the ground!"

"I told you I wouldn't."

"How can I trust you?"

I shrugged in frustration. "If I want to wreck this thing, I could just throw it against the wall!"

He jerked as if I had been spitting in his face. It was entirely possible that I had. I was disoriented from being tired, dirty and hungry.

Li-min backed off and retreated to his chair. He issued me a final warning before resuming his game. "Don't fuck up. Ju-lan will literally kill you." After a moment, he added, "Probably kill me, too, after."

I calmly nodded. It was good to know the animosity between them wasn't play.

I flipped out both touchscreens and realized that the camera wasn't registering the taps from my fingers. Then I noticed a small pop-up message: *If you are setting up for the first time or resetting, press and hold the black buttons behind each touchscreen.*

Ah, so that's what tripped him up. I'll bet half the camera's users missed the pop-up. I held down the buttons and the camera beeped.

"What did you do?" Li-min asked in a threatening manner.

"I'm initializing the flash drive," I said. He grumbled because, as I expected, he had no idea what I was talking about.

A menu prompted me to enter the date, time and location. I was about to ask Li-min what time it was when I noticed another small message: *Click here to connect to WiFi and autofill this form.*

I clicked on it and several networks popped up. Some personal ones. A few cafés. But the network with the strongest signal was the one with the name that interested me the most: Taipei 101 Parking.

I tapped the network and after two cycles of a digital globe, the forms autofilled. For GPS location, it filled out 25°2'1"N, 121°33'54"E. I licked my lips. I wished I was some map geek who knew where that was. Was I currently in the parking garage beneath the landmark building or in a space near it?

To frustrate me even more, the camera also filled out, "Taipei, China." I tried to change the country manually, but the scrolling list went from "Syrian Arab Republic" straight to "Tajikistan." No "Taiwan." Well, I'd have to live with it. The key point being that I planned to continue living past this hardship.

I went through the rest of the setup menu. Maybe there was some way I could send a message out to let people know that I was being held somewhere near Taipei 101. If I managed to get out even the most hopelessly vague signal, I had to hope that Frankie was out there watching and would be able to decode it.

I selected only the second-highest resolution for the livestreaming function because I figured it would help save battery power. This camera was going to be my lifeline out to the world, one way or another, and I wanted it to function as long and steadily as possible.

The camera prompted me for an account for streaming. That would be good for me to know.

"Uh, Li-min, I need some information."

"What?"

"What site are you going to use for streaming and what is your account and password?"

He shook his head and smiled. "I wouldn't tell you if I knew. That's something Ju-lan is going to enter herself. Are you done, already?"

"No, I still have a little ways to go."

"Well, just skip that step. How much longer are you going to take?"

"It's hard to say. I have to make these annoying adjustments."

"Well, don't take too long."

I planned to drag this out as long as possible to learn as much as I could about the device. Once I handed it back, I might never have my hands on it again.

"Sure," I told Li-min. "I'll finish up as soon as I can."

I opened the advanced settings menu and as a set of options unfurled across both touchscreens, I became hopeful. There had to be something that could help me.

Slow-motion mode adjustment? Not quite.

Calibrate display? No, thank you.

Motion adjustment? What exactly did that mean?

I tapped it, revealing an option for the camera to activate upon detecting a movement. That might be what I needed! I toggled it on. When Ju-lan or Li-min were gone or asleep, I could activate the camera and send out a desperate SOS.

I exited out of the submenu and scanned the main settings. Give me something to save myself with!

Energy-saver settings. I tapped it and discovered an adjustment that proved to me that a higher power truly did exist. *Turn off indicator lights* it read. I tapped "Off." That way the camera could be on and streaming and neither Ju-lan nor Li-min would be the wiser.

I handed the camera back to Li-min and tried out my sincere pitching voice.

"When you're done filming, put this setting on 'standby.' If you put it on 'off,' then all the settings will get zapped and you'll have to start all over again."

I said it with the soothing timbre I used with wary tourists.

Li-min responded as if I had allayed his fears of all technology. "Thank you, Jing-nan. I really appreciate it." To show how grateful he was, he promptly went back to gaming.

I bent my knees. All this standing wasn't good for my legs. "Say, Li-min, could you do me a favor? How about a stool or a crate to sit on?"

Li-min tapped his game on pause and raised an eyebrow. "I'm not supposed to let you have anything."

"You let me have the tarp."

He snorted. "I can't let you have anything that you could use as a weapon."

"I promise if you give me a chair, I won't attack you with it."

He looked thoughtful. "How about this. I'll let you have a stool, but when Ju-lan shows up, you have to give it back so she doesn't catch you with it."

"Sure," I said, even as I schemed. "I promise."

He went over to the store of stuff while I imagined a scenario where I could slam the backrest of a metal folding chair against his forehead. I certainly had nothing personal against him. I was starting to like him a lot.

He came back and slid a child's plastic stool over to me. It made a farting sound as it scraped along.

"I can barely fit my ass on that thing," I said.

"Take it or leave it."

I righted it and sat down. It was better than sitting on the ground like a stray dog.

CHAPTER 16

We both heard the sound of a car idling near the hidden entrance. Wordlessly, I handed the plastic stool back to Li-min. That thing had zero potential as a weapon. It was more hazardous to sit on it than to get hit with it.

The door slid open and admitted Ju-lan's sedan. She shut the car off but didn't exit until the entrance was closed once more. This time she had driven herself. She had rested and changed her clothes. As she approached us, she reminded me of a mean teacher.

"Li-min, how are things?" she asked vacantly.

He scratched his knees. "Good. I've got the camera all set up."

Doubting him, she picked up the camera and checked the settings. "Have you done some test shots?"

Li-min stood on his toes. "No, I didn't. I forgot to."

Ju-lan's shoulder slumped. "Li-min, I hope you didn't put this camera online." She casually tapped through the menu, presumably to kill the WiFi connection, and my lifeline. "We're going to record here and then upload the file from a VPN so they can't tell where we are."

"Ah, got it," said Li-min.

Ju-lan raised an eyebrow. "Do you know what a VPN is?"

"Vietnamese something-something."

Ju-lan quickly calculated that it wasn't even worth educating him on the subject. She closed out the menu and set the camera on the tripod.

"Excuse me," I said. "What do you plan on doing?"

"Mind your own business, Jing-nan!" she snapped.

I had nothing to lose by pressing her buttons. "I was minding my own business until you kidnapped me," I said. She looked at me and coughed into her fist. "Look, maybe we can help each other out here if you let me in on it a little. I'm a captive audience here."

She crossed her arms and considered the possibilities. "Okay," she said slowly. "You are smarter than Li-min. Let's see if you're more useful. I'm trying to use your life to bargain for my safe passage to China. You're close to Tong-tong and his influence could surely make things happen. Oh, I've been spying for China, if you haven't guessed yet. I was tipped off early this morning that my information had been compromised, so I took off."

"*Ma de*!" I said.

"I figured that you were the closest person to Tong-tong that I knew. I wanted to grab you for a bargaining chip."

"How did you know where I lived?"

She laughed. "Please, it was so easy to kidnap you, Jing-nan!" Someone else had said that before. Peggy! Something about how my schedule was so consistent, it was easy to shadow me. Damn.

"You know what's funny, Jing-nan? I have the chip design everyone was looking for." She leaned over and pressed her right index finger against my forehead.

"How did you get the chip design?" I asked.

"I made the fucking chip!" she roared. "I only gave it to Ah-tien because the system here is so biased against women. There's no way I could have gotten investors on my own. Ah-tien was my front. Other people used him as well, unfortunately. He was a front guy and a fall guy." She put her hand on her heart. "To be honest, he really doesn't know what the hell happened. I'm sure he's innocent of all charges."

"You could have helped him."

"He could have helped me. I pulled a move the Americans call 'schmuck insurance.' I left out one little component in my design, just in case Ah-tien tried to cut me out of the deal. And then he did try to cut me out!"

"The chip in his version of the plan couldn't work," I said.

Ju-lan smiled with genuine appreciation. "Exactly. You are smarter than Li-min. I was supposed to be at the final meeting with Tong-tong." She shook her head. "I was going to show them all the real final design. But Ah-tien never called me. He tried to play it off like he'd built it on his own. After that, the waters were a little poisoned. It wasn't like I could find someone else to make the same pitch." She smoothed out her sleeves with gentle hands. "Until now. I'm making the ultimate pitch for money and my freedom in China."

"Freedom in China?" I asked. "Aren't you deluding yourself? They just let that Nobel Prize–winner die in jail from liver cancer."

"He played it dumb. I'm gonna play it smart. I'm just going to live like a rich woman and not talk politics."

"How the hell are you going to get to China?"

"Tong-tong's going to get the military to fly me to Thailand, and from there the Chinese can pick me up." She paused to dramatically put her hand under her chin. "Oh, I'm assuming he wouldn't want you to die. Do you think he'd want to save your life?"

Would he? Had he felt slighted by the counter-protest at my night-market stand? By my trying to secretly record his daughter in an effort to gather material about his company, his business practices and overly cushy relationship with the police? By my meddling at his warehouse, which ended up revealing potentially embarrassing information about his captivity? Most recently, he had taken offense to me yawning while he held the floor at the air force auditorium.

"Of course he'd save me," I said. "He would do anything to help me."

She frowned. "I hope so," Ju-lan said. "You better hope so, too." Ju-lan walked back to the car and brought back a clear plastic bag that held two plastic containers of noodle soup with spoons and disposable chopsticks.

"Wait, Ju-lan, if you have the chip design the Chinese government has wanted all along, then why didn't they just get it from you?"

The bag swayed slightly in her hands as she spoke excitedly. "I work through the disinformation network of China's propaganda wing. That idiot who got caught was under the military's spy operations. I didn't even know they wanted the chip. All these divisions are run by stupid men who don't communicate with each other, even though they share information about where their assets are! Which is how I was compromised!" She looked around for a target for her frustration. It didn't take long to find. "Li-min!"

He jumped slightly. "What?"

"One's chicken and one's pork," she barked as she set the bag down by his feet.

"I'll take the pork," he said.

She crossed her arms. "What are you talking about?"

"He can have the chicken one," he said, stupidly pointing at me.

"Hell, no," she said. "They're both for you. One's your dinner."

"Dinner? I'm supposed to stay again tonight? I thought we were taking turns watching."

Ju-lan unzipped her purse and rummaged for something. Her gun? "You expected to leave a defenseless woman alone with a man?" she said, avoiding looking at him. "Anyway, this will probably be the only night we have with Jing-nan." She finally found what she had been looking for. A Samsung mobile phone that was popular probably five years ago, and modified to be difficult to trace, no doubt. To herself she said, "Just want to make sure this camera can sync."

Ju-lan walked to the tripod and flipped through the camera menu. Li-min, sensing it was best to eat and not talk, hoisted up one of the soups and peeled off the lid.

He was only about 10 feet away and the smell of salt wafted over to me. She had gone to one of those cheapo outlets that oversalt their broth instead of taking the time to simmer up a proper base with bones. I was pissed at myself for salivating. Ordinarily I would find that smell utterly repulsive. I looked at Ju-lan, trying to solicit some sympathy.

"Maybe you could get me a soup, too," I said weakly.

She finished up with the camera and chuckled lightly. "Jing-nan, you don't want to eat soup. It's dehydrating." She pointed at the small pail by the wall. "Li-min, did you empty his pail?"

Li-min's chopsticks paused on the way up to his mouth and the noodles were left twisting in the wind. "No," he said as he observed his container of yellow soup.

"It's not a big deal," I said. "I've only pissed twice."

Ju-lan dropped her phone back into her purse and zipped it shut. "Not a big deal? Your waste pail should be emptied with regularity. I don't want bad smells to attract attention." Damn, I wish I had thought about that!

Li-min looked around the room. "Where am I supposed to empty it?"

"Take your pick," said Ju-lan as she kicked one foot toward a corner. "There are some pipe openings over there."

"Is it all right to use them?"

"Who cares? It's just a few times. Like I said, if everything goes all right, this is his only night." Ju-lan swept her hair over both ears and stood in front of the camera. "Ready, Li-min?"

"You want to film right now?"

"Yeah, I don't have all day! You can finish eating after!"

He groaned and wiped his palms against each other. Ju-lan flattened her blouse and pants.

"Ju-lan," said Li-min, "maybe you should rehearse one time before I start shooting."

I added, "Maybe you should take some acting classes first."

"Shut up, Jing-nan!" she said. "You'd better stay quiet while I'm filming. Li-min? I will do a practice take before you shoot."

He put his hands on his knees and bent over so he was looking directly at the display screen. "I'll hit record when you do this again, but pretend I'm recording now in three, two, one . . ."

Ju-lan cleared her throat. "Hello, Tong-tong. I'm Liu Ju-lan, the real designer of that low-power chip. I want sixty million New Taiwan dollars from you and a flight to Bangkok with my special passenger here." She swept her head toward me. "You know Chen Jing-nan, right? Your daughter's class-mate and also a friend of yours. If you don't get me out of this country, you can . . . oh shit!" Ju-lan began laughing. "Oh, shit, I forgot something!" She jogged to her car and retrieved the gun.

"Ju-lan," I said. "I don't want to go to Bangkok."

She blew imaginary dust off the gun. "You're not going. I'm going to do a switcheroo of you and Li-min. I just need you to be my human shield until the last minute so they don't try to take me out with a headshot." She flicked the safety off and back on. "Li-min, forget the practice, let's shoot the real one right now."

I was extremely uncomfortable hearing her say that word while wielding a gun.

Li-min hunched over the camera and flashed fingers at Ju-lan. "Ready in three, two and one!"

Ju-lan took her talk from the top. When she got to the part where she gestured to me, she narrowed her eyes. "If you don't get me out of this country, you can plan Jing-nan's funeral."

She merely lifted the gun and held it limply. It was fully unnecessary to actually point it at me, I believed, and I was glad she did, too. That would have been overkill.

"Let me know soon, Tong-tong," she said. "I'm not going to give you my personal information. Just put up a response video. By nine A.M."

Ju-lan drew her hand across her neck and Li-min dutifully cut.

"Now what do we do?" he asked.

Ju-lan checked the camera and then hoisted it off the tripod. "You guys stay here until I come back."

Li-min rubbed his nose in irritation. "So, I'm a prisoner, too?"

Ju-lan had already made her way to the car. "How are you a prisoner? I'm paying you and I'm feeding you! You're not chained up like him!" She hopped in her car.

"*Ma de,*" Li-min muttered bitterly to his feet. "Motherfuck this shit."

"Ju-lan," I called. "If you're not going to give me something to eat, could you at least let me drink something?"

She leaned out of the car and grabbed the door handle. "I don't have access to my bank account anymore and I don't have much cash on hand. You'll have all you need soon enough." Ju-lan swung the door halfway shut before addressing Li-min. "If you're dumb enough to share your food with him, I don't want to hear that you've gone hungry."

After Ju-lan left, Li-min consoled himself by gorging himself. He polished off both soup containers, as his inner sorrows outweighed any consideration of me. When he had slurped up everything but the plastic, he ambled over to his inflatable bed, plopped down and resumed his phone game.

I made like a zoo animal and paced the length of my chain as quietly as possible, examining the floor and walls for a doorknob. No matter where I stood, I could hear Li-min sucking his teeth noisily as he continued to play.

I didn't have my phone and the camera was gone. I had no way to get online. Unless I had Li-min's phone. I shouldn't even bother asking him for it. He wasn't dumb enough to hand it over, and the request would only put him on guard.

Maybe he sensed that I was thinking of him because suddenly he asked, "Jing-nan, do you want the stool again?"

"Oh," I said. I had been so preoccupied by thinking, sitting hadn't occurred to me. I didn't need to sit now, but I should never say no to having another object in my possession. "Sure, I'll take it."

He pocketed his phone and ambled over with the stool. I drew a hand across the links in my chain. If I were quick, I could get the chain around his neck. But I'd never be strong enough mentally or physically to hold on and choke him to death. I let the chain fall slack as Li-min drew closer and put the stool beside me.

"Here you go, pal," he said with a sigh. "How about I empty your pail, too?"

"Yeah, sure," I said. "I'd really appreciate that. I'd appreciate some more water even more."

He kept his eyes on me as he grabbed the pail. "I'm sorry, Jing-nan. It's all gone." He sucked in both his lips and closed his mouth.

"Do you want to go to Bangkok?" I asked him.

"Hell, no," he said as he walked away. "But I won't be able to stay here, either. Wish I could." Halfway to his intended target, an open pipe against the far wall, he set down the pail and mightily relieved himself into it.

Then he zipped up and resumed the journey. I heard his plodding footsteps turn into small splashes. I guess the floor was wet with seeping groundwater over there. Li-min expressed disgust audibly but without language.

I watched him hoist up the bucket and heard hollow echoes as he poured our blended urine into the pipe opening.

Then the plastic bucket fell with a toy thud and Li-min began to do a bizarre dance. He wriggled furiously, keeping his feet grounded and pressing his arms flat against his sides. He didn't seem to have a good sense of rhythm but I had to admire his sheer physical exertion, even if it was completely uncalled for. I couldn't hear any music at all, but his body seemed to be responding to something tangible. He was moving as if no one were watching, completely free. I didn't think the big guy had it in him to express himself that way.

It wasn't until after he made a final full-body jolt and collapsed that I smelled something burning. Hair?

I coughed as the stench passed over me.

Li-min had been electrocuted.

Was he dead or just knocked out?

"Hey, Li-min!" I called to him to see if he could respond. "You must've been a cheerleader in high school, right?"

He remained completely still and didn't make a sound.

Now was my best chance to break out. I walked to the wall, took the chain in both hands and planted my foot against the wall as if I were about to scale it, then pulled as hard as I could.

Nothing happened.

I knelt down and examined the padlock that held the end of the chain to the lag eye bolted to the wall. It looked pretty solid. If I only had something to try to pick it with.

I dropped to my hands and knees and crawled along the wall to the right. I came across crumbled cement and incredibly a 50NT coin, which I promptly pocketed.

As I reached the end of my chain, I saw two things nestled against the wall only a few feet away—a thin nail and a dead coffee-bean shaped bug on top of it.

I stretched both my arms as wide as possible and closed the fingers of my right hand on the nail. Just as I did, the bug jumped on to the back of my hand. Startled, I dropped the nail. It bounced on the ground and rolled a few inches. It was probably out of reach now.

I lay flat on the floor on my stomach. I inhaled and stretched all four limbs out. I flattened my chest and heard my shoulder joints crack. I managed to touch my right pinky fingertip on the sharp end of the nail. I couldn't quite encourage the nail closer.

My body contracted. I had become accustomed to the smell of mold but being on the floor made me confront that odor anew. I turned my head and looked at the nail. It looked like a boat on the horizon about to disappear.

I thought about my family and how I wasn't celebrating Double Ninth with them. We never did when they were alive and well. "Do tourists know about Double Ninth?" I can hear my father say about any holiday, really. "Do you want to lose their business?"

We celebrated the holidays by working, which is a little odd because my parents were also devoted to paying homage to the divine and ancestors. There wasn't one morning that didn't start with bows at the temple. All that dedication to business and worship came at the expense of the family.

Why couldn't my mother and father both been a little taller? Why couldn't my arms be a little longer?

Double Ninth celebrates senior citizens, which my parents never became. My mother and father had died at 60 and 61, respectively. The fact was, they weren't my family anymore. They were now my ancestors, people who came before me and sacrificed so I would have a better life.

They sure would be disappointed if I couldn't get that fucking nail.

I took a deep breath and held it. I clenched my stomach, my hands and even my butt cheeks. I wasn't sure if failure would lead to my demise, but nonetheless I wanted to get out now, had to get out right now. Had to get that nail now.

Just missed it.

I exhaled and my breath was hot and wet on my sticky arms.

I shook my head to clear my mind. I'm going to reach out, grab that nail and get back to Nancy, in that order. I felt my heart swell and I trembled as adrenaline streamed through my body.

I grunted and whipped my right arm out like I was throwing the last pitch of my life. Which it could be.

This time I managed to slide my index finger against the nail. I nudged it back until I held it in the palm of my hand.

I inched myself off the floor into a crawling position. My knees and my arms shook as I stood up and walked. I grabbed the padlock and turned it over. The nail fit easily in the keyhole.

I had never picked a lock before. I put the nail in my mouth to wet it with my saliva. You know, for luck. As I sucked on the nail, I glanced to the left and saw a small pile of the same nails only a few steps away. I was already so relieved to have gotten my one nail, the sight only made me grin. Well, if I broke this one, I had plenty of backups.

I spat the nail into my right hand and jammed the sharp end into the lock. I poked the nail around. Something rattled inside, but I couldn't turn the cylinder of the lock. I made like a dentist scraping the plaque off molars. I thought I heard something snap, but the padlock still held.

I pulled the nail to one side, trying to break the cylinder, but instead the nail got stuck. I picked up another nail and stuck it into the other side of the keyhole. I grabbed both nail heads and twisted them. To my surprise, the cylinder popped out and the padlock came away from its shackle.

I was free.

As I gathered the loose chain in my hands, I thought about that Velvet Underground song, "I'm Set Free," and Lou Reed's bitter lyric about being set free only to find you've been tricked again.

I wasn't sure what my next step was, but man, this chain was five pounds of weight I didn't need on my left wrist. I stuck a nail in the handcuff keyhole and rattled it around. When nothing came out of it, I stuck in another. The handcuffs hadn't looked as well-made as the padlock, but it held better. I'd bet the key was probably a cheap piece of crap stamped out of a metal sheet.

The key! It must be in Li-min's pocket!

As I made my way over to his prone figure, the burning smell grew progressively worse. It went from smelling like electric piss to charred chicken thighs. Nothing smelled worse to my nose than overcooked food.

Maybe it was Li-min's thighs that were overcooked. I stood at a healthy distance from his body. If he were breathing, it was too shallow to be visible. His shirt seemed to be tighter than before. I squatted and rubbed my fingers against my palms and tried to discern what was in the scene before me. I didn't worry about losing my balance and tumbling forward. My squat was rock-solid. I'm from Taipei and I work in a night market.

His body lay on its back in a pool of water so thin even the most playful toddler would barely get a splash out of it. His clothes were essentially dry, apart from a big wet patch around his crotch. Li-min's eyes were wide open in shock. Some saliva bubbles had formed between his lips, which looked bluish and very dead.

Was there a live current running through his body? If I touched him and felt a shock, would I be able to retreat, or would I be unable to break away from the dance of death?

I returned to the area of my former captivity and came back with a handful of nails. I stood on a dry section of the floor and threw a nail that glanced off his shoulder. I didn't see any sparks.

I've been pretty lucky so far, and if the ancestors were indeed supporting me, I didn't think my streak was about to end here. I held my breath and quickly jabbed Li-min's arm. It was as stiff as a statue, and luckily it didn't electrocute me. I pressed my entire hand flat against it. Nothing.

Li-min was definitely dead. I began to feel a little creeped out that I had touched a dead body. I had never done that. "Sorry, Li-min," I whispered. He might have done a lot of bad in his life, but he was kind to me. Well, he did still owe me from knocking me out.

Newly galvanized, I slid my hand down his chest, aiming for his right front pocket. The second I felt anything like a tingle or even a static shock, I was going to leap back and roll away. Lessons learned in grade-school calisthenics would serve me well.

My fingers crossed the belt and entered the pocket, encountering something bulky. I pulled out a thin wallet without much fuss, impressing myself. I could have been an accomplished pickpocket.

I flipped open the wallet. Li-min had about NT$300 and an MRT card. His government ID was made out to Liu Li-min. Was he Ju-lan's brother, or another relative? That would account for her contempt for him and his ability to absorb the blows without reaction.

My sleeping shorts had one pocket and I shoved the wallet into it.

I crouched down and sent my fingers into his pocket again. I encountered a second object—his phone!

I was so excited that my hand and then my entire arm began trembling. Wait, that wasn't my nerves. Or rather, it was my nerves, but it was a live current making my arm jerk uncontrollably.

I think my hand was clamped tightly around the phone, making my fist a little too large to pull out of the pocket. I felt my heart speed up.

With all my strength, I pushed off my legs. My hand tore free and the phone went flying. As I crashed hard on my left shoulder, I watched the phone smash against the fake wall that concealed the exit. I heard it hit the ground and the faint echo of a piece of plastic breaking off and coming loose.

I stood up and looked at the body. The key was probably in his other pocket or a back pocket, but there was no way to check them safely. I walked slowly to the phone, delaying disappointment.

It was worse than I thought. The entire plastic backplate

of the phone lay about a foot away from the unit itself. I picked up the partially exposed phone gingerly in case it had a residual charge. Then I pressed the power button.

The screen lit up to the game that Li-min had been playing. He didn't have a password lock on it. I exited the game. He didn't have a browser on this stupid thing but at least a text-messaging app was here.

It was no surprise there wasn't phone reception. My only hope was getting on WiFi. I recalled that Li-min wasn't a tech-savvy guy. I opened up the phone's settings and it asked if I wanted to set up email on the device. Instead, I went to the WiFi option and connected to the Taipei 101 Parking network I had discovered earlier.

When I had that connection secured I opened the messenger app. The phone emitted a doorbell—Li-min's alert sound—and a message popped up. *Battery at 5%.*

Gan!

I opened the chat window and punched in Nancy's number. Shit, were her last two digits 89 or 98? I hadn't had to type them because my phone knew them, freeing extra brain cells to store more music. I paused for a moment. I had entered her phone number in my contacts on our first date. I hadn't punched them in since.

I wrote, NANCY ITS JING-NAN I AM BEING HELD IN AN UNDERGROUND GARAGE NEAR TAIPEI 101 NOT SURE WHERE BUT TRACK THE SIGNAL IN THIS TEXT LOVE YOU and sent it to both numbers.

I then sent a second message, I WAS KIDNAPPED BY THAT WOMAN JU-LAN THE B&B WOMAN!

A message popped back from the 89 number as the power level ticked down to 1 percent: WE SAW THE VIDEO, FRANKIE IS HELPING THEM LOOK FOR YOU.

Then the phone died.

GOING THROUGH THE DEAD man's bundle of belongings gave me a ghoulish thrill. I found the phone AC adaptor in the right pocket of his jacket and separate bags of baby carrots and peanuts in the left.

Charging the phone was a necessity but I lost my mind a little bit when I saw the food.

I ate the warm and slimy carrots first. A piece got stuck in my windpipe and I coughed until I managed to spit out the phlegm-covered offending bit. Then I resumed eating, even though my throat was sore, because I was so famished. Carrots never tasted so sweet and yet when I broke into the peanuts, I found that I was much more hungry for protein. Peanuts were something I had banned from my kitchen years ago. Tourists have all kinds of allergies and the peanut ones were the worst. Consequently, I haven't eaten peanuts in ages. Wow, they were good!

I was a little thirsty after so I sucked out the last drops of moisture from the carrot bag.

I took the charging cord from the jacket and tried to match the plug to the port in the phone. There didn't seem to be a port. I had a thought and picked up the phone's backplate. The port was attached to its bottom panel.

I put the phone back together and squeezed. I felt it snap together in one section but as I opened my hand, it came apart and a fingernail-sized curved wire fell out into my palm. I hoped it wasn't important.

There were plenty of four-cluster outlets around the garage. I wasn't really sure why. Did they expect people to charge things as they stood by their parked cars? Or maybe the construction company owed an electronics supplier a favor and overbought. I held the phone together in one hand and plugged in the prongs with the other.

Either the phone couldn't be charged, which was entirely

possible, or the outlets were dead, also entirely possible. I moved on to the second and third clusters. Maybe they were all dead.

Just to exhaust all possibilities, I unplugged the cord from the phone port and cautiously touched it to my tongue while the other end was plugged into the wall. Another shock to my system wouldn't mean anything at this point.

Nothing. No spark, no shock. What could I do at this point? It was not like I could pull the fake wall open.

Or could I?

I walked up to the wall and quickly found the seam of the moving door. I pressed against it and I swore I could feel it give just the slightest. I managed to get a fingerhold in. I wedged in one hand and pulled like I wanted to tear my arm off. It squeaked open an inch more. I stuck in my other hand and encouraged it to open another inch. Now a small but thick metal tab stuck out from the sliding wall. I peeked in and saw that it was connected with the mechanism within the door itself.

I wound my chain around the tab and grabbed the ends like reins. I thought about the long arc of my short life so far. It wasn't going to end now. I was going to pull this fucking door open all the way. I pulled the ends of the chain as if I were endowed with the strength of every water buffalo that strained to pull a plow to feed all my ancestors in Taiwan.

The wall inched along until I heard something inside it crack like a metal bone. I stumbled as everything came to a halt. I resumed the stance and pulled until the chain links burned angry red Olympics logos into my hands but I made no progress. A little more than a foot was all I was going to get. Actually less, when you took into account the random tabs of metal that stuck out from both the sliding door and its sheath.

Was there anything I should grab before attempting to leave the room for good? My eye went to Li-min's jacket. Why not? I could always ditch it if I didn't need it.

I tossed it through the gap in the door. I also passed through the tarp I had slept on. I wanted to push out the inflatable mattress as well, but reconsidered. I'd have to deflate it to get it through and there was no way I was going to waste my breath reinflating the whole thing again.

I looked through the gap at the jacket and the tarp. The gap itself was probably only two feet long. Shit, what if I couldn't get through it? I cracked my knuckles. No. I would make it out.

I gathered up the chain and tossed it underhand through the gap and began to slide out my body, leading with my left side.

Something sharp drew across my abdomen and my calves. This was just the beginning of my passage and I could only hope that minor superficial pains would be all I experienced. I pushed on and I got to an area that opened up slightly. I began to breathe easier. Then I encountered similar obstructions in my midsection and legs. Then my left leg stepped through to the other side.

I heard something from above. Was that a car? It could be anybody, not just Ju-lan. Then again, this garage didn't seem to get much traffic.

I became frantic and pushed my body against the pain. The car was getting louder. I was almost entirely free when my shirt got caught above my right shoulder blade. It hurt more when I tried to go down so I stood on my toes and tried to cartwheel out. My shirt began to tear. I got both arms out on the other side and pulled myself through. My shirt tore.

The car sounded like it was right on top of me. It was relatively dim and this room was twice as big as the one I had left. Two vehicles were parked here. One was a hatchback and a delivery truck was parked directly in front of it. I gathered up the jacket and the tarp and decided to head for the hatchback.

Wait! The sliding wall was still a little open! I didn't want Ju-lan to know right away that I had escaped. I shoved the door back but it wouldn't budge. Then I slammed my body against it and the wall snapped shut. I bolted for the hatchback as I heard the car make that final turn.

CHAPTER 17

I crouched behind the hatchback. The area was greasy with motor fluids. I lay down the jacket and tarp to prepare for another night on the floor.

Ju-lan's car pulled up and stopped at the door. I saw her reach up and press something above the shade.

The door made a loud clanking sound but to my relief it still opened smoothly all the way. She drove in and killed the engine before the door shut.

Maybe I should run up and out of the garage. But the time it took the sliding door to open might not give me enough of a lead to reach the ground level. I also might not be able to reach an exit.

I heard a dull thud as she closed the driver's door. I heard her shout, followed a few seconds later by a scream. Maybe she would touch Li-min's body and get electrocuted herself.

Maybe I should run down, not up. She'd never look for me on a lower level. As I prepared to make a move, I heard footsteps and clanking on my side of the barrier. Two men were chatting in the spirited way that men do when work is over.

Ju-lan screamed again. "Li-min! Li-min!" I could make out her words clearly through the wall.

Damn, I hadn't even considered yelling for help when I had managed to pick my lock. Someone could've given me a hand with that sliding wall.

A mechanical motor fired up and I crouched even lower behind the hatchback. The wall slid open and Ju-lan stepped through.

"Jing-nan! What did you do to Li-min!" she cried. The men I'd heard approaching came into view as they ran up to Ju-lan. They were uniformed delivery guys and the clanking sound I'd heard was from their two hand trucks.

They approached Ju-lan without caution.

"Is there something we can help you with, madam?" one of them asked.

"Oh, fuck!" said the other. "This is the kidnapper who put out that video threatening Tong-tong! I saw it on my fucking phone!"

"What! She kidnapped someone?"

Ju-lan responded by sticking her gun in their faces. "Did you see anyone coming out of here?" she demanded.

"No, no."

"We didn't see nothing!"

"Then get the fuck out of here!" She jerked her head toward the up ramp. The men jogged away with their machines. They jumped into their truck and lurched out. I was glad I had chosen the hatchback to hide behind.

But why was Ju-lan letting them go? Why not hold them hostage, too? She leaned against the wall and stared at the ceiling. I know the feeling of when your plans have been completely demolished. Evil plans, to be sure, but plans nonetheless.

I hoped she thought that I was long gone. Maybe I was back home by now. She shouldn't stay here now because it made no sense for either of us. Staying here was taking a risk; the cops were on their way, and I couldn't leave until she did go. Ju-lan remained stuck to the wall. How long could she keep this up?

Suddenly she shook her head. I thought she looked directly at me. I gasped silently. Had she guessed my hiding space? She took a few steps toward my position but then paused.

We both heard something coming. A few cars that were already in the garage were roaring their way down to our level, sounding like rain clouds moving in.

I was being rescued! It sure sounded like a rescue! Maybe the guys who took off in the truck called the cops or maybe Frankie helped find me!

Ju-lan retreated through the sliding door, although she didn't close it. Headlights streamed across the walls like ghosts and the vehicles stopped short, out of my view. I heard a number of doors open and close. And heavy boots! A bull-horn cracked and Tong-tong's voice, thick with phlegm and drenched with irritation, barked out.

"Liu Ju-lan! Are you still here?"

"Yes, I am!" was her defiant reply.

"Is Jing-nan here?"

"No!"

"Are you sure?"

"Yes!"

"Well, where is he?"

"I don't know!" Her voice cracked as she added, "He killed my husband!"

My legs jerked in surprise, rattling my chain. I'd had no idea, but when I looked back at the apparent enmity between them, of course they had to be closer than mere blood relatives. And she had had to pay him to do this work.

I thought about Nancy and wondered if we'd ever be close enough to kidnap someone to help secure our future.

"How did he kill your husband?" Tong-tong demanded to know.

"He electrocuted him!" she sobbed.

"*Ma de*!" The bullhorn broke off with a squawk. "Listen, Ju-lan. I have a proposal for you. How about you stay here in Taiwan and we go into business together, forty-nine fifty-one, and we make your goddamned chip? I won't press any charges against you!"

Still sniffling, Ju-lan asked, "Won't Jing-nan accuse me of kidnapping him?"

"No way. I'll take care of him."

What a presumptuous asshole! It seemed to reassure her, though.

"Who is the forty-nine?" she asked hopefully. "Me or you?"

"Ah, that would have to be you. I need to have the majority. That's how I do business. When I negotiate—on both of our behalves—I can't be hampered by waiting for someone else's approval before I execute."

"Okay," she said. Mustering some pride, she added, "I do have some provisions, though."

"Yes, let's talk about it. Come out with your hands up and we can talk about anything. Leave the gun on the floor."

Ju-lan emerged, her hands held high. The sleeves seemed a little short.

"Hey," she said. "No tricks!"

They turned out to be her last words.

Two shots zipped through the air and her head nodded hard twice. Her body folded into a widening pool of blood. Both my captors were now dead. Three soldiers armed with rifles charged in. They used their mounted flashlights to comb the nearby area. Two of them charged into the room.

Oh, shit! They didn't know I was here by the hatchback! What if they shot me by accident?

"Hey!" I cried out. My voice was ragged and unrecognizable to me. "It's Jing-nan! I'm here!"

"Jing-nan! Is that you?" Tong-tong snarled.

"Yes!"

"How do we know it's you?"

"It's me, I swear!"

The three men with rifles were reassembled near Ju-lan's body, looking attentive. "There's one down inside the room," a soldier said.

"Come out with your hands up, Jing-nan!"

"No way! I saw how that worked out for Ju-lan! Come down here yourself and see who I am!"

"It's him!" That was Nancy's voice. It wasn't as loud as Tong-tong's because she was yelling without a bullhorn. "It's Jing-nan!"

"It sure as hell doesn't sound like him," Tong-tong barked unnecessarily through the bullhorn. "Why would I go down there so he could get a good shot at me? I was dumb enough to get kidnapped. I'm not gonna have another lapse in judgment!" Then to me he growled, "Listen, if you're really Jing-nan, tell me something about my daughter that only Jing-nan would know."

I thought for a bit. "She brought a jade pendant of a bird into school, and gave it to a boy," I said. "The boy found out that it was a priceless antique and gave it back to her."

"Stand down!" yelled Tong-tong. The three soldiers shouldered their rifles. "Jing-nan! Come over here!"

I stood up and staggered forward. I saw Nancy running toward me and the chain sloshed in my hands as I rushed forward to meet her.

IT WAS ALL ARMY personnel who had come to rescue me. The two men Ju-lan had run out of the parking lot went and called Tong-tong's company rather than the police. That kindly old bastard had set up a hotline for me with a sizable reward.

My reunion with Nancy was brief. They had separated us to treat my wounds.

A soldier handed me a canteen of water and I drank the entire thing.

"You look like shit," he told me.

"Oh, I'm really all right," I said as I tapped my bandaged abdomen. Squeezing through the movable wall had left me looking like I'd been teethed by a Tyranosaur.

The soldier handed me a small mirror. "Look at your face," he said.

I tilted it at my eyes and saw a great purple continent was geographically centered on my right cheek. Some blood had pooled around the eye.

"*Gan*!" I exclaimed.

They laid me down in a truck while a medic checked my vitals. "What about my face?" I asked the canvas roof.

Tong-tong approached and stared down at me. "It's a badge of honor," he said. "Why cover it up?"

"Who are these people?" I asked.

"These guys are all off-duty. They're volunteering their time."

I wondered how they could be off-duty considering they were in uniform, driving Republic of China vehicles and certainly using military-issued rifles. An armband around my left bicep inflated and I felt my pulse racing.

"Tong-tong," I said. "You didn't have to kill her."

He turned his head so he could narrow his eyes and give me an evil sideways look. "What are you talking about, Jing-nan? She was holding you hostage with a gun to your head."

"She wasn't!"

Tong-tong nodded and tapped the roof of the car in

frustration. He looked around and spotted something out of my view. "Bring that here! Yes, right here." He reached out and when he turned back to me he was holding a pair of bolt cutters. He climbed in and at first I thought he was going for my throat. "Hold up your arm." I did as I was told and he clipped the chain one link under my cuff.

"Thank you, Tong-tong," I said. The beak end of the bolt cutter wavered by my left ear.

"You know, Jing-nan, the cops are on their way over. We should have our stories straight. If you were to say that your life wasn't in danger and that Ju-lan was shot in cold blood, well, you'd be setting up some of our young soldiers for murder charges when they had laid their lives on the line to rescue you."

I slumped in resignation. "What do you want me to say?"

He pulled away the bolt cutters and noisily ran his tongue over his teeth. "You know what? How about you and Nancy just get out of here and leave it to me. Don't talk to anybody. Seriously. Got it?"

I nodded. I sat up and tore off the band around my arm but found an IV stuck near the crook of my elbow.

"Can you get the medic over here to finish this up?" I asked.

"I got this," said Tong-tong as he reached in and yanked it out. "You're good. Now go."

They had been holding Nancy in another vehicle. When I stepped out of the back of the truck, someone brought me to her. I held her tight and felt the world spin.

"You didn't tell me about the bruise on my face," I grunted in her ear.

"I didn't even notice it," she said.

NANCY AND I TOOK a cab to her place because her couch was bigger and way better than mine.

A home should always have at least two servings of beef stew in the freezer. It is one of the few kinds of foods that improve in the storage and reheating process. Water molecules expand when they turn into ice, breaking down the beef and the vegetables. The meat softens and more of the essence of the onions, garlic and potatoes is released into the liquid as the stew is reheated.

I lay flat on the couch with my head in Nancy's lap as I gave her the full version of what happened to me. Our stews were spinning in tandem in the microwave on a low setting. We both ignored exasperated texts from Peggy asking where we were. I took for granted that when Tong-tong said not to contact anyone, he included his daughter, my old classmate.

"Jing-nan," Nancy said, "when you disappeared, I thought you were getting something for us and you were stuck in line somewhere."

"Something?" I asked. "You mean bringing back breakfast?"

"Maybe, or another surprise."

This was confusing. "Did you want a surprise?" I asked tentatively.

"Well, honestly, anything would have surprised me because I didn't think you'd remember."

Ma de!

"Your birthday," I said. I added sheepishly, "I'd forgotten."

She gave a little fake laugh. "It's not a big deal. It doesn't mean anything to me, really."

I sat up and held her hands. "It is a big deal. I should have remembered. Thanks to my kidnapping, I will never forget again." The microwave let out a plaintive beep to punctuate my vow.

Nancy got up and retrieved our dinner. I regarded the steaming bowls placed side-by-side on the cork tiles of the coffee table. "This is how old married couples eat dinner," I said.

"You mean when they don't have anything to say to each other, so they watch TV while they eat?" Nancy asked.

"We usually only watch TV when we eat, though."

Nancy cracked up and slapped my right thigh hard. "Jing-nan, you did surprise me on my birthday! I was eating and yes, watching TV, when I saw your hostage video!"

Her amusement irked me. "Weren't you freaked out? Weren't you worried about me?"

She touched my shoulder. "I was! I told Frankie and Dwayne right away. They were out looking for you so hard, you know, Jing-nan?"

"I could tell by their texts. I wish I could write them back and let them know I am safe."

Nancy shrugged, picked up her bowl and blew on it lightly. "I already did."

"Shit, Nancy!"

"He didn't say *I* couldn't contact anyone. And you want them to operate Unknown Pleasures tonight instead of still searching for you, right?"

"I guess so." I picked up my bowl and stirred the stew. The onions practically disintegrated at the touch. It was beautiful.

I hadn't even been gone for twenty-four hours but my ordeal stretched for days in my mind. Now that I was truly out of danger, I was hungry but I also felt uneasy. I wanted to be at work. I wanted to create great food. And there weren't any fresh ingredients today because I was kidnapped before I could hit the market. Dammit!

"Jing-nan," said Nancy. "Your legs are jumping. You're going to make me spill the stew."

"How is it?"

"It's great."

"Can you give me more detailed feedback?"

She raised an eyebrow at me. "I'll tell you one thing. Charring the beef was a great call. It provides a canvas for the flavors to drip on."

"I love that. I'm going to put that in the next review I write about Unknown Pleasures."

"You said you've stopped posting fake reviews?"

I ate half a spoon of stew. Nancy was absolutely right. The only problem was we were eating with metal spoons, which added a grey note to the taste. Plastic spoons would, oddly enough, be better. After I swallowed, I raised a finger to make a point.

"The names are fake, but the reviews aren't." I touched her arm. "And I did stop. I'm just kidding."

Peggy sent a text to both our phones that was marked with some finality. NEVER MIND. TONG-TONG JUST FILLED ME IN. HE'S GOING TO BE ON WOLF TV SOON.

"We should probably watch," I said. Nancy snapped on the television and had to use the guide to find the channel.

Little Brother was on, a show for people to call in and bitch about stuff. A caller was going off about how young people didn't respect their elders, not even on Double-9 anymore. A middle-aged anchor nodded with measured concern. A pop-up in the top right corner warned viewers that the show was going to a live police press conference imminently.

Someone off-screen cued the anchor and the caller was cut off mid-sentence.

"And now let's go to that press conference," the anchor said.

The riser behind the podium of the Taipei Police Department was crowded with people. The police spokesman was at the microphones, but he kept glancing at Tong-tong, who remained standing near the back, stone-faced.

"We have rescued the hostage Chen Jing-nan from the heavily armed kidnapper Liu Ju-lan," the spokesman declared. "The police department received a tip from an anonymous person that Ju-lan was hiding in a certain underground garage. When we responded to the call, we happened to run into a group of off-duty army officers, who provided back up. We also anticipated difficulty so we dispatched two specially armed officers to the scene.

"When we arrived, we found that Ju-lan was holding a gun to Jing-nan's head. She refused to lay down her weapon. We had no choice but to shoot and kill her."

Reporters in the room gasped. It was much more common for suspects to kill themselves, or at least have the police say the suspects killed themselves.

The spokesman put on a grim smile. "We deeply regret that there was a loss of life. On the other hand, Chen Jing-nan is now safe and we released him after a full evaluation of his health."

"Where was the garage?" asked Wolf TV's correspondent.

"In Taipei. That's all I can say."

"Was Ju-lan acting alone?" asked another reporter.

"As far as we can tell."

Another question came forth. "How come they didn't put Jing-nan in a dog cage?"

"Well, all kidnappers have their own style."

"Why is Tong-tong here, standing in the back? Did he poop his pants?"

No one dared to laugh. The spokesman cautiously looked back to Tong-tong who refused to give the slightest reaction to the heckler. The spokesman rubbed his nose before responding. "Tong-tong is here to offer support for Jing-nan, who is a classmate of his own daughter." Tong-tong grunted and stepped down to the front. He waved away the spokesman with both hands and approached the micro-phones himself.

"Chen Jing-nan is a very brave young man," declared Tong-tong. "I wish my daughter could find a man like him."

Nancy and I shared a look and shook our heads.

Tong-tong continued. "I'm personally grateful to him for his support in the days when I was rescued from kidnappers. I'm glad to return the favor.

"Taiwan has gone through a shock, marring our Double Ninth Festival. I am offering free bottles of chrysanthemum wine for every family. Please pick one up at any of my hotel properties."

"Is it true, Tong-tong, that you're donating a billion NT to Taida University to create scholarships for study in China?" asked a young man with a Japanese network. He was one of the few at the press conference who didn't wear glasses.

Tong-tong laughed but couldn't prevent his face from turning into an open-mouthed door-guardian frown. He was clearly wondering who the reporter's source was. "It's some-thing I've been evaluating," Tong-tong said slowly. "I've had some talks, but no commitment, of course."

An anxious middle-aged man pointed at Tong-tong with a pen.

"Didn't Jing-nan also hold a rally to counter your rac-ist remarks? And didn't one of your sons attack you at that rally?"

Tong-tong nodded slowly. "Jing-nan did hold a counter-rally, didn't he? Well, good for him and good for the country, too. We have a democracy. Everybody should be allowed to say what they think." He bowed his head slightly as he straightened his back. "Even if you only have stupid things to say." Tong-tong yielded the mic back to the police spokes-man.

A reporter called out from offscreen, "Have you found the people who kidnapped Tong-tong yet?"

A pained look came over the spokesman's face. Was he uncomfortable that he knew the truth or uncomfortable that he didn't? "We have not yet apprehended the suspects," he managed to say. "It's still an open case." The spokesman looked to Tong-tong, who mouthed something. "I should add that regarding Tong-tong's kidnappers, we don't know for certain anything about their backgrounds, so nobody should view foreigners in particular as potential culprits. Thank you."

As the spokesman essentially ran away, I saw Tong-tong step to the left, where he was met by his son Er-ming, who had voiced opposition to his father's anti-immigrant stance as "Erwin Lee." Tong-tong patted Er-ming's shoulder.

The spokesman had provided a lame walkback, a small repudiation of Tong-tong's earlier remarks. It was a coup for Tong-tong, though. He saved face because he didn't have to say it himself and yet the words were enough to satisfy Er-ming.

I scraped my spoon along the bottom of the bowl and slipped the last smile of stew into my mouth.

Nancy muted the television as it went to commercials.

"Do you want to rest early tonight, Jing-nan? You've been through a lot."

"I don't know," I said. "It's weird to be sitting at home this time of night."

"You're not thinking of going to Unknown Pleasures, are you?" She grabbed my left hand and turned it over. "You still have cuff marks on your wrist!"

"They don't hurt."

"I think you should take it easy."

I thought about the stall. I used to hate being there as a

kid because I had nothing personally invested in the business, money or otherwise. Now it was my rocket ship that could go anywhere.

"It's easier for me being there." I got up off the couch and picked up the empty bowls. As I walked to the kitchen, I felt a nagging ache in my calves. I was sure it would go away soon. Couldn't say the same for my abdomen. It had looked pretty bad before they wrapped me up. But nothing looked worse than my eye, which was truly gruesome. I returned to the living room.

"You have work to do tonight, don't you?" In Taipei there's so much work to be done it's like oxygen all around, simultaneously fueling and exhausting us.

"I could read some scientific journals," Nancy offered. I knew she loved to and she could only do so when I was asleep or at work.

"There we go," I said. I picked up my phone.

"Don't get kidnapped," she said.

"I won't." I typed a message to Dwayne and Frankie: I'M COMING TONIGHT.

GLAD YOU'RE OKAY, wrote Dwayne.

YOU WEREN'T GOING TO COME IN? asked Frankie.

I held my phone out to Nancy. "Take a picture," I told her. "I need it to post online."

She took my phone and I turned my face to her, bruise-first.

"You look like you're undead," said Nancy as she snapped away.

I took a look and laughed. "I'm not even going to use a filter on these!" I looked beaten up and thrilled. I posted the best one and hoped the enthusiasm was contagious.

"Tonight's vegan special: Black-and-blue fruit," I wrote for a caption.

I giddily slipped on my shoes. Nancy gave me a loving hug as strong as a heat rub, and closed the door behind me. I took the stairs, walked through the gauzy night air, and swayed in the MRT car that would bring me back to work.

We emerged from the tunnel and shot over the Tamsui River for the final stretch. I looked down and saw a dim, riderless train keeping even with us as it rippled across the stretch of dark water.

ACKNOWLEDGMENTS

I continue to be fueled by the love and support of my amazing wife, Cindy Cheung. Some of the childish behavior in this book was inspired by the tireless genius, Walter Lin.

I've set aside the best bowl of beef noodle soup for my agent, the great Kirby Kim.

I am nothing without Soho Crime. Juliet Grames keeps interfering in my mission to make myself sound as dumb as possible. Bronwen Hruska is kind enough to render my work into beautiful books. Paul Oliver, Abby Koski, Rudy Martinez and Amara Hoshijo are some of my favorite people in the world.

www.edlinforpresident.com

Other Titles in the Soho Crime Series

Michael Genelin
(Slovakia)
Siren of the Waters
Dark Dreams
The Magician's Accomplice
Requiem for a Gypsy

Timothy Hallinan
(Thailand)
The Fear Artist
For the Dead
The Hot Countries
Fools' River

(Los Angeles)
Crashed
Little Elvises
The Fame Thief
Herbie's Game
King Maybe
Fields Where They Lay
Nighttown

Mette Ivie Harrison
(Mormon Utah)
The Bishop's Wife
His Right Hand
For Time and All Eternities
Not of This Fold

Mick Herron
(England)
Slow Horses
Dead Lions
Real Tigers
Spook Street
London Rules
Joe Country

Down Cemetery Road
The Last Voice You Hear
Why We Die
Smoke and Whispers

Reconstruction
Nobody Walks
This Is What Happened

Stan Jones
(Alaska)
White Sky, Black Ice
Shaman Pass

Stan Jones cont.
Frozen Sun
Village of the Ghost Bears
Tundra Kill
The Big Empty

**Lene Kaaberbøl &
Agnete Friis**
(Denmark)
The Boy in the Suitcase
Invisible Murder
Death of a Nightingale
The Considerate Killer

Martin Limón
(South Korea)
Jade Lady Burning
Slicky Boys
Buddha's Money
The Door to Bitterness
The Wandering Ghost
G.I. Bones
Mr. Kill
The Joy Brigade
Nightmare Range
The Iron Sickle
The Ville Rat
Ping-Pong Heart
The Nine-Tailed Fox
The Line
GI Confidential

Ed Lin
(Taiwan)
Ghost Month
Incensed
99 Ways to Die

Peter Lovesey
(England)
The Circle
The Headhunters
False Inspector Dew
Rough Cider
On the Edge
The Reaper

(Bath, England)
The Last Detective
Diamond Solitaire
The Summons

Peter Lovesey cont.
Bloodhounds
Upon a Dark Night
The Vault
Diamond Dust
The House Sitter
The Secret Hangman
Skeleton Hill
Stagestruck
Cop to Corpse
The Tooth Tattoo
The Stone Wife
*Down Among
the Dead Men*
Another One Goes Tonight
Beau Death
Killing with Confetti

(London, England)
Wobble to Death
*The Detective Wore
Silk Drawers*
Abracadaver
Mad Hatter's Holiday
The Tick of Death
A Case of Spirits
Swing, Swing Together
Waxwork

Jassy Mackenzie
(South Africa)
Random Violence
Stolen Lives
The Fallen
Pale Horses
Bad Seeds

Sujata Massey
(1920s Bombay)
The Widows of Malabar Hill
The Satapur Moonstone

Francine Mathews
(Nantucket)
Death in the Off-Season
Death in Rough Water
Death in a Mood Indigo
Death in a Cold Hard Light
Death on Nantucket

Seichō Matsumoto
(Japan)
*Inspector Imanishi
Investigates*

Magdalen Nabb
(Italy)
*Death of an Englishman
Death of a Dutchman
Death in Springtime
Death in Autumn
The Marshal and
the Murderer
The Marshal and
the Madwoman
The Marshal's Own Case
The Marshal Makes
His Report
The Marshal
at the Villa Torrini
Property of Blood
Some Bitter Taste
The Innocent
Vita Nuova
The Monster of Florence*

Fuminori Nakamura
(Japan)
*The Thief
Evil and the Mask
Last Winter, We Parted
The Kingdom
The Boy in the Earth
Cult X*

Stuart Neville
(Northern Ireland)
*The Ghosts of Belfast
Collusion
Stolen Souls
The Final Silence
Those We Left Behind
So Say the Fallen*

(Dublin)
Ratlines

Rebecca Pawel
(1930s Spain)
*Death of a Nationalist
Law of Return
The Watcher in the Pine
The Summer Snow*

Kwei Quartey
(Ghana)
*Murder at Cape
Three Points
Gold of Our Fathers
Death by His Grace*

Qiu Xiaolong
(China)
*Death of a Red Heroine
A Loyal Character Dancer
When Red Is Black*

James Sallis
(New Orleans)
*The Long-Legged Fly
Moth
Black Hornet
Eye of the Cricket
Bluebottle
Ghost of a Flea*

Sarah Jane

John Straley
(Sitka, Alaska)
*The Woman Who
Married a Bear
The Curious Eat Themselves
The Music of What Happens
Death and the Language
of Happiness
The Angels Will Not Care
Cold Water Burning
Baby's First Felony*

(Cold Storage, Alaska)
*The Big Both Ways
Cold Storage, Alaska*

Akimitsu Takagi
(Japan)
*The Tattoo Murder Case
Honeymoon to Nowhere
The Informer*

Helene Tursten
(Sweden)
*Detective Inspector Huss
The Torso
The Glass Devil
Night Rounds
The Golden Calf
The Fire Dance
The Beige Man
The Treacherous Net
Who Watcheth
Protected by the Shadows*

Hunting Game

*An Elderly Lady Is Up to
No Good*

**Janwillem van de
Wetering**
(Holland)
*Outsider in Amsterdam
Tumbleweed
The Corpse on the Dike
Death of a Hawker
The Japanese Corpse
The Blond Baboon
The Maine Massacre
The Mind-Murders
The Streetbird
The Rattle-Rat
Hard Rain
Just a Corpse at Twilight
Hollow-Eyed Angel
The Perfidious Parrot
The Sergeant's Cat:
Collected Stories*

Jacqueline Winspear
(1920s England)
*Maisie Dobbs
Birds of a Feather*